An Unconventional
Mr. Peadlebody

D.L. Gardner

An Unconventional Mr. Peadlebody

More works by the author as well as video and audio are listed on the author's website. https://gardnersart.com

Dedicated

...to all the slightly dysfunctional families
who, when all is said and done,
when dull tooth meets the sharpened tongue,
forget their grievance against each other
and in distress, they help their brother!

The Late Rockford Peadlebody

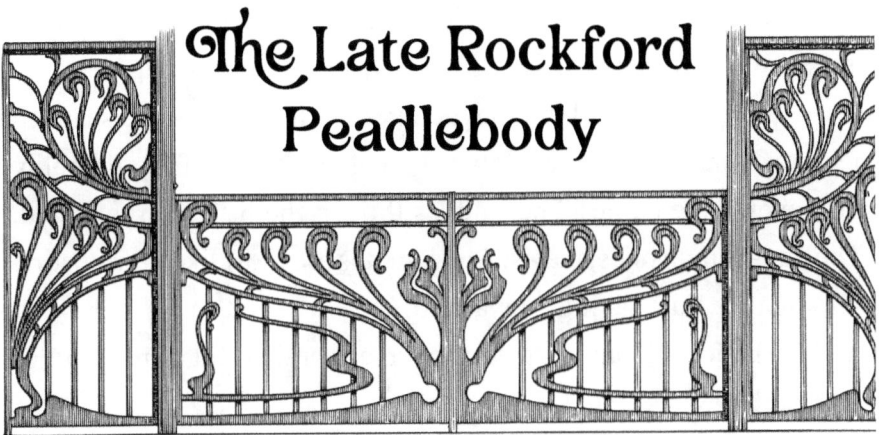

S unlight filtered into the church lobby and rested on the backs of—and Raymond Peadlebody counted them—a hundred-and-thirty-one people. He also attempted to count the lint particles as they floated in the atmosphere. However, in the act of calculating, a surge of guests passed by. Cologne, minty mouthwash, and body odors made him sneeze, sending even more dust into the ozone.

Raymond pulled a handkerchief from his suit pocket, held it to his nose, and blew. If there was one thing he hated, it was being in a room crammed with strangers, especially strangers that reeked. Fortunately, no one seemed to notice his allergy to humans as he pushed through the assembly and tucked himself in a far corner of the lobby.

Shaking his handkerchief, he tucked it back into his vest pocket, leaned against the wall, and scratched the stubble on his chin, fighting the urge to tap his foot. "No," he scolded himself under his breath. "Remain calm under all circumstances." The words passed through his teeth like steam from a teakettle. "If they suspect who I am, it'd be a social disaster.

No social disaster!"

The guest book lay open on the desk next to him, unsigned, pen covered and unused. A doily laced the linen tabletop and provided a cushion for the leather-bound journal. A silver vase with a single white rose cast a faint shadow onto the empty pages.

Raymond rolled his tongue over his left fang as he scanned the crowd and then glanced down at the guest book. "They probably don't even have names," he said, as though the little journal cared. "The non-human ones, that is. And humans are most likely protecting their identity. Just saying," he added.

The journal lay muted, of course, but that didn't make it, or Raymond, any less lonely.

The guests continued to arrive, ushering in a wave of cool autumn air whenever the door was opened. One woman, who obviously didn't feel the same way he did about being noticed, strolled into the lobby smacking with arrogance. Red high heels made her tall and lanky body tower above the crowd. A flowered scarf twisted into a red and yellow turban on her head looked like a beach ball bouncing over a sea of black felt hats.

No one else in the room wore such bright colors. Black suits and ties enmeshed both men and women into a dark shadow that buzzed about the church foyer like a swarm of flies. What made this middle-aged female think she can come to his father's interment dressed like a fashion queen?

Her pale face was buffed bright with powder and blush. Her thick red lips emphasized her pout. The most puzzling accessory was the pointed sunglasses she hadn't bothered to take off, despite the dimly lit room. With barely enough daylight to read the order of service, why did she wear sunglasses? Humans have no manners at all, wearing shades in church! Then again, maybe she wasn't human.

A crude lot of miscreants, their high heel shoes and patent

leather loafers tracked over the plush red carpet carelessly. Each face pale and sickly, all of them framed by dark brows and slick black hair. Raymond had seen none of these individuals before, although the night before his mother had assured him only relatives would come to the funeral. Blood relations that came out of the woodwork, probably literally, simply because the rumor swept through Mason County that his father had died.

"That's what vampires do for half-bloods," his mum had explained the day before when they unpacked their suitcases in their stuffy motel room. "Half-bloods like you and me and your father— those who aren't privileged enough to be pure-blooded vampires."

Raymond had snuffed his mother's explanation, caring little about being a half-blood, much less a vampire. He hated his father, Rockford Peadlebody, who now lay resting in the casket in the sanctuary. The man was the eldest son of Benjamin Peadlebody, the last pure-blooded vampire in his family. His grandmother was an elf. He never met either of his grandparents.

Raymond had even less vampire blood in him. His father married Ginger, who had been human before he came into her life. Raymond was born twenty years ago in swampland along the Mississippi River. His father hid him away as a child. Home-schooled. His dad thought him a mistake. He didn't care. Mum loved him. He was confident of that. Mum was human before his dad changed her and that's why she had a heart. Raymond wished he had been born normal like her. Humanity was the lineage that he lay claim to.

He pushed a curly black lock of hair behind his ear and glanced at his watch, pulled up his already too short coat sleeve and mumbled to himself. "Fifteen minutes. Mum, where are you?"

He dreaded walking into the sanctuary by himself. He'd be expected to sit in the front pew and to do that he'd have to walk past all these ruffians. He fastened his collar again. His slender fingers moved deftly and inconspicuously as he straightened his bowtie, all the while scrutinizing the individuals that now closed in on one another as the room filled. Everyone waited for the double doors to open. Soon, the swarm will pack into the sanctuary like a flock of crows, black as night and just as ravenous.

His gaze drifted to the woman with the turban. She stood close enough that the scent of her perfume gagged him. He coughed into his handkerchief and tucked it back in the pocket on the inside of his coat. She looked at him. He gave her a cordial smile, which she did not return.

She stepped up to the refreshment table and leaned over the elaborate centerpiece as though enjoying the flowers. She didn't sniff them, though. She picked at them with long pointed fingernails painted fire-engine red. Raymond grimaced as he watched, completely entranced. She reached into the center of a gladiola and pulled out an earwig. She didn't fuss, nor did she drop the bug. Instead, she held the struggling creature by its pincers, and with the other hand, she lifted her sunglasses ever so slightly.

Raymond's heart stopped as he watched in shock. The bug turned white. She dropped it. When the insect hit the table, it broke into a thousand tiny chips, as if it were a delicate porcelain statuette shattering on a tile floor. The woman quickly brushed the splinters onto the carpet.

She turned sharply and looked at Raymond. Her glasses were back on again and there was a nasty smile on her face as she lifted a glass of punch to her ruby red lips.

"What are you staring at, mortal?" Her words struck him like a lightning bolt. Her wicked grin sent chills down his spine.

He shut his mouth, which had been hanging open, and he looked away just as his mother burst through the double doors. A timely interruption!

He left the turban lady and pushed through the crowd to get

to the short, red-hair woman he so lovingly called Mum.

Ginger Peadlebody was nothing special in anyone's eyes but her son's. Most guests turned their heads away when she entered as she was not particularly attractive. Just the opposite! It wasn't her fault. Raymond, Uncle Gerald, and Mum had arrived a day ago from a long train trip from Mississippi. The river had flooded and had washed away all their belongings, except for a few rags Ginger had pulled out of the muck. Today she wore one of her faded, mud-stained house dresses, and wrapped a crochet shawl over her shoulders. The only funeral-appropriate apparel that adorned her was the black box hat with a polka-dotted veil. She bee-lined across the room to Raymond and grabbed his shirtsleeve. "There you are!"

Raymond's shoulders relaxed and he smiled a greeting. "Mum! Finally!"

"Why are you still in the lobby? You should be in the sanctuary."

Before Raymond could answer, Ginger pulled him through the crowd, intercepting the Turban Lady. He didn't mean to, but he bumped into her shoulder. The woman's glass flew from her hands and spun upside down, splattering bright red punch on her skirt.

"Oh! I'm sorry!" Indeed, he was more than sorry. He had no intention of crossing the woman, not with the superpowers he had witnessed earlier. He would have stopped to help pick up her glass and clean up, except that his mother tugged him away. He glanced over his shoulder. He should help her. His thoughts changed as soon as she adjusted her sunglasses. Whether she was going to take them off, he didn't know, nor did he care to find out. He turned away and peeled his mother's hands off his shirt, clasping them gently.

"Mum, please, I'm a grown man. I can walk on my own."

"I know Raymond. Just hurry and get clear of these hoodlums. I worry about you around them."

"Why?"

"You're so—I don't—vulnerable."

"Hush, Mum. Don't say that!" Vulnerable was the last thing he wanted these hungry, wicked predators to think. They wouldn't attack a pure-blood, but Raymond was less than a half-blood. He adjusted his bowtie again as he walked. Everyone in the room looked at him. Everyone. Their faces somber, emotionless. Intimidating.

"Don't let them see you!" his mother whispered as she ushered him along.

"How are they not going to see me? You rammed me right into that lady with the turban and made me spill her drink. You know she's going to confront us at the reception, don't you? Who was she, anyway? She called me a mortal."

"She doesn't know you from Adam. Did you say anything to her?"

"Just that I was sorry."

"Sorry?" Ginger rolled her eyes.

Raymond skirted ahead of his mother to avoid her jostling. When he came to the end of the aisle, he halted. Ginger bumped into him, knocking him forward and into the casket. He caught the spray of roses before they hit the floor and placed them on the dark cherry wood cover. He froze when he saw the body inside.

"That's not him!" The corpse's face was powdered with too much makeup. The pits that had once marred Rockford's skin were now filled with foundation. His thick black hair lay starched and plastered in waves against his swollen temple.

Worse, his mouth was sewn shut.

Dead as dead, he looked human, not at all like a vampire.

His mother's lips trembled under the veil and her gloved fingers fidgeted nervously before she linked arms with Raymond. She drew him away from the casket and spoke slowly, as if telling a prologue to a ghost story. "They changed him." She looked over her shoulder, then quickly hustled Raymond to the front pew. "Sit down."

"Who did?"

"Cousins! They're all in cahoots. They hired the mortician to change him. We'll talk later."

As soon as they sat in the front row pew, four photographers hurried down the aisle. Two were young men a little older than Raymond, one in a pinstripe suit, his hair cut on a flattop which did nothing more for his appearance than to show off his enormous ears. The other men dressed more conservatively, though acted aggressively. Black silk suits and flashy silk ties shouted "PRESS" louder than their badges did.

Cameras flashed as the men dodged around the casket. The number of images they added to their portfolio was beyond counting, though Raymond tried. A vampire always counts, always keeps track, even if he doesn't want to, even if he shuns his bloodline and renounces his heritage. Counting was an instinct that took more discipline than it was worth to curtail. When his mother lifted her veil and gave him an abrasive nudge, he stopped.

"What are you doing?"

"Nothing," Raymond lied.

"Don't count. Your lips are moving."

Raymond slumped back against the hardwood seat. His mother sat as straight as an organ pipe, giving little mind to the dawdling reporters and all the impending news coverage—press that would make even a celebrity edgy. She pulled the dark veil over her eyes. Still, Raymond could see her face under it. Her lips were formed to a "Shh" as if she sensed the question Raymond wanted to ask.

"Why let these jokers take photographs?" he thought. He didn't speak the words, though. This was Mum's day to call the shots. If anyone should object to the press taking photos of Rockford Peadlebody's body, it would be the widow. There was no protest coming from Ginger, and no tears either. When the photographers finally found their way back down the aisle, cameras strapped to their backs and notepads tucked away into leather briefcases and slung over their shoulders, she whispered.

"Let them report your father's death from one end of the country to the next." Her lips puckered, her eyes narrowed as she looked at her son. "The plan was to leave those horrid fangs intact. The world should know what he was, not just speculate. Your cousins sabotaged me."

"You hired them?" Raymond asked.

"Plan didn't work out well," she grumbled.

"Mum, the world thinks vampires dissipate when they die," Raymond said quietly, whispering into her ear. "No one's going to believe those stories."

"They would have!"

He glanced over his shoulder at the reporters, hesitant to agree with his mother's agenda. Ginger Peadlebody wanted revenge and satisfaction for the years she suffered as a vampire's wife, hoarded away in the bayou by her madman husband. If his father's true species were exposed, the entire room of hoodlums would be incriminated. So would Raymond! If that happened, any chance of having a normal life would be utterly ruined. That is, if there were a chance for him to have a normal life. "How could you?" he asked.

"You're safe with me. Don't worry."

The monkey-eared cameraman shot him a smile before he walked out the door. Raymond scoffed at him, wondering what was going on in that kid's mind, taking photos of a corpse. He wondered too what the tabloids were going to read in the morning. "Rockford Peadlebody the Vampire Man gets Clean Bill of Health at Funeral?"

"Tuck your lips together, Raymond. Your teeth are beginning to show." He heeded his mum's warning immediately, hoping no one else would see. It'd be criminal if the monkey eared news reporter noticed his teeth! How he hated these fangs. They poked his lips when he wasn't deliberately tucking them into his mouth. Rarely did he smile when humans were near. Now that he was in the city, and once he found his mother a proper place to live, he would get rid of these tusks permanently.

"Mum?" Raymond muttered.

"What?"

"You'll probably think I'm crazy, but what do you know about gorgons?"

"What do you mean?"

"Gorgons? The monsters that can turn things into stone." She lifted her veil slightly and looked him dead in the eye.

"There's one here. I swear," he said.

She leaned close. "Don't say a word about it. Don't look at it. I have no idea what gorgons can do to vampires, if anything."

Raymond settled against the hardwood pew and watched the rest of the attendees take their seats. The church was packed. For a man who kept his family hidden in the back-country, Rockford Peadlebody sure had a lot of relatives.

Individuals shuffled into the stuffy room, fanning themselves, coughing genially as though that was proper protocol, folding their gloved hands on their laps as they settled. Some of the people looked normal, like humans. Several stood out from the others, such as the robust, heavy weight man with the curly white hair and gray-checkered suit. He ushered the woman Raymond had bumped into, the one with the scarf turban who called him a mortal, and who had a red stain on her skirt. The one who had turned an earwig to porcelain. Raymond shifted uncomfortably.

The last folk to enter were the most frightening. They reminded Raymond of the crows that had congregated in the grocery store parking lot that morning. They filed in as one shadowy flock. Raymond had never seen so much black. The men wore black silk suits. The women wore black straw hats with black veils. They all wore black leather gloves. One man even had a black cane and made eye contact with him just before sitting down, his black eyebrows furrowed in his pale face.

Raymond turned around quickly and held his breath, wondering if those were the cousins that spoiled his mother's plans.

"Those are the ones!" She nudged him. "They'll destroy your life if you ever cross them. Don't make eye contact with any of them!" She patted his knee.

Raymond spotted a red exit sign near their seats. "Why are we even here?"

Ginger snapped him a quick grimace.

"I mean why are we going to stay at grandfather's estate? From what Gerald says, it's barely livable. There's a hole in the roof, you know?" He never met his grandfather, but the thought of living in a pureblooded vampire's house gave Raymond the willies. "Why don't we just take a bus downtown, rent a house and start our lives all over? We could live like human beings."

"We've got your uncle to take care of. He needs us." Ginger looked over her shoulder again. "Here he comes now. Scoot over and make room for him."

Gerald Peadlebody was an upright sort, well dressed in his Sunday best, with enough of a mustache to cover his canine teeth. His salt and pepper hair was plastered in waves on one side of his part, the side that his smile bent toward. He walked casually down the aisle, nodding at the ladies. He'd taken one leather glove off to shake hands with the men. When he greeted the fellow with the black cane, Raymond groaned. "He doesn't actually know those people, does he?"

"Just remember your uncle lived here before you were born. He knows these sidewinders. No shame on his part. He can't help it. He's got to acknowledge them."

"He doesn't expect us to be friendly, does he?"

"What do I care what Gerald expects? We aren't here for him, or them."

"Then why are we here?"

"I told you. Your uncle needs us. He can't survive without us. Your father took care of him all his life. Now it's our turn."

"You aren't serious. We can't feed him."

"I'll find a way. I have a plan."

Whatever his mother's plan was, Raymond doubted it would work. She had never been successful getting his father to drink from a cup, regardless of what was in it. Surely, she didn't expect Uncle Gerald to fight his instincts.

"We're better off leaving the whole lot of them, Mum. Let's just get away."

Ginger straightened the crochet shawl on her shoulders as Gerald approached, and Raymond's voice vaporized into the heated room.

"Raymond! Good afternoon. Ginger!" Gerald nodded to the two and pulled his wool scarf from around his neck as he sat down, tossing it over his knee. Raymond didn't return the greeting. Their eyes met, though, and Gerald's mustache twitched.

"I see your father's looking quite the gentleman." Gerald nodded.

Raymond inched away from his uncle suddenly aware of the rising temperature in the room.

"He's not himself," Raymond responded.

Gerald snorted.

Raymond continued. "None of these rogues knew Dad much less were they a part of his life. If they're ashamed of him, why didn't they just stay home? What business do they have here?"

"They just want to make sure your father has a proper burial, Raymond." Gerald said.

"Shh," Ginger interrupted. "According to these vampires, this has to be done. When a half-blood dies he's given a human burial. Some sort of dumb tradition to protect the species."

"Who told you that?"

"Your father. For all the things he didn't do, he did give me fair warning of what to expect if he ever passed. Told me the proper way to bury him, but what do I care about their traditions? If I had my way, I'd shine a spotlight on the whole lot of them!"

Gerald cleared his throat in protest.

Raymond peered over his shoulder again, prompting a jab in the ribs by his mother.

"Don't stare."

The last of the attendees entered and the doors were closed. The warmth of the room peaked. Raymond yawned. Soon this would be over and he and his mother could get on with their lives.

What kind of life? He wasn't sure. If he had a say, he'd be living a completely unique existence from the one he just left. Watching his home float down the muddy waters left him feeling abandoned, yet in another sense, liberated. That little rambler spinning in the current had been his life. He'd been born and raised in that house. That house was his childhood.

Not a happy one either. Mum had been his only friend. Though he'd meet neighborhood children, he could never play with them. Mum's orders, not his father's. She kept him away from all human beings. When he asked why, Mum explained it was for the neighborhood children's safety as well as his. He never inquired further, although he sensed the danger had something to do with his father.

Rockford was a scary man. Raymond never liked him. Never.

"A filthy vampire," his mother would call him when they were alone. He couldn't remember her ever saying anything good about him. Rockford was seldom home and when he was home he spent his time in his study, or bedroom, or some secluded cubbyhole.

If Raymond bothered him, he was scolded. His father's chastising was scary. His lips would curl; his teeth would show. His eyes lit up with fire. Raymond learned not to seek him out for any kind of companionship or advice.

When Raymond learned to read, he spent time in his mother's library. He loved books and he loved learning about the world. Mum had many books, most of them were about vampires. Raymond read every one of them, spending long hours of sleepless nights turning through pages of legends, facts, and fiction regarding his bloodline. Books also became his only connection to the outside world and to humanity. In that, he and his mother shared their passion. Books taught him who he was, and why he was isolated.

The vampire books sank to the bottom of the river the day of the flood. Maybe they were in the belly of a giant catfish, still the horror written on their pages remained with Raymond.

Raymond, Gerald and Mum gathered what belongings they could find along the bank—some of their wardrobe and a few treasures Mum had salvaged and filled three tattered suitcases. His father met them on the road later with four train tickets to Cincinnati.

"We'll move in with old Benjamin Peadlebody!" he said, slapping Raymond on the back as though they were best friends. "You hear that, Son? You never met your grandpa. It's time. You're a man now. Time to get in with the big boys. See what actual vampires can do! Teach you to hunt and pounce on prey. No more listening to your mother and drinking out of a cup! Time to grow up. My dad will be the best teacher you can get!"

The thought both terrified and repulsed Raymond. He had no desire to feed on humans. He liked people. He felt a bond with people. Raymond swore he'd escape his father's scheme and now look — Providence provided his way out.

Raymond's lips curled into a smile as he stared at the body

lying in the casket. Fortune had been with him on the long train ride from Louisiana to Ohio—a derailment that shook the nation. The authorities found Rockford's body alongside the tracks near the engine, a splinter of railroad tie pinned through his heart.

Raymond was liberated!

The tabloids claimed Rockford Peadlebody caused the accident. Rumors spread that he had been a vampire. Mum took advantage of the rumors and had the press come to the funeral. That's why the cousins had Rockford's mouth sewn shut.

Even more bizarre than his father's death was the news that Benjamin Peadlebody, Raymond's grandfather, had faced a similar calamity the week before. Benjamin's fate was due to a storm, and a fallen tree, a caved-in roof, and again, a stab in the heart.

Peculiar coincidences, completely unrelated and life-changing for Raymond and his mother. In one week, Raymond attended two formal services. First, his grandfather's wake, now his father's funeral.

Hopefully, these fluke events were over and marked an end to the traumatic years of Raymond's life. He was ready for something new, something ordinary.

With Rockford dead, Uncle Gerald, was now heir to the Peadlebody estate. He had been hinting that Ginger stay with him under the custom of taking care of a brother's widow. If Raymond had his way, he'd refuse any inheritance, get a job, provide for Mum, and ditch Uncle Gerald. He could find a modest house somewhere in a quiet neighborhood far away from the Peadlebody Manor and forget the cousins he never knew.

The service started. The organ music increased in volume as Reverend Black stepped up to the podium and folded his hands. He waited for the final chorus of the hymn, Rock of Ages to blare out a musical 'amen'. After which his sermon on being thankful was long winded. Raymond grunted to himself. Being thankful seemed an appropriate theme for the occasion, one with which he could happily agree. Rockford Peadlebody was dead. Add alleluia!

Between the smell of the lilies surrounding the altar, his father's Old Spice seeping from the casket, and his uncle's cologne, Raymond's stomach rolled and begged to release its contents. When the call for eulogies finally came, Raymond stood.

Surprised that a steady line of people came forward, yet not surprised his mother remained seated, Raymond straightened his coat and nodded at Mum. She lifted her veil, her eyes popped open. Raymond met her gape with a twisted smile and instead of walking on stage like all the other phony mourners, he pivoted on his patent leather shoe and stepped out the exit.

The walk in the fresh air was exhilarating. Thirteen quick laps around the funeral home's finely manicured garden woke him up and settled his stomach. On the fourteenth round, he tired and strolled to a park bench by a rose garden, surrounded by neatly pruned shrubbery, and where he had a clear view of the chapel. There he waited until the two limousines and a hearse filed out of the driveway.

He'd meet his mother at the graveyard and walk a mile with her to the motel, gather their things and hit the road. That was his plan.

The Will

Gerald loosened the yellow wool scarf from around his neck. Whether it was the temperature of the day and lack of air in the parlor, or his anxiety over meeting the probate lawyer, the scarf was much too warm. He eyed Ginger critically. Tacky black bobby pins pulled her red hair behind her ears and under the boxed hat with the polka dot veil—a clashing decoration to her faded house dress that had been pulled out of the mud in Louisiana. At least she washed it. He never understood what his brother saw in the woman.

A wretched being, he thought, yet if he didn't look at her he'd be forced to look in the mirrors behind her. If he did that, he'd be reminded of his condition. He'd see his reflection, knowing that if he were a real vampire, he wouldn't. He hated being reminded of who he was not.

Gerald lowered his gaze, keeping his focus below the wainscoting. He had no desire to see how drained and pale his flesh was. The last two weeks had been exhausting and he must have lost thirty pounds. He cleared his throat and addressed Ginger. "Where's Raymond?"

"He's outside."

"Shouldn't he be in here?"

"You tell him. He's a mind of his own."

Gerald shifted restlessly on the camel back sofa and stilled when he heard a crack come from under the upholstery. He glanced anxiously at the stiff collared butler across from him.

"The furniture is in want of repair, sir. I suggest you sit over the leg." The servant nodded toward Gerald's right and so Gerald slid over, nearer the window where he could see his nephew pacing back and forth in the driveway.

Voices came from the stairwell, and then the lawyer's reflection appeared. Madison T. Ferguson's face was buried in his notebook and he stood to Gerald's left at the threshold of the parlor, forcing Gerald to look in the mirror to see him. Ferguson was not a large man. He was, in fact, thinner and shorter than Gerald. His wiriness was disguised by thick shoulder pads that held up his suit coat, and the oversized tie that covered his starched shirt. Gerald sat quietly when Ferguson made his appearance. There was no handshake, no cordial greeting.

The secretary, a young pale woman, whose dark hair was swept onto her head in a neat little hive, stood next to Ferguson. She was the epitome of fashion, with her fitted wool suit and lace gloves. She would have been more attractive if her ruby lips hadn't been twisted into a snicker. Gerald wondered what her species was, for though she paraded great beauty, the glint in her eye could have been that of an evil beast. Perhaps a sorceress of some sort. She had that sharp edge.

Observing the secretary, or more specifically the secretary's neck, marked the first time since his brother's death that Gerald's stomach growled. He had to wipe drool from the corner of his mouth with his scarf.

"Are we all here and accounted for?" Ferguson gave them

the courtesy of looking up. Once.

"My son is outside." Ginger commented.

"Your son? I wasn't aware..."

"Raymond Peadlebody."

"Raymond..." Ferguson shuffled through his papers.

"My father's grandson." Gerald's irritation was taking root.

"Cottlebone, would you call him in, please? I'm not sure if he's mentioned in the Will, still it seems we should have an account of all family members." Ferguson addressed the butler put his papers back in order. "No one told me about a grandson," he grumbled under his breath, causing Gerald to glance up.

"Yes, sir." The man named Cottlebone left the room. Gerald watched the well-built servant stroll out the door. Though his collar was buttoned to the top, the tip of a tattoo peeked out from under his chin. His head was bald and a ring adorned his left ear.

Gerald watched through the window as Raymond was summoned.

His nephew rolled his eyes and followed Cottlebone back into the house. The door slammed, footsteps sounded in the entryway, and the scent of fresh morning air followed Raymond into the room. The young man pushed past Ferguson and stopped.

"Well don't just stand there, sit down!" Gerald said. "You should have come in with the rest of us. You're holding up this parlay."

Raymond looked at the furniture, choosing the space next to Gerald. He sat down so forcefully that another sound of splitting wood underneath Gerald broke the silence.

Ginger gasped.

"Where are your wits? Move over and sit on top of the leg of the sofa!" Gerald urged him to the far side of the davenport with a wave of his hand. Once Raymond was settled, Ferguson looked up again.

"Are we ready?"

"Can we get this over with quickly?" Gerald asked, fanning himself, once with his hand and again with the edge of his scarf.

Ferguson began his discourse, a mouthful of legal jargon that took more than a patient's cry of time to deliver. Halfway through, Raymond raised his hand and, without waiting to be called on, interrupted.

"Before you get into all that, why don't you just come out and say it? Uncle Gerald is the man getting the bucks, right? Can we get to the important issues? What does he have to do now? Sign papers? What?"

Ferguson looked up from his paperwork. "Mr. Gerald Peadlebody inherits the manor. Yes, he needs to sign the papers that I laid out for him on the kitchen table. He also inherits the manor's servant, Mr. Richard Cottlebone."

Gerald's eyes widened and he and Cottlebone exchanged glances. Raymond broke the tension with a hearty laugh. "That's ludicrous. How can you inherit a servant? Slavery was abolished a century ago, or thereabouts."

"Mr. Cottlebone had an eternal agreement with Benjamin Peadlebody. His room and board continue with the estate. He's here to stay."

Raymond laughed again, holding his hand over his mouth after Ginger made a gesture that his teeth were showing.

"Raymond, stop laughing. The man needs a place to live and good heavens there must be a hundred rooms in this house." Ginger pulled up the veil from her hat, offering a cordial smile to Mr. Cottlebone. With all the mirrors in the room, Gerald wondered why she hadn't noticed her lipstick was smeared.

"Twenty-eight, is all, Mrs. Peadlebody," Cottlebone corrected.

"Cottlebone knows the manor inside out. He will be an asset

to you, Gerald." Ferguson offered.

Gerald waved away any concern. "It's fine by me."

"I'm an excellent cook." Cottlebone assured him.

"Stupendous! Not that it makes much difference with my diet," Gerald said.

Ginger released an audible, "Tsk," most likely meant for Gerald only. Raymond moaned and Cottlebone winced.

Ferguson returned to his papers and thumbed through them, mumbling aloud, apparently reading. He tapped his finger on the document several times when he came to what he was looking for. "The clause concerning Benjamin's bank account. Gerald will be the heir of all of Benjamin's property, including his money."

"What's the catch?" Raymond asked.

"Catch, sir?" Ferguson grumbled.

"All of this goes to Uncle Gerald. What's the catch? What skeleton is hidden in the closet?"

"Raymond!" Ginger glared at her son.

Ferguson's face suddenly turned red. He pulled his hankie from his pocket and dabbed at his face. "I'm sorry. I don't understand what you're trying to say. Everything is in the paperwork. You're welcome to read it. If you'd like to sell, Mr. Peadlebody," For the first time Ferguson made eye contact with Gerald. "I have a cash buyer. The transaction would be swift and clean, with no effort on your part. You won't even have to move your grandfather's clutter. This buyer will take it all and pay you generously." Gerald sat up straight.

Raymond laughed again without showing his teeth and clapped his hands in triumph. "We'll take it!"

Gerald scowled at his nephew and the snarky attitude that emanated from him. "Nonsense. This is a perfect place for us to live. There's plenty of room for the entire family."

"What entire family?" Raymond's face paled and his eyes

popped open.

"You know. The three of us."

"I'm not living here, Uncle. You can bet your bottom boots that Mum and I are hightailing it out of here as soon as this is settled. Tomorrow will be too late."

"Not so fast, Raymond," Ginger interrupted. "I never said any such thing."

"If I heard correctly the estate was willed to me," Gerald said. "So, it's my decision what becomes of this house. We have no intentions of selling. I promised my brother that I would take care of his wife and family if anything ever happened to him."

"You're not taking care of me!" The couch bent when Raymond shifted, drawing all eyes to him. "I can take care of myself."

"You choose to disown us?" Gerald lifted his chin. He and Raymond never got along before. This was breaking the camel's back, or the camel back's armature in any case.

"Yes. Of course! I chose to disown you and my father a long time ago. I don't want anything to do with you vamp..." Raymond bit his tongue and looked at Ferguson, the secretary, and Cottlebone. He stopped mid-sentence.

"I'll let you folks hash this over. Mr. Peadlebody, if we're done here the papers are in the kitchen. We can discuss the sale of your property later when you're alone." He nodded nervously at Gerald, took his secretary's arm and escorted her to the kitchen.

Gerald rose, letting the weight of the couch collapse under Raymond, who ended on the floor. Gerald paused for a moment and watched his nephew struggle to get up. He sighed and offered Raymond a hand. The young man refused his help, so Gerald turned and followed Ferguson.

Heir to What?

The day settled into evening, the work was done and the papers signed. Ready for a new life as a homeowner, Gerald stepped out on the porch and watched Madison Ferguson and his succulent secretary drive off in the lawyer's sports car. With Ginger and Raymond already on a trolley to gather their belongings from the hotel in the city, Gerald was left behind at the manor with only the servant and an enormous, unkempt home.

As Ferguson's car disappeared down the gravel drive, the smell of its fuel dissipated into the atmosphere, replaced by the fragrance of rose from a scanty bush growing near the steps. Sweet as the flower smelled, the bush had barely a leaf left from black spot. Its spindly branches balanced loose clusters of pink petals that fell to the ground as forlornly as autumn leaves.

Amazed that the wretched plant had any scent at all, Gerald breathed a frustrated sigh. The Peadlebody estate direly needed workers, including a gardener.

From the looks of the grounds, Cottlebone was obviously

inept at outside chores. Raymond wasn't going to cooperate, so Gerald would have to hire a landscaper once his finances were in order.

Upkeep of the manor was just one of the many issues he'd have to manage now that his brother and Benjamin Peadlebody were gone. The idea of overseeing something as huge as his father's home frightened him. What an overwhelming task! Gerald never had lived up to his father's expectations. To fail in caring for the estate would be to fail at life! What if he squandered the money, or somehow bungled the renovation of the home?

With a heavy heart, Gerald turned and faced the door of the manor. Memories immobilized him as his fingers grasped the cold brass knob. His image danced and divided through the red and blue glass of the door window. An image that today was a middle-aged man, but had once been young, Raymond's age. Not that many years ago, twenty-one to be exact, and his numbers were always exact.

Rockford had convinced Gerald to leave, and it hadn't been a hard sell. Gerald was not his father's favorite son by any means. He could still hear the disgruntled sire calling out to Rockford.

"Teach him to hunt while you're in the bayou Rockford, my boy! Make an honest vampire out of him."

Gerald never learned. He never pleased his father. Still, he would have liked to have seen the old fellow before he was set in the ground to apologize for being so inadequate.

That there were very few details about Benjamin's death kept Gerald uneasy. The lawyer had mentioned something about a storm, a fallen tree, and a hole in the roof. Gerald inquired for additional information from the law office, but no one seemed to have any, or else they were keeping it secret. Though legend told that vampires dissolve into thin air rather than die bodily, it still would have been satisfying to have seen his remains, or some proof of his final departure.

"Well, enough of that!" Gerald mumbled as he opened the door. "He's obviously gone or he would not let anyone take over his household."

Gerald stepped inside. His stomach groaned, reminding him of the one personal problem he'd been unable to solve since his brother's death.

Hunger.

A wave of emptiness swept over him. Seven days had gone by since he'd eaten and he was feeling the effects. How he longed for the courage to hunt. More so, how he yearned for his brother to hunt for him. Rockford never let Gerald go hungry, not one day.

When they were children, the two would wander the alleys downtown together in search of dinner. Rockford was always the one to pounce on their prey and quiet them so that Gerald could take a drink. Even when they were young men in Louisiana, Rockford provided for his younger brother. Now that Rockford was dead, Gerald was at a loss on how to sustain himself.

Cottlebone, on the other hand, as mysterious as he is, had been his father's servant. Is there a chance that he served his father in the most substantial way possible? Did Benjamin feed off Cottlebone?

Gerald stepped quietly into the hall and flipped the light switch to 'off'. He'd been secretly eyeing Cottlebone during the entire reading of the will. The servant's skin may be tough, but Gerald's teeth had not been used for quite some time, and had plenty of point.

He licked his lips at the thought of fresh blood and took another careful step. He'd been waiting for the house to empty to make his move. Cottlebone was a large man, twice Gerald's weight. Tackling him would be difficult. Gerald would have to outsmart Cottlebone, or come up from behind with a candlestick or something.

No matter the difficulty of the struggle, the feast afterward would be well worth the effort. What a perfect situation if Gerald could feed on the servant's blood for evening dinners, and possibly for breakfast as well. Cottlebone would indeed be a loyal servant!

Gerald quietly shut the door, his ear keen on any noise that might reveal Cottlebone's whereabouts. Not a sound, but the beating of his own heart. It didn't matter where the servant was now. The man would eventually appear. He had to. Gerald wrestled with whether to wait, or to seek him out.

This would be a first solo feed, an event both exciting and terrifying. He carefully took his scarf from around his neck and hung it on the coat rack so that his clothing wouldn't get in the way. He thought twice about removing his coat since the house bore an empty chill, but peeled his leather gloves from his boney fingers, tucked them into his pocket, and rubbed his hands together as he sauntered down the hall.

One peek into the room where Benjamin Peadlebody's last Will and Testament had been read, the 'parlor' as Cottlebone called it, assured Gerald it was empty. The rest of the manor, aside from the kitchen where he had signed Ferguson's papers, was unfamiliar to him.

Cottlebone was not in the kitchen, so Gerald followed the hall past a junction that veered into the dark. Several doors along that corridor, all closed tight, reflected light on their thresholds. None of those doors gave the appearance that anyone had walked through them recently, and Gerald, skittish about his own agenda, was not about to explore the unknown. The other passage led to a spacious living area.

Several old and worn area rugs stretched across a dull hardwood floor in dire need of waxing. A crystal chandelier dangled from the cathedral ceiling, its prisms coated with dust and cobwebs.

Heavy black drapes covered the windows and prevented daylight from leaking into the room. Several antique chairs were pushed up against the wall, and the stone fireplace stood cold and abandoned. "Does Cottlebone not work inside either?" Gerald whispered to himself.

The only movement exhibited in that room besides his own was a constant clicking of his father's clocks. Shelved on the mantle and hanging on the walls were timepieces each ticking their own beat, each counting a different hour in the day. Antique clocks that had clearly been birthed at the turn of the century shared wall space with modern sunbursts. Gerald didn't remember this collection and wondered why his father had gathered them.

He would have inspected the timepieces further if he hadn't heard footsteps coming down the spiral staircase. Gerald dodged under the stairwell and held his breath, looking feverishly for something to use as a weapon. To his pleasure, several books lay on a den table next to him. He grabbed the thickest with both hands.

Richard Cottlebone strolled, stepping one foot at a time on the carpeted rungs while Gerald waited in the shadows against the wall under the stairs, visualizing his plan of attack. He would knock him on the head with the book to stun him and then grab the man's throat, as he'd seen Rockford do so many times. He'd pinch Cottlebone's neck, just under his jaw where the jugular vein is, and hold him until he cannot breathe, then tackle him to the floor and bite.

The whole scenario would be over quickly and poor Richard Cottlebone wouldn't know what had drained him whilst Gerald would be fully nourished.

"And I will make him comfortable as he recuperates!" Gerald thought. The whole scenario intrigued him. His heart thumped against his chest. Cold sweat trickled down his brow. He held his breath to keep from hyperventilating. The wait was too intense.

What took him so long? Cottlebone's steps slowed the closer he neared, but finally there he was. His shoes in view on the step above him, Gerald froze as he watched Cottlebone's black Wincklepickers appear. Gerald waited a moment longer, until he saw the man's shoulder, his neck, his head.

He lunged.

Cottlebone swung.

Gerald flew across the room and landed on his back. Cottlebone was on him, holding his shoulders down, his wide lips in a regal frown, his brow furrowed.

"Mr. Peadlebody," Cottlebone said in a rough and vicious voice. "I know who and what you are." Cottlebone unbuttoned his collar and loosed his tie with one hand, his other hand, and his body weight pinned Gerald to the floor. The butler's bare skin flexed as the tattoos flashed in Gerald's face.

The half-blood whimpered and turned away. Cottlebone took Gerald's jaw in one hand and turned his face again, his beady red eyes narrow and thirsty. Surely, Gerald was a dead man!

"You see this?" Cottlebone popped another button on his shirt as he yanked it open. The tattoos glowed. Crosses adorned his neck and his chest.

Gerald grimaced. "Yes! Yes, I see. Don't make me look!" A pain shot through Gerald's gut. Cottlebone's hold grew tighter around his neck.

"I lived with your father. I know what he was and what you are. I was his servant and his bodyguard. My blood is not for drinking," he said.

Gerald's chest caved under Cottlebone's weight. "Okay, I understand. I see!"

Cottlebone kneed him in the stomach. "Never."

"Never. I won't ever attack you. What a stupid idea! I don't know what got into me." Gerald hoped this was not his end. A coward he'd been with his brother, a coward he'd remain, but wiser now.

"As long as we have an understanding."

"We do! I swear, we do."

Cottlebone studied Gerald for a moment before he stood. Noticing the missing button, he tore the shirt off his shoulders, mumbling a profanity that Gerald could not understand. Gerald remained on the ground, stunned. Not until he was offered help up did he come to his senses. Surprised, Gerald took Cottlebone's hand, and shivered when the man's brawny fingers engulfed his.

"What was I thinking," Gerald mumbled to himself.

"We will maintain a professional relationship from here on out?" Cottlebone asked as he pulled Gerald to his feet with one quick sweep and then reached over quickly to pick something off the floor. A small red book of some sort had fallen out of the servant's shirt. Cottlebone's face flushed as he retrieved it and quickly tucked the journal into his pant pocket.

"Yes, yes of course." Gerald watched the servant saying nothing, though he wondered why the embarrassed expression. He dusted his sleeves and breathed deeply. "Now then, what did you say?" Gerald stared into the servant's eyes, recollecting what he had heard. "Bodyguard?

What is this about being a bodyguard? For my father?"

Cottlebone did not answer right away. Instead, his cold eyes bore a hole through Gerald, a look he could barely decipher, so Gerald asked again. "Why did my father need a bodyguard?"

"I'm not at liberty to say."

"Heavens, Cottlebone! You're my servant. You lived with my father. We have no secrets!"

Cottlebone only swallowed. The tattoo in his neck made a leap over the lump in his throat.

"Tell me. What kind of trouble had my father been in that he needed help?"

"No trouble, sir."

"Then why did he need a bodyguard?" Cottlebone's silence

provoked Gerald's anger, and fear. "These rumors about his death? Are they true?

How did my father die?"

"You heard the story. The lawyer told you."

"Of course, I heard and I find it hard to believe. Did you see the hole in the roof? Did you come upon the body?"

"Your father was a vampire, and as all true vampires do, Benjamin Peadlebody dissipated."

"Did you see the hole in the roof?"

Still, the man did not soften, but stood rigid, holding tight to his story, and to his silence. "The roof is fine, sir. There are no leaks, now."

"Was my father murdered?"

Cottlebone threw his shirt over his arm, turned his back on Gerald, and walked down the dark hallway.

Gerald called after him. "Was my father murdered?"

"Your bedroom is ready for you. Up the stairs the third door to the left." That was all the man offered.

He watched the husky servant promenade into the depths of the manor, leaving Gerald certain that his father's death had not been an accident, and that this tattooed servant knew more than he was letting on.

Atop the Trees

top the Trees

A month passed.

Raymond kept his promise and moved to town. Ginger spent two days in the manor and decided she'd be happier in the tree house out back. In a way, the arrangement was a welcome relief for Gerald. Ginger was a strange little woman with mothering instincts that wouldn't stop. Her logic threw both him and Cottlebone into chaos. Though Gerald had promised his brother he'd take care of her for the rest of his life, he soon regretted that vow.

Ginger's move to the tree house was not an uncomfortable choice for Gerald. Raymond came around often enough to modernize his mother's home and the arrangement kept her out of his hair.

Today, a slight breeze hinted of an approaching winter as Gerald stepped out his front door. He fixed his scarf up over his neck, filled his lungs with cold crisp air, and hurried around back. There he eyed Ginger high on her porch, beating an area rug. Crows flew over her head and she waved them away with angry shouts.

He snickered at her scrawny profile and the tasteless clothes she wore. The faded dress was acceptable he supposed, but why must she always wear mismatched socks?

Was she blind? Today she wore one blue ankle sock on her left foot while a white knee-high stretched to the hem of her dress on her right. Their mates hung from a maple tree by her windowsill stuffed with thistle seeds, pecked apart by the creatures that she fed.

"Get out of here you flighty pests! That food belongs to the squirrels!" She jumped at a raven that slowly hopped out of her way.

Gerald wished the seed belonged to the birds and shuddered at the mention of squirrels. Ginger raised squirrels in the same way ranchers raise cattle—feeding them until they grow to a plump and ripe size ready for her. And most unfortunately, Gerald's breakfast, lunch, and dinner. A concoction Gerald hated with a passion.

Ginger's brew, and that he, Gerald Peadlebody, son of the great and infamous pureblooded vampire, Benjamin Peadlebody, had to drink squirrel blood out of a cup, was proof he had failed.

"You're heartless, Ginger. What's come of you?"

She chased a robin off the windowsill. "What? Why do you say that?" She scowled down at him.

Gerald scuffled up the wooden steps, avoiding the bird droppings on the railing along the way. "You've changed. Ever since we moved here you've become obsessed with those creatures."

"Ever since I married your brother I've been obsessed, period. Who can blame me? I was perfectly normal before that scoundrel ruined my life."

"Even so, you never raised squirrels in the bayou."

"Times were different then," Ginger said. "We had possums."

Gerald opened the screen door and let himself in. Ginger followed, broom in hand, letting the door slam and bounce twice behind them. One look at the kitchen table and the mountain of books that were stacked on it reminded him of her other obsession. Books.

"All those visits to the library—What for? Do you think you're going to discover something new?"

"I hope to. Hope to kick this curse out of my soul and all the way to the badlands," Ginger retorted.

"Curse!" Gerald scoffed. "I don't understand why you don't like being a vampire. Our lifestyle has a multitude of advantages over humans, you know."

Ginger moved from the door to the pantry and pulled out a pan. "You're one to talk. As if you even know anything about being a vampire!"

Gerald coughed forcefully and looked around the cluttered home. "I have something to discuss with you."

"Sit down then." She pulled a frozen package from the freezer. "What's so important? Did you solve your father's murder mystery?"

There were no empty chairs, all of them having stacks of dirty dishes, opened envelopes with colorful advertisements hanging out of them, and squirrel feed.

"Not yet," Gerald said. "I'm working on it. I'm reading past issues of local newspapers. There are quite a few articles that mention Benjamin Peadlebody."

"Your father made the news in this town? What did he do? Organize a church bazaar? Break par in a round of golf at a hospital fundraiser? Don't keep me in suspense."

Gerald dusted his shirtsleeve and swept his hair from his eyes. "Why do you mock me?"

"Because I find you absolutely hilarious, Gerald! Playing private eye like an old Dragnet of some sort. Your father died in a storm. No one could have killed him. How? How would someone have killed a full-blooded vampire without everyone in town talking about it?"

"I'm not sure they didn't talk about it. In every newspaper

41

I've read there has been some sort of uncanny event happen in this town, and much supposition as well."

"Such as?"

"People disappearing. Lots of them. This town has a history of tragic oddities. Twenty-four to be exact!" Gerald said.

"Does that seem absurd to you? Think about it, Gerald! A vampire lived here. What would you expect?"

Gerald wiped his brow with his woolen scarf as he watched the woman move about her kitchen. "Are you saying my father killed people?"

She spun around wide eyed, as if he knew the answer to that question.

His shoulders sank, somewhat defeated, knowing that perhaps she was right. She held up a finger. "My advice to you is to let this death of your father rest. You certainly don't want any more shenanigans happening. For all you know he could pop out of his grave." Ginger had brilliant blue eyes that shone almost white when the sun hit her freckled face. This morning, they were mere slits covered by blond lashes as she squinted at him.

"What a novel thought! "Gerald said. The idea of bringing Benjamin Peadlebody back to life never occurred to him. "I miss my father. I would love to see him again. I wonder if it's possible."

Ginger waved him off and opened the screen door to let a small varmint rush into the house. The chipmunk jumped over his feet and brushed against his pants. Dusty fit his name as the chipmunk had a habit of rolling on the ground and then trailing dirt into the house.

Dusty hopped on the kitchen table and picked at a pile of acorns that had been laid out for him, stuffing one in its cheek and nervously fingering another. He spat the shells about, scratched at the newspaper under his feet, tearing it into shreds, and stared at Gerald with his beady black eyes.

Gerald winced at the noise Ginger made, for he knew by the rattling of pans what she was doing. Fixing a meal for him. Squirrel blood! Ginger's professed remedy for vampire hunger, or at least a substitute for the real thing. A repulsive cocktail. He considered leaving, but before he could open the screen door, she spun around, a wide grin on her face.

"Look here! I've got some brew ready."

"No!" Gerald retorted. "No thank you. Not today!"

"What do you mean not today? You need to eat every day, Gerald. You'll get dizzy and weak and go on a rampage when you don't eat."

"I've made other dinner arrangements, and it won't be a rampage."

Ginger laughed at him.

"I'm serious. I will eat this evening, and I will dine as any good vampire ought to. Tonight, my plan will work." Gerald pulled the wooden chair from under the table and sat down, startling Dusty who scampered away and jumped on the refrigerator. With a sweep of his arm, Gerald pushed the shreds of torn newspaper, acorn shells, grocery wrappings, and birdseed to another spot, resting his elbow where the clutter had been.

"It smells in here, Ginger."

Ginger brushed her crimson curls away from the straight white hair that sprouted like straw above her forehead. "When has your plan ever worked? You've always been dependent on someone to feed you. Now that your brother is gone, you need my brew. Admit it!"

"Don't badger me, Ginger. It's you who needs me! After all, who is providing you with a roof over your head?" He looked up at the ceiling, verifying that he did, indeed, provide her with a roof.

"Squirrel's good for the gizzard and it will keep down your nasty hankering for bloody humans."

Gerald Peadlebody huffed at her remarks and fluffed the woolen scarf around his neck. "I am too sophisticated to continue pretending your brew is a substantial substitute for what I really need. I am a vampire, Ginger, from birth."

"No. What you are is starving." Ginger grunted and turned to the sink.

He had quite enough of her falsities, always denying the family name by refusing to drink the blood of humans. Worse was that she spent so much time flipping through pages of books, looking for potions that might turn her into a mortal again. "You need to be more grateful, Ginger. Not everyone is as privileged as we are. Remember, we are immortal."

"Not my heritage," she murmured as she wiped her fingers on her apron leaving long red streaks in a pattern that could be mistaken for Sumi art. "I never asked to be one of you. And I certainly don't intend to be a vampire forever. I will find a means of escape."

"If you do become human again, you'll have to leave this little house I allowed you and your son to build."

"Maybe I'll leave or maybe I won't. Maybe I'll turn you into a human being. How would you like that?"

"You dare? Not only am I a vampire but this family boasts a long line of other," he searched for words. "—peculiar beings, every one of them a predator of humans. It would be sacrilege to change into something that my family feeds on. They'd disown me, if any of them were alive."

"I thought your family was immortal."

Gerald peered out the window, a twitch shaking his right eyebrow. Who knows where gorgons go when they turn as brittle as their prey? His great grandmother could very well be camouflaged in the rock wall that hedges the garden. Maybe his two werewolf uncles, Sam, and Wishbone, simply morphed into the neighbor's Chihuahuas, spying on him every time their wet little noses sniffed under the fence. That crow on Ginger's porch could have been Aunt Elsie leaving behind her two cents. She'd never been worth much more than that. The whole family for ten generations could be alive and reconnoitering—eavesdropping on this very conversation.

"What you suggest would be highly inappropriate." Gerald spoke loud enough that any ghosts lurking nearby would hear him and absolve him from any wrongdoing. Or wrong thinking.

"Say you don't drink my brew today. What sort of fool plan do you have instead?" She carried two cups to the table and set one in front of him. "You aren't going to chase one of those janitors at Raymond's office again like you did yesterday, are you?"

Gerald huffed at the suggestion. Raymond's workplace was on the third floor of the Charles Mueller Building downtown in a tiny office hidden in a long gray hall set aside for small transient businesses such as the Gypsum Vacuum Cleaner Repair Shop. Vacant and eerie, the empty halls bothered Gerald. He had only gone to Raymond's place of employment once —and once was sufficient.

"Of course not! Although I was very near successful in capturing the rascal."

"It would have been your first catch."

"Come, now Ginger, I'm not that bad of a hunter."

"You're not a hunter at all."

Gerald huffed. "The brute put on quite the chase. I would have caught the wiry little devil if he hadn't dodged behind the dumpster in the alley. I was not going to be caught behind a trash can feasting on a human. The very thought is repulsive!"

Ginger rolled her eyes.

"I have other plans for the day. Today I begin interrogating people about the murder of my father."

"What? Who are you going to interrogate?

"Cottlebone for one."

"Good luck with that."

45

"He'll talk. I plan on having a heart to heart with him."

Ginger laughed and set her cup down. "So, you decided not to let your cousins scare you into dismissing Benjamin's death as an accident?"

"I suspect they had a part in whatever devious and guileful mishap is behind my father's death."

Ginger grunted. It was obvious she cared little what had happened to his father. "All the man was good for was that weather-worn manor."

"Which could have been your home! You could have had a room upstairs and enjoyed the services of Cottlebone, but that wasn't good enough for you."

"No, it isn't. The floor creaks, the wainscoting is moldy, and the draft made me sneeze. And that dumb Cottlebone is a thickset old meddler that has none of his own business to tend to so he minds the business of everyone else. You can keep your old shanty."

"You prefer the woods and marshes over a mansion? Besides, Cottlebone says there are no leaks."

"No leaks? How about where the tree crashed through the roof?"

"The stairway to the north tower is sealed off."

Ginger had been staring at Gerald's hands and when, out of curiosity, he followed her gaze he realized his long slender fingers rattled like a snake's tail.

"Shame?" she asked.

"What?"

"That's shame rattling your bones, isn't it? You hate what you are don't you? Just like I hate what you are and what your brother was. Your father couldn't have been any better." Drool foamed at the corner of her mouth.

"I don't hate."

Ginger raised her brow and her cup along with it. "Then

46

cheers to you, brother-in-law Gerald. Drink up before you die a ghoul of a leech. You've not a drop of vampire gumption in you. Your race is perishing, and I'm not diminishing with you. I'll be out of this rat's mess before you can shake a fang at your next victim."

He watched her guzzle the dark liquid; head held back, eyes closed. If he didn't know better she seemed to enjoy herself. When her cup was empty, she wiped her mouth with her sleeve. After a long and obnoxious release of acidic air, she nodded to his cup.

Gerald pushed his mug to the center of the table and stood despite her glower. He would not give in. Not this time. Even though his stomach was so empty, it felt like a locomotive racing along a track during an earthquake. He was going to follow his plan and consume his nutrients the way a good vampire was made to consume them.

"You're starving," she reminded him. Again.

Very well. If that's all she could say she could nag at his back, she could tell the screen door as it slammed, and she could tell the white drippings of bird poop along the railing after he took a step off the last stair. He wasn't going to listen.

Raymond

Raymond peeked out the window, checking the weather to make sure he was dressed properly. A cool breeze floated over a chilly Ohio morning and there was just enough wind to warrant wearing the sweater-vest Raymond's mum had made. She'd spun and knitted the vest out of squirrel down. Natural gray with puffs of white wool gave the pullover a scratchy texture, but by wearing his turtleneck underneath, he barely felt the fibers.

Raymond took one last look in the mirror, checking that the whites around his dark eyes were still white and not the gruesome gray color of his uncle's. Uncle Gerald had warned him that on his twenty-first birthday his entire face might turn morbidly pale, or worse, he might grow unwanted hair in grotesque places like on his forehead, or out his ears.

There was another possibility, too. He might lose his reflection altogether, like his grandfather who, being invisible, had slithered into so many victims' rooms unnoticed and exsanguinated them to satisfy his appetite. So terrifying was the vampire of Mason County, that the entire village held special services to ward off his presence.

Raymond knew. In a month's time, he'd been around enough humans to hear the stories. He'd seen the song sheets posted on the bulletin board outside the chapel on Main Street. Directly under them hung a shadow box which held the memorial candles used in prayer vigils for the deceased who had disappeared so mysteriously.

Raymond's grandfather had made quite a name for himself, though his reputation was spread by gossip and sealed with presumption. No other descendant of his could live up to such horrific accusations, since they had either intermarried with other species, or, like his uncle, lacked tenacity.

Raymond's chances of losing his soul and becoming invisible were highly unlikely. In a way, he was disappointed. Invisibility was a gift that could be used much to his advantage. Losing his soul? Well, it seemed that having his soul caused him so much misery.

If he couldn't be invisible like his grandfather, why then would he grow hair like his werewolf relations? Uncle Gerald had been foretelling doom ever since Raymond refused to live at the manor. If any of the freak things Gerald predicted came true, Raymond would be forced to quit his job as a vacuum cleaner repair man. Perhaps Gerald's plan was to badger him until he quit.

Or perchance Uncle Gerald was trying to live his aspirations through Raymond. No one could be a worse vampire than Uncle Gerald. As much as Raymond hated his bloodline, at least his father was good at who he was.

"He can't even feed himself!" Raymond whispered to the mirror. "If he thinks he's going to live his life through me he's got a lesson or two to learn! Never, even if Mum doesn't find a cure for the curse!"

Dismantling vacuum cleaners wasn't the greatest job in the world. It was a dirty and thankless occupation. Still, he liked where he worked. If he were ever forced to leave the Charles Mueller Building, he'd die. Literally. There would be no reason to take another breath because it was in the Charles Mueller Building that Amber Fay Richardson worked. Amber was a courier for the law offices at the end of the hall. He sighed when he thought of her. She was perfection. Not only beautiful, but sweet and kind, soft-spoken and intelligent. Not only that, but she had a dimple in the middle of her chin. Amber was special.

Raymond searched the medicine cabinet, his long slender fingers running quickly over the metal shelves until he found the package of files. He leaned over the sink, and with his mouth open, breathing hot air into the looking glass he filed the points of his fangs. Raymond was religious with his daily manicure. But today was special and he wanted to make sure there was nothing about him that might appear unusual. Today Amber Fay was going to stop by the shop and wish him a happy birthday. How did he know? He offered to walk her home after work.

She said yes.

He smiled as he grated the enamel off his teeth, shaping them flat, using the file as a level to make sure the fangs matched shape and size of the other teeth. He stared at the inside of his mouth, but he saw Amber in his mind, her hazel eyes, curly brown hair, and the candy-apple red of her lipstick. Raymond brushed tooth-dust off the turtleneck and switched his attention to the other side of his mouth, stretching his tongue over his bottom lip. The abrasive sawing felt like sandpaper to his insides as he worked, but he'd grown used to the vibration. All this effort was for a worthy cause! He sneezed once from tooth particles that went up his nose.

He didn't care. He had to win Amber's heart and if rasping away at his teeth was a step toward a wedding threshold, then he'd rasp away.

Maybe he wouldn't propose today. Hearts like Amber's aren't won in a day. She had only actually spoken words to him for the first time yesterday.

She smiled at him when she said yes. How sweet was that one brief word? A wink, her dimple, and a twist of her lips. She even had a twinkle in her eye he knew was meant for him only because it sent a tickle through his body. That tickle made him feel more human that he'd ever felt before. And he was, after all, part human.

"There mustn't be even a hint of a point in this mouth. Not one hint!" he whispered to the mirror. He had to look human.

He put his lips together and looked at himself somberly. "Mum has to find the secret to sealing our humanity. How can I ever have a wife? I'd have to sneak in the bathroom to file my teeth every morning. I'm not a sneak, nor am I a liar. My wife would find out. And then she'd ask questions. Lots of them."

The curl over his brow hung low and he brushed it away from his eyes. "Are you ready for that kind of confrontation, Raymond Peadlebody?

Could you tell Amber you're a vampire? Seriously?" The answer was no. Never. The thought of having to talk about his bloodline made him shudder. "When she learns what I am, she'll be afraid. She'll leave me. I'm destined for despair if Mum doesn't find a cure!"

Lost in his world of primping, he failed to hear the knock at the door. He flinched when he saw the reflection of his uncle in the mirror. Gerald stood at the entryway, directly at the end of the hall from the bathroom.

Raymond spun around as Gerald cleared his throat. The man's grin was so wide that the rays of sunlight seeping through the bathroom window landed on his fangs. His canine teeth glistened brightly, blinding Raymond for half a second and leaving spots in his eyes afterward.

"Raymond, Nephew!" Gerald had taken several steps down the narrow corridor, blocking Raymond's passage to the rest of the house.

Raymond's forehead beaded with sweat. Normally he paid little mind to his uncle and his horrific smile, except that some days the man looked paler than usual. And hungry. Today was such a day. Vampires don't approach a relative when they're hungry. Tradition, Mum said. But Gerald had been acting strangely ever since Raymond's father died.

"Good morning, Uncle." Raymond stuttered. He was trapped in the bathroom. The window was too small to jump through, and there were no other exits. Gerald continued his slow march up the hallway. Raymond panicked.

"Uncle Gerald!"

The man's eyes glazed over in a trance. He didn't respond to Raymond's voice. He simply smiled that sickly vampire smile.

Raymond's only escape was the front door behind Gerald. To get there he'd have to walk, or run, past his uncle. He drew in his breath and took a step forward, pressed his body against the wall, and slithered past Gerald's shoulder. The man's overcoat and scarf smelled warm from the morning sun and fresh from the autumn breeze. Raymond yearned to be outside himself, especially at that moment.

"What brings you here this morning?" Raymond asked nonchalantly, but loud enough to wake his uncle from his trance-like state.

"I'm on a mission. Foraging you might say. I thought I'd stop by and see how my favorite nephew was." He grabbed Raymond's arm before the young man could weasel away from him. Gerald's mustache tickled Raymond's cheek as he leaned close. His hands trembled as he pulled Raymond nearer still. His breath smelled bad, like his stomach was empty.

Like bile.

Raymond pushed his uncle away, though the man didn't let go of his sleeve but rather followed him down the hall pulling the vest loose from his shoulder. Raymond reached the living room.

"Stop it, Uncle! I might be your favorite nephew but that's because I'm your only nephew. The only one you have! Take note, you have no other. If I weren't alive, you would have no nephew at all! Think about that!"

"Yes. Yes, I know. However, you're looking very much like you aren't my nephew, if you know what I mean."

"No. I don't know what you mean."

"I don't see a blood resemblance right now." The hairs of his mustache bent upward, and his teeth showed. "You're looking very human today."

"It's the light uncle, that's all. There's a glow in this house that makes everything look warmer than it really is." Raymond loosened his uncle's fingers from his sweater and shoved him aside, dodging behind the couch.

Gerald followed, his footsteps slow and short. "You shouldn't run from me. I know what you're trying to be. You're trying to be human, and you do a really good job of it." He grinned. "Raymond the human."

Raymond picked up his coat that was slung over the couch, grabbed his lunchbox from the coffee table, and scrambled for the door. "You know I'm only half human, Uncle. My blood's not warm. It's cold. Sometimes. You don't want my blood, I swear. It's as rotten as yours."

Gerald ruffled the scarf around neck. His hands shook as he wiped his brow. "Oh my! What's come over me?" His voice trembled and he gave Raymond a pathetic tilt of his head.

Raymond sighed, glad his uncle was coming to his senses. "You're sick? Why are you here? Didn't Mum feed you breakfast? Didn't you drink your tonic this morning?"

Mr. Gerald Peadlebody straightened, his smile vanished, and his lips stretched over his fangs much like a hound dog's cheeks droop. "I went to see your mother, but I didn't drink her brew. I've decided to be who I am, not who she wants me to be."

"Oh, good grief! Don't think like that. Do us all a favor and forget who you are and try to be something you're not. Try to be human. Otherwise, everyone in the family will suffer. You'll suffer. Mum will suffer. So, will I if they find out what we are."

"Who?"

"The world. The cops. Whoever it is that cares."

"Don't be inane. You underestimate our bloodline. We're invisible when we aspire to be. We've never been caught. Benjamin Peadlebody was never captured! No one even knows we exist except for a few screenwriters and legend makers, describing our kind behind a velvet curtain as some breed of invisible phantoms, or ghosts. They have no idea what we are. And whatever they think we might be they're dead wrong. Dead wrong!"

He chuckled at his use of words. When sweat formed again on his forehead, he wiped his brow with his sleeve. "Besides, humans are too frightened of vampires to do anything about us. What would they do? Arrest us?" His face sobered, his confidence faded with the drop of his shoulders. "I've tried to be someone else ever since Rockford died. It's not working. It never works." Gerald pulled the end of his scarf out of his coat and daubed his face with it. "Oh, don't worry. I'm not going to feed on my only nephew."

"Are you sure?"

"Of course, I'm sure. I didn't mean to scare you just then. Sorry." He snickered to himself. "At least I still have the ability to terrorize."

Raymond glanced at the hands on his watch, pulling the wristband free from the hairs on end. "I've got to go. Don't follow me today, okay? Just stay away from the Charles Mueller Building today. Promise me?"

"I'm not going to be chasing any janitors, if that's what

you mean." "No. I mean stay away from the building. Stay away from downtown. Don't go anywhere I go. Go home and talk to my mother."

"But it's the first of October."

Raymond rolled his eyes and checked his watch again. "That it is."

"There, see? It's your birthday if I remember right."

"Birthdays don't mean anything anymore. Not at my age."

"Twenty-one, isn't it? That's a special age. A turning point for vampires, you know."

"You told me that before. But I'm not a vampire."

"Bah!" Gerald's face paled to a gaunt and deadly guise. He stared at Raymond as though something sinister budded in his mind. "That's not what you just told me. You said you were cold blooded. Which is it? Human or not?"

"I said my blood was as black as yours. I'm your kin but I'm not a vampire. Nor am I a werewolf, a warlock, a gorgon, or an elf. None of those."

"You're all those things. You're family, aren't you? Twenty-one years ago, you were born in a little shanty by the river. And I was there. Outside on the porch, but I was there. My brother and your mother, both vampires. One by birth, one by blood. What else could that make you?"

It was the rotten truth, though Mum never admitted to being one of 'them'. If Raymond denied being a vampire in front of his uncle, he'd have to fight his uncle off, a struggle he'd rather not have. Gerald was already over the edge with hunger and obsession. And he was still his uncle, his father's brother. Raymond could outrun Gerald Peadlebody, true. However, vampires are sneaky and active in the middle of the night. Who could trust one, even one so inept as Uncle Gerald? Raymond needed to sleep at night without worrying about being bitten by a relative.

He sighed, his shoulders sinking in surrender. "All right. I concede. I'm family. I'm what you say I am. Now please, just stay here today."

"I can't come with you?"

"No!" Raymond balked and rushed toward the door. "Stay here. Listen to the radio. Heck, grab my cards and play solitaire. I'll come home after work and then we can celebrate my birthday."

"Oh joy. How drab will my day be sitting here all alone?"

"Then go see Mum."

"I'd rather go with you."

"No! Never come to my work again Uncle. Please? This job means too much to me."

The last time Gerald Peadlebody had shown up at Raymond's work place he claimed his vacuum cleaner was broken. Even though Raymond insisted he could fix the machine at home, his uncle stayed. What a mistake that had been. Uncle Gerald had taken pleasure in scrutinizing his coworkers while waiting for the belt to be replaced. Most of Raymond's friends had dodged into the supply room, commenting on the man's peculiarities. A complete embarrassment for Raymond. When the janitor walked in unannounced, Gerald was on the poor soul like a wasp on a plum tree.

Raymond opened the door but stopped before he went outside. His uncle looked pathetic. Sickly. Anemic. Not only were his eyes pale, but his eye sockets were bluer than his irises. The only color on his face was the red of his nose, which he had been pinching to keep tears from flowing. Raymond felt bad for him. "You look awful, Uncle Gerald."

"I'm just hungry is all."

"Okay, we can fix that. Stay here. I'll call Mum and have her bring you tea. And tonic. When I get home, we'll have a party."

Gerald spit out a "Pfft' and sat on the couch. He pulled his scarf from around his neck and tossed it to the floor. "Don't send your mother. I don't want to see her, nor do I want to drink her tonic. Just go, go, let me collect my thoughts. You'll not see me until my flesh has got its color back, birthday or not. Now go!"

Gerald Takes a Stroll

Gerald pretended not to watch Raymond race out the door with his coat slung over his shoulder and his eyes on his watch. Once outside, Raymond was quite visible through the sheer lacey drapery that curtained the front window. The young man trotted down the driveway, clearly anxious about his tardiness. Gerald grunted and with a shudder, shook off the hungry thoughts that possessed him earlier. Sucking his nephew's blood would be sacrilege, a true disrespect to his grandfather's name. However, the boy should take life less seriously. Be more himself!

Raymond was the first and only person of the entire Peadlebody family who even had a job. What a fool. Why should a Peadlebody work? What could Raymond possibly buy that wasn't included in the estate? The family had become owners of a great deal of property in Mason County. Raymond had access to all of it, so there was no reason for him to get a job and buy a fixer-upper in a questionable neighborhood like this.

Gerald walked to the gold-framed mirror that hung at the corner of the hallway. Backlit by sunrays that shone through the picture window, he studied the image staring at him. With his shirt collar askew from having thrown off his scarf, and the top three buttons to his coat undone, his appearance lacked appeal. The only thing in place was his salt and pepper curls, which were plastered tightly against his head with two layers of hair gel.

He curled the ends of his mustache and lifted his double chin until the slight parting of his lips revealed his canine teeth.

Generations of coupling species with species, gorgon with elf, werewolf with vampire gave Gerald these hybrid tusks, pointed as sharp as a dog's tooth, and hard as the stone of the humans that accidentally looked into a gorgon's eyes. These were his pride, his heritage, and his legacy. He should use them for something besides cleaning his fingernails.

"It's time to get tough, Mr. Peadlebody."

The sunken eyes stared back at him, dull and unmotivated.

"Is it really food that you want? Or is there a more pressing matter? If my father were alive, I wouldn't be having this conversation with myself. Father would be teaching me to hunt. I'm ready now. I think."

As his mind filled with memories of his childhood, his eyes filled with tears and his vision blurred. He would frolic through the grassy fields with his brother, but when they came to the forest, he stopped. The edge of the meadow was as far as he'd go even when his dad called for him. He just couldn't bring himself to take that step into the dark. Rockford went every time. Gerald could still hear his father's voice when he'd hold up his prize, a rabbit, a cat, whatever they found. Gerald would stand wide-eyed, wishing he had gone with them.

"Shut your mouth, Gerry, you'll catch a fly!" And then his Benjamin would laugh or slap him on the back. "Come with us. There's nothing in these woods that will hurt you. Not my vampire boys!"

Rockford would come home, hot and sweaty, his shirt

unbuttoned, sometimes his pants rolled up to his knees from wading in the marshes, but full of energy. He relayed the day's adventure to Gerald—how much fun he and dad had, the tasty blood they feasted on. Rockford would demonstrate some of the jumps and lunges he learned.

Gerald watched quietly wishing he were Rockford, coveting Rockford's enthusiasm, admiring his brother's courage and mostly he envied the praise he received from their father. Those were the worst days for him because he'd be sick with regret. Even though Rockford begged Gerald to join them the next time, Gerald always refused. Why? Scared? Yes. And he lacked confidence. He hid in his room and made up six hundred and twenty-three excuses why he couldn't take part.

His father finally gave up. His brother enjoyed stalking and catching prey so much that he hunted for Gerald, too. Life was simple, and there was no need to change.

Except that Rockford died. And his father died too. Now neither his brother nor his father was here to help him.

Gerald's lips trembled and his heart grew black with an inner rage that had been bottled up inside. He spoke to the man in the mirror.

"Someone's lying to you, aren't they? Something brutal happened to Benjamin Peadlebody. Something or someone killed your dad, didn't they? And that being the case, they robbed you, Gerald!" Gerald pointed at his reflection. "You, Gerry boy, have got to do something about it! No one else is left to avenge your father." He scowled. "Prove yourself to your father and find the culprit."

The image nodded, prodded by the shaking of his head. Gerald adjusted his scarf one more time and left his reflection to its own musings, sealing Raymond's front door.

The air was fresh, and a bit of chill was in the breeze. A few maple leaves floated casually through the air, descending to their new home amongst the mud and mulch of lawns, street gutters, and sidewalk. Winter would come soon, and Gerald was glad of it. As much as he detested the sun, he was forced to linger in its rays until a more dismal and pleasing season.

Gerald could only imagine what poor grade of human blood lingered inside the homes in Raymond's neighborhood. Nor could he understand why the boy would want to live among humans. Unless Raymond were feeding, there was a certain danger in mingling with the species. Vampires had secrets. A vampire living in this middle-class neighborhood was akin to a wolf living in a chicken coop. Gerald laughed at the analogy.

"Ludicrous thought but true. I must say, Raymond lives in a very tasteless chicken coop at that!"

All the houses were fashioned alike, aside from their stucco walls, which had the color octave of foggy gray to mudflat brown. An occasional decoration on the garage door distinguished a few homes from the neighbors. However, if Gerald hadn't made a point of counting lawns beginning at the corner of Elm and 24th, and if his nephew didn't have his father's stone gargoyle in the garden, he'd never be able to tell where Raymond lived.

Gerald's soul searching in front of his nephew's mirror caused him to change his plans. Instead of following Raymond to the Charles Mueller Building, he took 24th Street to Mission Lane and headed to the probate lawyer's office. He had unfinished business with Madison T. Ferguson.

The lawyer's stopover to the estate had been quick, vague and discourteous. Granted, his nephew's attitude had some influence on the duration of the reading of the Will. Still, Ferguson had rushed the family through the processing of probate without answering one of Gerald's questions. Now that a month, four days, six hours and - he looked at his watch—thirty-six minutes had passed, it was time to reexamine his father's case. He would go to Ferguson and inquire anew.

Ferguson's office was a two-story house, painted sparkling white with shiny black trim around the windows and the porch banister. At the end of the walkway facing Mission Lane, a huge wooden sign, black on gold in curly font, heralded the lawyer's name. Gerald grunted. The front of the office was friendly and personal, giving the impression that Ferguson was everyone's favorite neighbor and best friend; a good marketing tactic if nothing more-and a lie!

Friendly and personable was not the impression Gerald had of the lawyer. Not once did Ferguson give the Peadlebody family a sympathetic word on the passing of a family member? Nor had he offered condolences at the funeral. In fact, since Ferguson was cold and impersonal to the Peadlebody's, why had he been placed in charge of his family's accounts at all?

Gerald held his knuckles to the door, about to knock when he thought better. This was a place of business, and the sign already welcomed him. He didn't need to knock. Gerald lifted his chin, twisted the knob, and pushed the door open with his shoulder.

"Yes?" a woman's voice shrieked in surprise.

"I'm sorry. Is this Madison T. Ferguson's office?"

"It is. Do you have an appointment?"

He recognized the woman once he stepped inside. The dark-haired secretary again! The pretty one. Gerald smiled and counted thirty-four years to her liking, no more and perhaps less. She wore glasses, but they framed her face nicely. Her dark hair was pulled up on her head in a bun again, just as it had been the day of the reading. The sight sent a burning sensation down his spine as he rested his gaze on her exposed neck. Exceptionally smooth and delicate, Gerald could see the veins under her skin.

"You're Mr. Peadlebody, aren't you?"

Gerald cleared his throat and wiped his brow with his scarf. "You remembered?"

"How could I forget? You're the man with the insolent nephew and the broken furniture."

Gerald flushed. "That's how you remember me?"

"I could go on, but I don't think you want me to. Your case was closed a month ago."

"Not a month. One month, four days, six hours and—" he looked at his watch, "— oh, I am sorry, seven hours and fourteen minutes."

She stared at him, her mouth cracked. He was tempted to say something about catching a fly, but he restrained himself and chuckled instead. "I just need some questions answered," he continued, choosing to ignore the glare in her eyes.

"What sort of questions?"

"About my father."

She smiled, but her grin was slanted and snarky. "You probably know more about your father than anyone else."

"I don't know how he died."

The woman's expression changed, inviting a stony silence into the room. She stood and reached in her desk drawer, for what Gerald didn't know. He watched her hands, but she didn't reveal whatever she fiddled with.

"We told you."

"What I mean is, did the hole get repaired?'"

"What hole?"

"The one that was made when the tree limb was struck by lightning and crashed through the roof and landed in my father's—" He cleared his throat again. It was an absurd thing to recount, much less to have happened. He licked his lips as they were becoming parched. No longer did the woman's neck attract him, it was what she was fidgeting with in the drawer that drew his focus.

"Mr. Ferguson gave a very accurate and complete report of your father's death."

"Yes, well he didn't show any of that report to me."

"It's available at the coroner's office."

Gerald held out his hands. "Where?"

"And you'll find all the information about your estate at the assessor's office, along with the title to your mansion and other probate documents that were submitted by Mr. Gainsworthy."

"Who's Mr. Gainsworthy?"

"The realtor."

"What realtor?"

"Look," she glanced down at her hands. Was she loading a gun? "I know who and what you Peadlebodys are. You should consider yourself fortunate to have Mr. Ferguson represent you. You have your house. If you're worried about its condition, I would suggest that you climb on top of your roof and see for yourself if the hole's been fixed."

Gerald took his turn to open his mouth, but no words were ready to come out.

"You may leave, Sir. Now."

"I just wanted to talk to Mr. Ferguson."

"I said now."

Gerald took a step to the door and slid outside.

He didn't know for sure if the receptionist was really reaching for a gun. He didn't know if Mr. Ferguson was in the building, or if anyone knew his father was a vampire. He certainly didn't know a Mr. Gainsworthy. Perhaps his own insecurities made the situation look much worse than it was.

Or not.

He'd been told that the only way a vampire could die was if a stake was driven through its heart. But what about a half-blood? What about someone whose mother was an elf? Could a bullet kill them? Gerald wasn't ready to die so he left, like the lady asked.

Raymond and Amber

Only one person was in the Gypsum Vacuum Repair office when Raymond arrived. Beverly Woods, a middle-aged woman who had worked with Gypsum Vacuum for 22 years. Beverly was the receptionist who greeted customers with a pasted smile as they came in and saluted them as they left. She was anything but anti-social. In fact, Raymond heard all about Beverly's three daughters and their tragic love affairs, Beverly's fatherless grandchildren, the family feuds between her and her in-laws, and the medical records of all her cats.

"Good morning!" Raymond walked past Beverly's desk and peeked through the double doors that opened to the shop. "Where is everyone?"

"You're late." Beverly didn't look up from her typewriter. She took another bite of apple, set it down, and returned the carriage.

"The street sweeper held up traffic. Bumper to bumper. I would have had to jump on cars to get across to get here on time. I didn't wear my jumping shoes." Raymond explained.

"Do I look like a timecard? What do I care? You're here. That's all that counts. Now, anyway."

"You know it's my birthday?"

"I know? But what do you want at eight-o-five in the morning?" Beverly spat apple peeling in the wastebasket by her knees, looked up at him and smiled. "Happy birthday."

"Thanks."

"Someone's even going to get you a cake later this afternoon so be patient and act surprised. Just remember this isn't a national holiday. Just another employee's birthday. K?"

Her grin pinched her cheeks where the dimples met her mouth. Raymond had never really examined Beverly's face before. She kept it sealed behind financial journals, primping mirrors, or her typewriter. This morning the sunlight from the hallway lit up her small brown eyes as they peeked out from curly brown mascara. Her pudgy cheeks were dusted with too much rouge. The mix of rose and bayberry reeked from her blouse as she shook the fabric to cool her overweight body, directing a scent of perspiration into the already overbearing fragrance.

Raymond coughed. "Yeah. K."

He pushed through the swinging doors and stepped into the back room where a pile of vacuum parts was strewn across his workbench. New tags tied to his schedule meant four hours of work and the shop wasn't even open yet. With slumped shoulders, he shoved his lunchbox into the fridge, took off his sweater and rolled up his sleeves.

The day was not turning out the way he expected. First, his very own uncle accosted him, and now a workload instead of a celebration. What else could go wrong?

The jingle of a bell announced the arrival of a customer. Raymond cracked open the door, dreading another order so early.

His heart palpitated when he saw the glowing face of his favorite human.

"Is Raymond around?" Amber asked.

"Raymond!" Beverly's voice pierced his ears. He was standing right behind her when she yelled. "Oops. That was fast! I didn't see you."

"Hello Amber." He locked eyes with her. Amber's perfume permeated the room and Raymond breathed in deeply. He hated perfume, but he loved Amber's fragrance. He hoped to get near enough that the scent would rub off on his shirt and perhaps he'd have a token of her presence to drown out the smell of dirty vacuum cleaners.

"Hello Raymond. I baked some cupcakes for your party and thought I'd drop them by this morning. I'm not sure if I can come later this afternoon."

"Oh?" Stunned, Raymond took a moment to process the rejection. "You can't? Sorry to hear that."

They stared at one another in an awkward silence. She held the cupcakes out, but he didn't take them. Instead, Raymond exhaled, debating whether Amber's perfume smelled more like vinegar.

Beverly cleared her throat.

"So," Raymond began, dreading asking and dreading the answer even more. "If you can't make it to the party, that doesn't mean we're off for tonight, does it? I mean, our walk home?"

Amber shifted her weight and glanced at Beverly for a split second.

Enough of a glance for Raymond to guess the answer.

"I'm sorry," she said.

Raymond's heart sunk into his bowels. That was the worst news ever. So much for a happy day, he might as well go home and call in sick.

"I'm not walking home tonight, after all. I have an early

dinner date tonight," she said, unashamed.

"You have a dinner date?" Beverly was quick to ask.

Raymond cringed.

Amber smiled when she answered Beverly. The two exchanged a twinkle in the eye that Raymond had thought belonged to him. "Tom Rutherford asked me out."

Beverly squealed with joy and Amber's excitement heightened as they talked.

So, it's not everyday Amber got to go on a date with the Sheriff's son, apparently. As Raymond listened, his insides turned upside down. He tried to ignore the wink of Amber's eye and the shrug of her shoulder, but the giggle made Raymond sick to his stomach.

And why wouldn't he be?

That was worse than the worst news he could ever hear on his twenty-first birthday. Raymond's attempted indifference to the announcement proved pitiful.

"Oh, well no sense in ruining your appetite with some silly birthday cake." He shrugged and rummaged through some paperwork on Beverly's desk. The receptionist slapped her hand on his and looked him in the eye. "I was actually thinking of going home early, too," Raymond told Beverly.

"You were?" Both Beverly and Amber chorused.

"I don't think you'll be done with your work early Raymond," the receptionist said with a scowl on her face. "There are some appointments coming in this afternoon with a rush tag."

"Oh! Well, I mean after work. Early after work."

Amber shrugged and handed him her gift without looking Raymond in the eyes——without a twinkle or a smile or any kind of signal that made him tickle inside. "In any case here are your cupcakes," she said.

"Thanks. I bet they're really good." He would never find out because, of course, he had no intention of eating them.

"I hope so. I'll try to stop in later if I can."

"Yeah, do that. If you can. If you aren't busy." he mumbled and waved after she left. With a thick silence and a broken heart, Raymond glared at Beverly.

Suddenly Beverly gasped and then exhaled a look of late wisdom on her face. He set the cupcakes on her desk.

"Oh, my heavens to Betsy! I get it!"

"Get what?"

"You know!" she winked.

Raymond put on the best façade he could- a scowl and a pout.

"What?"

"Oh, don't play naive." She pointed her finger at him and shook it. A grin beamed across her face. "You like her, don't you?" She clapped her hands.

Raymond stepped back.

Beverly appeared as though she would soon jump over the desk and pounce on him. "You two would make a hot item if Tom Rutherford doesn't snatch her first."

Raymond calmly slipped his hands in his pockets, though the thought of being hooked up with Amber made his heart race. "Right. Well, evidently Tom Rutherford already has snatched her. So, all I need to do is find a legal way to beat off the sheriff's son. So that's that!" He gave Beverly a curt smile. "I've been mulling around long enough. Time to get to work."

The old vacuum leaning against the wall would be his first victim. He grabbed the handle and dragged it through the double doors to his bench.

Unfortunately, Beverly didn't mind talking through the walls. Her voice became a machine gun, drilling holes into his gut. "I know that look on your face! There's enough drama going on in my house to not know lovesick when I see it."

He nearly stripped the screw head out of its socket before prying the canister loose. Gray dust puffed into his face as he removed the paper bag from its container. Still, Beverly's voice blared from the other room.

"How was she to know you like her if you don't say it? When you get that far in the dumps you need to speak up, Raymond. Don't hold it in. You'll just rot inside if you do. You wouldn't want rotten blood, now would you?"

He already had rotten blood. That's what he told his uncle this morning, and now his declaration was validated. Rotten blood can't mix with pristine blood like Amber's. Better to stew.

Soon as this work is done, Raymond will forget about being twenty-one years old and he'll go see his mum. She'll know what to do, what to tell him. Maybe she found the potion today, the magic that will change them both. Maybe the vampire curse will finally pass over him and he can turn into a human before his fangs grow back. Maybe any resemblance to his father or his uncle will disappear, and women will look at him like they do the sheriff's son.

"Whatever is bothering you, Raymond, stay strong. It's only one date that she's on with Tom, after all. Maybe she won't even like him. You just sweet talk her whenever you can and I bet she'll see you in a different light! You'll overcome this. Just be patient. I'm rooting for you!" Beverly laughed.

Overcome? What did it matter that he'd been raised in the backwoods along the river by a bloodthirsty father who imprisoned his mother with a bite and a curse? Maybe he can overcome his childhood and all the dark and dismal memories of never having friends, never playing baseball, or eating ice cream. Maybe. Not likely, though.

Raymond dissected the vacuum cleaner. The dark, empty shell reminded him of the coffin his father had been laid in. That white pasty face, the over pronounced nose. His dad had never looked more human than at his death. Raymond had almost thrown up when he saw his father lying in state. He was so not him!

Even his mother hated Rockford Peadlebody. If it weren't for his father, Raymond might already have found a girl. If it weren't for his father, Raymond wouldn't be a freak. If it weren't for his father, the sheriff's son wouldn't be a problem!

There was little hope. Amber must have read the tabloids headlines broadcasting that Rockford Peadlebody caused the train crash.

Eyewitnesses attested to his father's guilt.

Dust flew into his eyes as he pulled the bag from the canister. He coughed.

The stories were true. Raymond remembered his father mumbling something about being hungry and watched him leave the rail car they were in, open the door to the next car, and move on until he couldn't see him anymore. Shortly after that, maybe ten minutes, a loud screech filled his ears and people screamed. That's when the engine and three cars ahead of them derailed. The rest of that day was a blur. Mum made him stay where he was, and said he'd find out soon enough what happened. Somehow, she knew, just like he did.

Mum and Uncle Gerald and he had escaped without a scratch. His dad was dead, pierced in the heart by a slivered railroad tie. The newspapers reported that Rockford had robbed the conductor.

"Robbed!" Raymond snickered. "I guess you could call it robbery. Robbed his veins, no doubt."

Mum never said a word. Not to the police, or to the press except to have them take photos.

She wanted revenge, but all Raymond wanted was to be normal. He wanted to laugh and work and eat normal food like human beings. He was tired of squirrel blood, reheated from the cartons that were frozen in the fridge. He was tired of living in darkness. Of not having friends. Of not having a girlfriend.

He wanted someone to love. Really love. Not someone to crave for dinner. If he weren't a vampire, he might be able to pursue a relationship with a girl as beautiful as Amber.

His dream had almost come true. Until today, his birthday. Until Tom Rutherford, the sheriff's son, homed in on his prize. "It's not Tom's fault," he muttered. "It's just my fate."

Why even hope for a better life? His first romance was over before it began. Now all that was left was this broken vacuum clean.

Ginger's New Potion

Ginger slammed the cover of the book closed, blew out the candle, and leaned back in her chair with her eyes closed. A cool breeze blew in from the open window and passed over her cheeks, leaving the fragrance of new rain. She smiled. Living in a tree house wasn't so bad. She was close to nature; just like she had been in the bayou. She liked it here, much more than if she'd been living in that stuffy old manor with her cranky brother-in-law and the weirdo butler, Cottlebone. She enjoyed being alone too, not having to answer to anyone. Not having to answer to Rockford!

Her calm broke when the kettle overheated. Its rocking motion played a tap dance on the cast iron grate. With her book still on her lap, Ginger reached over and turned the burner off. "There!" Seeing it was too hot to drink, she pulled two ice cubes from the freezer and dropped them in the pan.

"One more cocktail of a bizarre combination of whatnots. I don't even remember what I put in it." She emptied the contents of a dirty cup into the sink and then poured her latest drink into the cup. "I don't know, Dusty."

No sooner was it in her mouth, it was back out again and all over the rest of the dirty dishes. "Oh, I hope this isn't the answer. It's putrid!"

Wiping her tongue with the hem of her apron, she then placed the pot back on the stove and turned the burner back on. "Maybe it's not done yet." Ginger sat and fingered through the pages of the tabletop edition of Witch's Concoctions.

"Where do people come up with these recipes?" she asked her chipmunk. "As much as I want to believe this stuff works, I wonder how many vampires rid themselves of the curse by sipping a rotten infusion. You'd think there'd be some reviews." She flipped to the index and skimmed the alphabetically arranged lists. Nothing under 'A' for assessment, nor 'R' for review.

"Seems odd no one wrote in to tell the author if it worked or not. Chance! Pure chance, I suppose. Unless—" She looked at her pet chipmunk. "Maybe they all died, the ones who drank this stuff."

Dusty gave her a curious tilt of his head. "Well, think of it this way. If it's so easy to turn a mortal person into an immortal beast, then why is it so hard to reverse the curse?"

Dusty cracked a nut and looked up at her with his beady black eyes, spinning the shell with his tiny fingers and nibbling the meat at the split.

"I envy you," she said. "Life's simple for you. Used to be for me too."

Ginger had made thirty-five trips to the library this last month. One hundred and thirty-two books on vampires, witches, brews, herbal remedies, and historical accounts of witchcraft. There were plenty of theories on the fountain of youth and looking for immortality, but she didn't want immortality. She had it. What she wanted was to be a person again. Sure, she could quit being a vampire if someone drove a stake through her heart, but she didn't want to die, not in this state! And she certainly didn't want to die and leave her precious son at the mercy of Gerald Peadlebody.

Raymond deserved better.

"So, what's the answer?"

The sun peeked through the window, casting a warm ray on her spider plants that curtained the sill. Long spindly branches swooped from out of their pots, over the shelf, teasing the sink with bundles of new buds sprouting the likeness of their mother. Not unlike the spindly course of her and her son's life. Oh, that Raymond would find a better rendering than what she offered!

The small brown chipmunk scurried onto the counter and sniffed the dirty cups, turning his nose up and baring his teeth at the smell. He flipped his stripped tail, sat up on his hind legs, and looked around. His quick movements, his bright eyes, and his constant chirp broke Ginger out of her melancholy.

"What? What are you trying to tell me?" Ginger sneered. "Never mind what's in those cups."

He rubbed his nose and moved along the sink ledge.

"I should be like you packing away food for winter. I should keep busy. Keep gathering what, though? Books from the library? I think I might've read them all, Dusty. I'm running out of genres. We've done mythology, Egyptian history, black magic, white magic. I even looked through some art books. Well!" She slapped her hands on her knees. "Library day! It's time to take these books back and try again."

She wiped her hands on her apron and gathered the volumes that were closest to her, stacking them in a pile on the table. Three books were still by her bedside, and one in the bathroom. The collection she had to take back today was exceptionally heavy. She had planned to leave early, at the break of dawn, so that she'd be walking in the day's cool before the sun was high.

"Got to go, Dusty. Take care of things for me." The chipmunk gnawed on an acorn he had found.

"What would you like from town? More acorns? I could stop at the oak tree by the park on my way home. That is if I don't have too many books with me on the way back."

Of course, the chipmunk didn't talk to her, but she kept her eyes on Dusty all the same. His toenails tapped against the chipped enamel as he landed in the basin and licked up droplets of tap water. Dusty was a fine-looking animal, furry, shiny coat. Healthy. Mortal.

Envious of his vitality, she could use his energy about now. She was exhausted having spent the entire night searching for a recipe and finally coming up with the infusion that she spat out all over the sink.

"Now I remember. St. John's Wort, Silver leaf, tonic water. A dash of red saffron and maple syrup. Must have been the St. John's Wort that tasted so bad."

She had hoped this would be the cocktail that would complete her transformation back to a human, but then, she had the same hope for all the mixtures she had brewed. So far, no success. How many magic infusions had she tried already? The most any of them had done for her was to give her an upset stomach. Vampirism was so complex, so dark, and so nasty.

Perhaps no one has ever returned.

She eyed the aluminum pot rocking on the stove as though some sleepy dragon were caught inside emitting puffs of anger in its captivity. Steam spewed out from under the lid threatening the flames that cradled the pan.

"Wait. That's not steam! It's smoke! Run Dusty!"

She jumped up. Dusty scurried to the door and nudged the screen open, but his toe got caught under the doorframe. Once Ginger freed him, the squealing chipmunk scrambled onto the porch railing and jumped into a tree, favoring his front foot. From there, he disappeared in the manor's direction.

Ginger rummaged through her cupboards, looking for a

potholder. Gagging and coughing as the room quickly filled up with smoke, she finally found her mitt.

"Keep calm, Ginger," she told herself as she walked carefully down the stairs with the smoldering saucepan. She placed the pot on the cobblestone walkway away from anything flammable and stepped back. Her eyes were still burning and so she wiped them with her apron and waved the putrid smell away from her face. There was no sense going back inside until the smoke cleared. She waited at the bottom of the stairs, breathing the fresh morning air until her eyes stopped burning and her tear ducts stopped leaking.

When all was calm, when Ginger's heart stopped racing and the sweet scent of the woods behind the manor returned, Ginger took in the morning's beauty. Clouds hung low. The tops of the maples were covered with blue mist. Moisture clung to Ginger's hair. So thick was the fog that it sealed in the silence. Only the sound of a bluebird could be heard. That and a muffled squeak of a tire.

A car?

Ginger flinched at the sound and searched for its source, not sure if the fumes from the concoction had scrambled her brain. Gerald had no car. Neither did Raymond. But sure as day, a bright shiny vehicle turned around in the manor's driveway.

One of the fanciest cars she ever laid eyes on made the loop around the driveway at a turtle's pace. Bright as a neon sign, chrome, and metallic shine against the forest backdrop, she was not mistaken. If she were close enough, she'd jot down the license plate number. Neither was there time to run up to the house and stop the car and inquire why it had come up a private road. All Ginger could do was stare at the chrome, the white walled tires, and the bright lights that stole its way through the fog.

Ferguson perhaps, but so early in the morning? She'd seen Ferguson's car. He had a blue hot rod. This wasn't a hot rod. This was a big car and the color of cream in coffee. Did Gerald know he had a visitor? How long had it been here? She didn't know the answer and she didn't like the intrusion of one iota.

Visitors were rare. Who would venture up the drive to a dilapidated old house? No one in Mason County! Not without an invitation or a specific purpose. Certainly not to sight-see. Neither she nor Gerald ever closed the old iron gate at the end of the driveway. There just had been no reason to.

"Well, that's going to change! It will be locked up from now on!" Ginger muttered as she watched the taillights fade into the fog. "The gall of those intruders!"

The Frog Prince

Ginger pushed the lever that opened the library door automatically while juggling a pile of books in her arms. Fully aware of the eyes that turned her way, she stumbled through the entry wondering if she had forgotten to wear lipstick.

"What the blazes does it matter? I didn't come here to impress these people," she mumbled in disgust. She dropped her heavy burden on the counter, creating a disturbance that turned heads at a nearby table. She scowled at the man and woman, daring them to complain. A librarian approached her.

"May I help you?"

"I certainly hope so," Ginger paused, out of breath, hot, and frustrated. The walk from the estate had been rough because of the heat, or the weight of the books, or maybe because she had inhaled so much smoke this morning. Perhaps the fatigue was due to the fact she had to stop twice on the way to pick up books that had fallen and landed all over the sidewalk. Bending and lifting had been way too much exercise for a lady her age. She fanned the neckline of her dress and waved air to her face. Once she gained her composure, she looked the librarian square in the face. It wasn't this young woman's fault, but Ginger couldn't hold back the angst.

"None of these books have any of the information that I'm looking for."

The librarian, a young lady in a pink tailored suit, painted fingernails, and a hairstyle that would have put Sandra Dee to shame, raised her eyebrow as she stacked the books neatly, turning each one right side up. She read the titles aloud, one by one, as she pulled the dated cards from the inside covers.

"Dark Magic and the Evil Thereof

Alchemy for Dummies

Infusions 101

Science and the Supernatural

Vampires and their Victims?" She looked up. Ginger shrugged.

"The Night of the Stalker."

When she had finished reading the titles, she gave Ginger a scowl.

"Just exactly what are you looking for?"

"Something simple."

"Simple?" the young lady repeated.

Ginger pushed the last four books toward the librarian with trembling hands. How does one explain her state of affairs without explaining her state of affairs?

"I need a magic book. Something simple."

"I see," the girl said as she stamped the index cards with 'returned,' and slipped them through a slot on the counter beside her. After she placed the pile of books on a cart, she turned and faced Ginger, folded her hands neatly in front of her and looked the woman in the eye. "Like what kind of magic? A fairy tale maybe? Fairy tales are simple."

"No fairies." Whereever would Ginger find a fairy? She needed a practical fix. If ingredients existed for transforming her and Raymond back into human form, they would have to be readily available and she'd have to be able to forage for them.

"Snow White and the Seven Dwarfs? There's magic in that story."

"No dwarves." Same problem. She might be able to find one dwarf, but seven? And what would she do with them once she found them?

"Okay, well, have you read The Frog Prince?"

"No. I don't read much."

The librarian eyed the pile of books on the cart that Ginger had just brought in. "No?" She peered at Ginger and did not wait for an answer. "I see. Well, I think you will like the story of The Frog Prince. It's an entertaining story. The only fairy that is mentioned is introduced at the beginning and she soon disappears. Her character has very little to do with the story after that. The important characters are a princess and a frog."

"Frogs? Yes! Frogs would be feasible." There are ponds everywhere, even in Madison Park, which is on the way home. Finding frogs would be easy. There are bullfrogs in the marsh around the pond. And the park has other kinds of frogs too. All sizes. Ginger had lots of experience frogging from her time living along the river. "Do you know what kind of frogs they're talking about in this story?"

The librarian shrugged her shoulders and looked deep into Ginger's eyes. "You know, I never really thought about what species the frog prince is. But honestly, I don't think it matters."

"That's encouraging. That gives me a good selection to choose from. So, what does the frog do in this story? What's his role?"

"The frog has a deep desire to turn into the prince that he once was."

"Oh, my goodness! That's perfect. Does he?"

83

"Do you want me to tell you the ending?"

"Yes! Please! Tell me how it ends."

For some reason, the girl was hesitant, but she kept a steady eye on Ginger. Leaning over the counter as if to tell a secret, and with a slow and drawn out voice, the girl spoke. "The frog turns into the most handsome prince any woman in the world would want to marry."

Ginger leaned opposite her, swallowing all that the girl had to say. Their faces almost touched they were so close. "A prince? Hence, The Frog Prince?"

The librarian winked and nodded. "You got it!"

"This is remarkable! For real? He turns from a frog into a prince?" This would be perfect for Raymond! It might even work for herself. "I need that book."

"Very well." The girl tossed her hair over her shoulder and stood upright. She walked around the counter, and taking Ginger by the arm, she guided her to the children's section. "Honestly I think this will be a much better read for you than those dark and disturbing books you just returned. It might bring some light into your life. And there are pictures in all of the editions as well."

The librarian pointed to where the different renditions of The Frog Prince were shelved. "There you go."

"There are so many!"

"Yes, well the story's been rewritten many times. Not all of them are the same, so you get to pick and choose which one you like best." She smiled sweetly.

"They aren't all the same stories?"

That complicated things. How would Ginger be able to figure out which one held the magic she was looking for? She turned to face the librarian, anxious. "I want to do this right, you know."

The girl smiled and winked. "They all have the same ending. You'll be fine."

Ginger grabbed every edition the library had and carried the books to the counter, salivating with delight.

The Frog Prince books were not nearly as large as the magic and alchemy books Ginger had carried down the hill from the manor. They were, after all, children's books, so they were made for small arms and miniature hands, a simple burden for the trip back up the hill. Simple was exactly what she had asked for. Because they were not a heavy burden, Ginger purposely took the long route home, turning on the street that passed the park. The day was so pleasant she wandered into the gardens and sat on a bench to read, and listen for a frog that might pipe in the reeds by the pond. She wouldn't try catching it in broad daylight, but she would do some spotting, which would make frogging much easier at night when the park was void of people and she had a flashlight in her hand.

Ginger opened each of the six books one at a time and looked for a publication date. Her intent was to read the oldest work first. That way, the original story would be infused in her brain, and she wouldn't lose track of the magic. Spells worked better when drawn from the source.

"So, we have a princess that doesn't like the frog, but he helps her get her bouncy ball out of the pond he lives in, in return for spending the night at her house. And when she shows him kindness, like letting him eat dinner with them and then what? Letting him sleep in her bed? As suggested by her father the king? That's what makes the frog turn into a prince?"

Ginger flipped back to the title page and read the author's name. "Brothers Grimm. I think I've read some of their stories. Not sure this one makes all that much sense but it's worth a shot. Being nice, give the frog a place to stay, some food." She scratched her chin. They eat bugs, I could catch some bugs I suppose. "I'd doubt they'd want squirrel blood. A warm house, I have that. They could sleep in the bathtub. I'm not so sure about having them sleep in my

85

bed. They're kind of slimy."

Ginger flipped through the book again, making careful note of the delicately drawn images on the pages, and then set the book down, leaned back on the bench, and closed her eyes.

Sunlight warmed her cheeks, the air so fresh and fragrant that Ginger fell asleep dreaming of frogs bouncing balls across the lawn in a game of foursquare. What fun they had, until the balls bounced harder and grew in size and then bounced on the heads of the other poor frogs, smashing them against the walkway. Her dream turned into a nightmare. She woke up screaming, "Stop!"

An elderly man and woman passed by and glanced at her. She stared back. Once they moved on, she gathered the books in her arms, and continued her journey home.

"When you dream about magic spells, it must mean something! I think I have us a winner."

Talk about love

"You're still here? I thought you went home." Gerald was the last person Raymond wanted to see and yet there he was sprawled over his couch, staring at the ceiling. Raymond tossed his coat on the arm of the easy chair across from Gerald.

"Were you aware there are six-hundred-and-twenty-two ceiling tiles hanging over you when you sit in this room? And you have a cobweb that stretches from that corner of your curtain all the way over—" Gerald pointed from the window to the archway that led into the kitchen. "—to there!"

"Why are you still here?"

"You told me to stay."

"It was a suggestion. You could have left. In fact, the way the day has been going it's probably better if you do." Raymond pulled his vest off and tossed it over his coat, loosened his tie and curled his hair behind his ear.

All Raymond wanted to do was sit and mope, but Gerald was in his space. He paced in front of his uncle, irritated.

Gerald pulled himself to a sitting position, landing his feet solidly on the floor. "Nonsense. It's your birthday."

"Big deal."

"And why aren't you excited? Life is opening its doors for you, Raymond! This is the year of change for you."

Raymond fell on the couch next to his uncle, yanked the overstuffed pillow from behind his back, and threw it on the floor. "Things aren't going well with Amber."

As soon as those words left his lips, he wished he could retract them. Did he really want to confide in his uncle about Amber? He examined Gerald from the corner of his eye, relieved the man was toying with his scarf as though he hadn't detected Raymond's despair, nor heard what he said.

Gerald huffed a laugh. "Things didn't go so well with the damsel I met today either."

"You? What damsel?'

Gerald shrugged. His face turned red. Raymond raised an eyebrow. "What? You couldn't catch yourself some dinner?"

"Well," Gerald brushed the wrinkle from his jacket and pulled off his scarf. "I didn't go there with the intention of having anything to eat, per se. Although I have to admit I was tempted." He sighed as he straightened the wool wrap by laying it on his knee and running his hand along the fold. "She had the most scrumptious looking veins, but I contained myself."

"Well, I'm proud of you, Uncle."

"Yes, well that wasn't the reason I went there."

"And where did you go?"

"Madison T. Ferguson's office. The lawyer that handled your grandfather's probate case."

"Why did you go there?"

"Information, dear Raymond. There are circumstances concerning your grandfather's death that I feel compelled to unravel."

"Oh?"

"I think Mr. Ferguson knows more about what happened than he's letting on."

"Did you learn anything?"

Gerald chuckled. "Oh yes! I learned the secretary probably has a gun in her drawer."

"Was that the same woman that came to your house to help Ferguson read the will?"

"The very one."

"I didn't like her." Raymond pulled himself up from his slouch and leaned toward his uncle. Gerald sucked in his lower lip, the tips of his fangs glistened in the ambient light. Raymond stared intently at his uncle's fingers as Gerald twiddled at the threads in his scarf. Red and blue yarn bouncing back and forth, mesmerizing Raymond until what his uncle said caught hold.

"Wait! She pulled a gun on you?"

"Well, almost. I think. Also, it occurs to me our secret is out. That woman, and Ferguson I suppose, knows that we are vampires. It's an assumption, but it's a valid assumption. Otherwise, why would she assault me?"

Raymond considered Gerald's accusation and corrected him. "On the contrary, they know you are a vampire. You, uncle. Not me. They know what your father was. What my father was. They don't know anything about me."

Gerald patted him on the knee, a condescending gesture that Raymond resented. "Keep telling yourself that, Raymond. You're guilty by association. By birth in fact. If Ferguson knew that my father was a vampire, I'm wondering who else knows. Why, everyone in this county could know! What might they do about it? My guess is we have enemies, Raymond. Cruel and wicked enemies. As a matter of fact, I don't buy the story of my father's death. I think he had an adversary. I think he was murdered."

Raymond leaned back again and stared out the picture window at the neighborhood he called home. The sun had disappeared behind a cloud, creating a premature darkness just before twilight. A bicyclist pedaled on the sidewalk across the street and a woman checked her mailbox before jogging back to her house. Signs of a simple, very human life. Raymond sighed. Would he ever be able to blend in? "The manner of grandfather's death did sound contrived, didn't it?"

"If someone killed him, they very well could mean to kill us."

That was a disturbing thought, but Uncle Gerald could be right. "Mum too?"

"I'm just speculating."

"Maybe Mum should come live with me. She'd be safer here."

"She's happy where she's at."

"Happy and vulnerable."

"Raymond, I am merely telling you that we need to find out how Benjamin Peadlebody died."

"What if it were a storm? What if a tree limb did fall through the roof? Wouldn't it make more sense to find out if that happened first rather than accusing a lawyer of murder?" Sometimes Gerald was naïve to the world. "Fighting a lawyer in court would be ludicrous."

"I did. On my way home from the Ferguson's I stopped at the newspaper office and requested a back issue of The Daily Press. You can read for yourself. It's the issue that was released the morning after my father died." He nodded at the pile of newspapers on the coffee table.

Raymond turned the pages to the headlines and shook his head. "Are you sure this is the right issue? There's nothing about a Peadlebody death."

"No, there isn't. With the fuss they made over Rockford, surely father's death would have been in the headlines, but it wasn't. The media made no mention. I'm assuming that's because he died after that issue came out. However, because I had the same thought you have, I checked the weather. Go ahead. Find the weather report and read it."

Puzzled, Raymond thumbed through the news until he came to the statistics under the colored image of a map of Mason County. "Weekly forecast. Clear skies, slightly windy, temperature 55 degrees." Raymond paused and looked at his uncle.

"Go on."

"Chance of precipitation, none."

"You see?"

"What?"

"Good grief, Raymond are you blind? There were no storms that day, nor the day before, nor the day after!"

"No storms?" The puzzle was coming together.

"No storms and no lightning," Gerald added.

"No lightning and no fallen tree? No hole in the roof, no branch piercing grandfather's heart?"

"Exactly."

Raymond thought. "He was murdered? Then your presumption is right?"

"Well, I'm not sure if this proves anything but I'm going to investigate." Gerald jumped from the couch, fixed the scarf around his neck again, and buttoned his coat. "Walk with me."

"Where to?"

"Does it matter? Let's just walk."

Raymond slipped on his vest again and threw his coat over his shoulder. He followed his uncle out the door toward Pine Street. The setting sun had peeked from under the clouds just in time to touch the horizon with a golden hue. Maple leaves floated along the quiet sidewalk at their feet. The air smelled crisp even though the breeze was warm.

"Tell me about your day. Why didn't things go well for you?" Uncle Gerald rested his hand on Raymond's shoulder with an unusually friendly pat.

"My day? You want to know about my day?" Raymond scratched his head, not sure where to start, or what he wanted his uncle to know.

The temperature fell once the sun sank beyond the horizon, so he put on his coat, pondering his uncle's request. Never once had he spoken man-to-man with his Uncle Gerald. Maybe he should, especially now that Gerald was inviting him to probe into the mystery of his grandfather's death. Maybe they needed to bond. Maybe if they were close, they could see each other better through their traumas. Maybe Raymond wouldn't hate Uncle Gerald so much. This could be a good thing. It might make life easier for the both of them.

"I really like Amber," Raymond began.

"Ah yes, the temptress. Say no more. I've got those same urges. Especially the ones that wear their hair up, their long pale neck pulsating with fresh rich veins."

"No, Uncle. Stop that! I don't see Amber like that."

"Nonsense. How else would you see her?"

"Like a person."

"That's what I mean."

"Never mind! There's no sense in talking to you." Raymond kicked at the sidewalk, scooting a stone into the street. "You'll always think like a vampire."

"I am a vampire."

"So, you'll never understand how I feel." Raymond sealed his lips along with the anger that boiled inside.

"Actually, that's why I wanted to talk. I'll try harder not

to interrupt. Go ahead. Tell me." Gerald led Raymond through the arched hedge that gated Madison Park. When they reached a quiet corner away from the light of the streetlamp, Gerald lowered himself onto a bench and patted the seat next to him.

Raymond hesitated to sit down. "What are we doing here?"

"We're going to work on our relationship. I've been thinking about things lately."

"Things like what?"

"Our family's predicament, about my father and yours and what ill fate has befallen them. I want to understand the human part of you, and what better place for a man-to-man than on a park bench, amidst the beauty of nature. Trees, flowers, a handsome fountain." He pointed to a statue of a woman pouring water from a pitcher into the pond.

Raymond had seen the statue many times before and never thought about her, but in the evening light, as the sun painted the clouds and the earth absorbed the colors, the statue took on a radiance. Her smooth alabaster skin, the soft look in her eyes and graceful posture, the dimple in her chin.

Tonight, the statue looked like Amber.

"A perfect setting to get to know my favorite nephew."

Raymond gave him a leery eye as Gerald patted the seat again.

"C'mon. Sit with me."

Raymond relented. How could he stay angry with Uncle Gerald? He took a place on the bench and listened to the babbling of the water that poured from the statue's vessel, the quiet chirping of frogs and a mourning dove cooing in a tree some distance from them.

"Raymond, my brother's son," Gerald sighed the words. "I sat in your house all day today thinking about you, my father, and the gun that was almost pulled on me. For a split second, I realized how vulnerable I really am. If I were shot, I could die."

"You could?"

"It's possible. My grandmother wasn't a vampire. She wasn't human either."

"What was she?"

"Some sort of elf. Who knows if a bullet could kill an elf? Or a half-blood."

"She was Dad's mother too?"

"Yes."

"So, I have even less vampire in me than I thought?"

"Yes, I suppose. The point is though, I had an opportunity to contemplate my possible mortality all because of how quickly that secretary in Ferguson's office reacted. I presume the woman was driven by fear. They say humans are deathly afraid of vampires."

"They have reason to be."

"Yes. Well, I thought I should try to understand the way human beings think. A revelation of such might reveal some clues as to how my father died."

"You're pretty sure he was murdered then."

"I am. And you can help me understand the motive."

"What makes you think a human killed him? Why not one of the cousins? Or some other creature?"

"There are far more humans who would have reason to kill a vampire than one of his own kind, I would think. Look at you! You, being partially human, have anxieties toward your family that I've yet to understand. If I could grasp your hostilities, it could well open up a door to the murderer's motive."

"And once there's a motive there's a suspect?"

"Exactly. So, tell me why you're so hostile toward your family."

"Really? I can just blurt out all the things I hate about my dad?" Raymond asked, amazed that Gerald would even want to know.

"I'm listening."

"That might make me look like a murderer."

"True. But you're not. Don't worry. I won't suspect you." Gerald gave him a patronizing grin.

"Well that's good to know."

"Although, you were on the same train as my brother when he died," his voice trailed.

Raymond sneered. "Really, Uncle? Could I have driven a railroad tie through my father's heart?"

"Not likely, you're right. On the other hand, I find it extremely odd that my father would die just before his eldest son, the heir, dies."

"Yes, I thought that kind of strange as well."

"So, it's obvious you didn't kill Benjamin Peadlebody."

"Gee thanks for letting me off the hook." Raymond leaned back on the bench and folded his arms across his chest.

"Not so obvious you didn't kill your father."

"What?"

Gerald patted Raymond's knee again, but Raymond pulled away.

"I'm just teasing you. Rockford gave you everything you could possibly have needed. And we were all on our way to live at the manor. So, money would not have been a motivation for murder."

"I didn't kill anyone."

"I know. The motive could have been revenge, or hate."

"Uncle Gerald, I didn't kill anyone."

"It's all right. I know."

"Then quit thinking up motives that I might have had."

"It's just the way my mind filters information."

"You have issues, Uncle Gerald." Raymond shifted his weight. "Living with grandpa was not something I ever wanted to do, anyway. Neither did I want to live in that dilapidated manor."

"What did you want to do?"

"Live a normal life. I want to forget about being related to my father, or you. I want to marry and have kids that are human, and live in an average neighborhood. I don't want grandpa's stuff, or his reputation."

"His stuff? I never thought about his belongings. That's not something vampires think about. They mostly think about food."

"Didn't you say the house was worth a lot of money?"

"I did. It is." Gerald scratched his chin and looked off into the distance.

"Don't you see? I wanted to get to know Amber better. As a person. As someone I could care for. I thought maybe she's the girl, the one I could live with for as long as my mortal life lasts." Raymond accented the word mortal, catching his uncle's attention.

"Mortal? That word has a new meaning to me. Tell me about this mortal, this girl."

"Amber?" Raymond lifted his chin to the wind and breathed deeply. The sun had set, the evening settled quietly around them. The scent of rose was in the air; the same sweet fragrance he had sensed on Amber that morning. Just as he was about to tell Gerald how beautiful she was, two people strolled into the park, arm, and arm. It wasn't until the light of the streetlamp shone on her face that Raymond recognized her. Amber and her friend Tom Rutherford. Raymond's heart skipped a beat, fluttered, and then stopped for a full second. Heat flushed into his face and rage steamed inside his gut so fiercely that when he dug his nails into his palms, he drew blood. How could a woman do that to him? It was as if a sword pierced his heart.

Beautiful Amber stood under the streetlamp, hand in hand with the sheriff's son. She smiled up at Tom as though he meant the world to her. So overwhelmed with jealousy, he didn't notice his uncle whip out a hankie from his pocket and throw the cloth over Raymond's fist, wiping the spot of blood from his fingers. Raymond glanced Gerald's way and cringed. As if the night couldn't get any worse, there was his Uncle Gerald with the hankie in his mouth, sucking like a baby on a bottle.

Raymond jumped up and heaved his uncle off the bench by his coat collar. The heat of his anger escaped through clenched teeth. "Get out of here, you leech!"

His voice must have carried on the breeze, because when he looked over his shoulder, Amber was staring at him. Raymond shuffled his uncle through the archway, behind the verge and down the street far from Madison Park.

Secret Findings

Gerald wasn't accustomed to being escorted home, and never in all his life had he been dragged. Raymond's strength surprised him. Who would have thought that the young man whose coats hang off his shoulders and whose pants fall below his waist without a tightly strapped belt, or a pair of suspenders, carried so much muscle power? Or was it that his own physical fortitude had been an illusion? Maybe Ginger was right, after all. Maybe he was starving.

Raymond lugged Gerald all the way to the Peadlebody gate, giving him no rest whatsoever.

"I don't see why you are pushing your weight around like this, Nephew. Is it because I tasted your blood?"

"Heaven's no, Uncle. Why would a fool thing like sucking my blood in public bother me?"

"Then why in the name of Dracula are you manhandling me?"

"Why? Because you made a fool of me in front of the girl I love. And you're repulsive!" Raymond let go of Gerald's now crumpled collar and the threads of his woolen scarf, but not without a final push. "Go inside the house and stay there. Drink the potions that Mum makes for you. Leave me alone."

Gerald caught his balance, adjusted his scarf and wiped his coat sleeve free of the wrinkles that Raymond had created. He drew in his breath and took a long look at his nephew. Raymond was the spitting image of his brother, exactly as he had remembered Rockford years ago on the day they left the manor for Louisiana. If this weren't Déjà vu, he didn't know what was. Pity this encounter was so hostile, standing under a darkened sky, breathing in the fragrance of musky soil and evergreen, facing each other at the end of the Peadlebody driveway both angry, both disheveled. "I was merely trying to bond with you."

"Bond? That's what you call bonding?"

"By 'that' if you mean what I did with my hankie, I was merely mending your wound."

"You were sucking my blood!"

"Not literally."

"Yes, literally!" Raymond rolled his eyes and turned to walk away. "You are sickening."

"You were the one that wanted to talk about your girlfriend."

Raymond stopped and glared at him. If Gerald hadn't known better, he would have sworn a bit of his father's high-strung temper possessed the boy. "She's not my girlfriend. If she were I wouldn't be standing here with you. I'd be with her. I'll tell you one thing though, if she ever is my girlfriend, I'm not bringing her anywhere near you."

Gerald huffed with indignation. "That's the thanks I get? For all I've done for you?"

"What have you done for me?"

Gerald snickered in disbelief. "I've offered you a home! One that you've been too stuck up to accept. That's what!"

Raymond spent a brief moment sighing, looking away, and sighing again and all the while Gerald stared at him. Youth these days are ungrateful and Raymond proved himself among the worse.

Gerald had never really observed his nephew, before. He had always seen him as his brother's child, a package of energy that was more of a bother than an asset. If it weren't for the fact that Raymond had the same handsome features his brother had, which kept the memory of Rockford alive, Gerald may have tried a long time ago to persuade his brother and Ginger to give the rug rat up for adoption.

"Thank you." Raymond finally looked him in the eye, though fire spat from his. "Thank you for dragging us to your father's estate and giving Mum a tree house to live in."

"She could have had the upstairs. She didn't want it. She has the same snobbish attitude that you do. She can live in the house. You can too."

"I don't want to live in your ghost ridden shanty. I want to live far away from you. Far away. If it weren't for Mum, you would never see me again. Ever!"

Again, human hostility played favor in Raymond's voice. This could be the moment of reckoning! If Gerald uses his cunning correctly, he could get Raymond to spit out the reason for that anger. What a revelation of human reasoning that would be! The exact ingredient to understanding, perhaps, why his father was murdered, and who may have murdered him.

That is, providing his father was murdered by a human.

Gerald lifted his chin and fuzzy goatee, pointing them at Raymond. His nostrils flared as he inhaled. "Very well, I understand that you don't want to live with the Peadlebodys. Why not?" he said bluntly, hoping for an equally candid response.

Raymond contorted his face in a ferocious squint, his teeth barred and with a hiss, he blurted, "Because you suck! Literally!"

With a puff of anger so furious that Gerald thought he saw smoke, his nephew pivoted on his heels and left him standing alone in front of the wrought-iron gate, somewhat bewildered, just as the first stars of the night speckled the ebon sky.

Gerald's ears rang with echoes of Raymond's rejection. Not only had he failed to get an intelligent answer out of Raymond, one that might give him some clues to a murder motive, but he seemed to have flared the boy's anger. For the first time in his life, Gerald felt remorse over the relationship, or lack of. The confrontation had been fruitless at best, devastating at worst.

If Gerald's eyes had not been opened wide, and his senses alert, he would have walked straight into the gate that spanned across the drive. Odd that this ornate piece of ironwork, which had stood off to the side as a decorated escort to the estate, now sealed its entrance. Gerald fumbled with the combination lock for a moment before he realized his thin stature could squeeze in between the rails. Once on the other side, he dusted his coat and began his trek up the driveway.

A dark and lonely trek, Gerald mused over what had happened, and wondered if he should tell Ginger. Her light was not on, however, and neither did the manor's porch light shine. Cottlebone either thought Gerald had come home already, or he was preoccupied in the kitchen, or asleep.

Not that Gerald cared about light. Being nocturnal by nature, he could see well in the dark. In fact, the dark to him meant that the world was at peace. Moonlight danced on the broadleaf shrubbery along the driveway, stones under his feet glowed gray and blue and the dark of the shadows they were cradled in bolstered his weary heart. However, having been humiliated by his nephew earlier, a 'welcome home' would have satisfied the elf blood in him.

Still overwhelmed with questions about his father's death, Gerald stepped onto the porch and opened the front door. He hadn't set foot inside the house when a light came on in the parlor and Mr. Cottlebone was by his side.

"I'm sorry, sir I thought you were in the den all this time." The servant took Gerald's coat and scarf, bowing slightly. "My apologies. Would you care for tea, sir? To calm your spirits? They do need calming, do they not?"

Gerald awed at the servant's perception. "Am I wearing my emotions on my sleeve like you wear your tattoos on your neck?"

Cottlebone hooked the coat over the coat rack and placed the hat above it. "Sir, you forget who trained me."

"Ah yes, my aristocrat father who knew all the ins and outs of rearing servants."

"Indeed."

"Yes, I could try some tea. Though tea scarcely satisfies the hunger I feel right now." Gerald eyed the tattoo that peeked out from under Cottlebone's collar, knowing that an even larger cross was tattooed on his chest. He wondered if his father forced those tattoos to be etched on Cottlebone to protect his servant from other vampires? Or had the servant come to Benjamin's service with the tattoos already? Or did Cottlebone discover his father was a vampire and had the tattoos made to protect himself? Whatever the reason, there was nothing Richard Cottlebone could do to appease Gerald's hunger for human blood. Gerald would never make the mistake of trying to overcome the servant again.

"Coming right up, sir."

"Richard?"

The servant turned.

"Why was the gate closed?"

"It's Madame Ginger, sir. She told me to keep it closed from now on."

"Ginger did? Why on earth?"

"I'm sure she'll tell you, sir." Cottlebone didn't stay to

explain but moved quickly to the kitchen in answer to a whistling teakettle.

"Odd." Gerald stepped farther into the parlor and surveyed the house with fresh eyes, eyes that might see as Raymond sees. Eyes that might wish his father ill. Dark maple wainscoting. Mirrors covered the paisley wallpaper, a cobweb coated chandelier, a few ornately framed portraits above the antique furniture, and an assortment of rare and unusual clocks on shelves, the mantel, and the curio, each timepiece stretching its delicate hands to different hours of the day. Once Gerald's heart slowed, he heard the clocks ticking, though not in unison. So much clatter filled the room that it was a miracle he hadn't gone crazy. Or maybe he had.

When Cottlebone returned with a cup filled with tea, he looked puzzled. "Sir, will you be in the parlor or at the table?"

"I need some answers, Richard."

Cottlebone cleared his throat, turned and walked to the table, setting the cup and saucer down. "I'm afraid I have none."

"Who does?"

"Your father."

"Explain yourself." Gerald had no time for riddles. His patience had already been tried by Raymond.

"I believe all your answers are written in his journals."

"Which are where?"

"In the basement."

"And is the entry to the basement locked, Cottlebone?"

"Yes, sir, but I can unlock it if you wish."

"Do so, then. Please." Gerald swallowed his tea in one gulp, forgetting that it was human food and not his own. Immediately, his reflexes tried to expel the liquid and he raced to the sink, releasing the foreign fluid. Cottlebone was by his side with a linen napkin and Gerald wiped his mouth.

Gerald looked up and when he did, their eyes locked. For

a moment, Gerald wanted to slap the servant. The tea had been Cottlebone's idea. He knew what it would do to him and yet he stood by his side waiting with a napkin, cold as steel.

"Unlock the basement. I have some research to do." Gerald tossed the napkin in the sink and followed the servant down the spiral stairs through a damp hallway. Cement walls surrounded them; walls which tapered off into foundation pillars and in some places, bare earth.

Aside from the few nightlights glowing at their feet, the cellar was dark and damp. A haunting atmosphere like this never bothered Gerald; in fact, he relished the mysterious quality of underground passageways and savored the dungeon-like ambiance. Raymond had once remarked how creepy the staircase was and turned his nose up at even descending the stairs. His loss, Gerald thought. Many a treasure lay underground. This basement was no exception.

When they came to the library entrance, Gerald waited as Cottlebone slipped the key into the lock and pushed the door open. A gust of dry, warm air met him. The library was heated by ducts above, preserving the precious books and manuscripts within.

"This is amazing!" Gerald had never been in the library before. He had only heard of its existence from his brother. The magnitude of the room alone was surprising.

"Your father had been, among other things, an avid reader. He collected books from all over the world on every subject." Cottlebone walked through the maze in front of Gerald, switching lights on as they roamed. "Novels, history, his interests embraced every genre written."

"I didn't know he was so well read."

Cottlebone laughed. "He read quickly, and he read everything. Fantasy, historical fiction, but his favorite genre was the study of human beings."

"That would make sense I guess, being as he fed on them.

Do you mean physiology?"

"No, no, he read some physiology and some psychology. However, he was interested in specific people. Anyone in the state of Ohio with a documented biography is represented in this room."

Cottlebone led him back to the entry where a small roll-top desk was nestled against the wall. "This library was also the site where Benjamin Peadlebody wrote seventeen volumes documenting his own life. He wrote right there at that desk, by hand. He never used a typewriter, not until he married again."

"Seventeen? I can't imagine having that much to say about myself."

"You forget, sir, your father was ageless."

Cottlebone knows much about his father, and yet he has no specifics to share? Gerald found the servant's manner both suspicious and frightening. The servant must have read his thoughts, for Cottlebone went on to explain.

"Maybe you didn't think I knew that your father was a full-blooded vampire, but I assure you, it would be impossible to live with him and not know, nor to cater to his needs."

"What needs?" That sparked Gerald's interest. Once again, he suspected that Benjamin fed on Cottlebone. The servant stiffened. Gerald waved the thought away. "Never mind. You don't want to talk about it."

"We had an agreement, you and I."

"Yes, we did. So, we'll forget about my father's 'needs'. Tell me instead what he was like."

Cottlebone laughed and crossed his arms over his chest. He shook his head, clearly lost for words. "You want to know what your father was like?

"You're his son. You should know."

"I knew him as a boy. That was a long time ago and my father didn't like me very much. Please just answer my questions."

"There are some things I wouldn't want to tell you and that's why I suggest you read his books. He wrote them for his sons. It's not my place to hold back what he wanted you to know."

Gerald resented Cottlebone's attitude. "All these books? That's a lot of reading."

"You have time." Cottlebone's answer was too quick. Gerald felt as though the man was testing him. Maybe he was questioning his mortality.

"I'll read. But at the moment I prefer to know what others thought of him, such as yourself?"

Cottlebone took a moment to clear his throat, his arms still crossed, but he relaxed as he spoke as if remembering his father gave him a certain comfort.

"Benjamin Peadlebody was a master at life and a maestro at death. Never once did he disrespect his victims. He studied them, their genealogy, their attributes, their weaknesses and strengths, before he took them on. Once the initial contact was made, they came to him. They would ask him to, well, to take them."

When Gerald didn't respond for quite a long time, but rather stared into the servant's rather pale eyes, Cottlebone coughed politely. Gerald shook his head in bewilderment. What Cottlebone had just described was not how he remembered his brother's method of hunting. Rockford never premeditated his moves, nor did he know who he'd prey on before sneaking up on the poor souls. Certainly none of his subjects asked Rockford to 'take them'. And yet Rockford had been trained by his father.

"I find that hard to believe." Gerald finally said.

"Why is that?"

"Well because I have other recollections of him."

Cottlebone shrugged off his response. "Is there something else I can help you with, Mr. Peadlebody?" the servant asked. "I've read many of these books myself and I have a photographic memory.

I know which book would have the answer to any of your questions."

Regarding the number of books on the hundreds of shelves, and the size of the bookshelves stretching across the entire perimeter of the vault, Gerald liked the idea of using Cottlebone as a resource. "Well, actually yes there is something you can help me with. I'm looking for information about recent events, you know, like in the last year or two. You say my father has written a detailed autobiography. I would like to see it."

Cottlebone scratched his head. "I see, sir. I can start you with volume one, but that book covers nothing about his later years. Although it might give you some clues as to how he thinks, the source of his powers, that sort of thing." Mr. Cottlebone grabbed a step stool by the door.

"I suppose the first volume would be an appropriate place to start." "Very well."

Before Cottlebone walked too far into the labyrinth of shelves, Gerald changed his mind. "Wait! Where does Volume One begin? If it starts while he was a baby, maybe that would be going back a little too far. For now, I mean, I want to read it sometime in the future but there are pressing matters. I think something more recent."

"Volume one begins before conception, sir."

"And up to what age?"

"Whose age, sir?"

"My father, of course."

"Oh, I'm sorry Mr. Peadlebody. Your father isn't in volume one."

"But you said he was?"

"No. I said it would give insight to how he thinks. Volume One is written before conception when he was still a spirit being, he was just space, not in his body. There's no age and it's mostly a transcription of—" Mr. Cottlebone coughed again, holding his hand over his mouth as he cleared his throat. "Of the Rule of Vampirism as told to him by his great grandmother while they were both in spirit form. I'm not sure you would enjoy it though as it's rather dry."

The concept sounded fascinating, but Gerald doubted he would discover who murdered his father by reading some kind of ancient 'spirit' scroll. "When does my father as a—" he stuttered, not sure what the term would be. "As a non-spirit being come into the picture?"

"He was always made up of spirit, sir."

"Yes, but when does he take on flesh, if that's what he was made of?"

"Volume Five, sir, approximately chapter thirteen."

"Thirteen, that would make sense, wouldn't it? Very well, bring me Volume Five."

Cottlebone grabbed his stepstool and disappeared into the corridor of bookshelves. He called back to Gerald through the many stacks and heaps of pages. "There are also recent journals you might be interested in. And telephone books with hundreds of his client's numbers."

"Clients?" Gerald was not aware that his father had a business. Cottlebone cleared his throat again, loud enough for Gerald to hear all the way down the hall.

"Oh right! Victims. You just told me about that. No, I won't need any phone numbers yet. The journals may be what I'm looking for, though. What else?"

"Not all clients were victims. But regardless, I won't trouble you with the contact numbers. One moment please." Mr. Cottlebone shuffled off his stool, slid it along the aisle and then climbed again. "There are several more recent journals that aren't filled in completely."

"Excellent! Bring those as well. This reading will keep me

busy for quite some time."

"Very well, sir." Mr. Cottlebone disappeared down another aisle of bookshelves.

"What else? Recent?"

"Most recent would be the real estate listings, sir."

"Seriously? Real estate?" Odd. No one said anything about his father being in real estate. "I suppose you could bring me one or two of those."

Gerald scrutinized the room more while he waited. He had never been in here when he was a boy. Perhaps the trek down the stairs had been another obstacle that Gerald, in his youth, refused to conquer.

Not surprising! Gerald spent his early years alone in his room, counting and calculating. Math had always been his forte rather than literature. Reading gave him a headache and made him fall asleep. When he and Rockford moved to the river after Rockford married, Ginger hoarded all the books. Gerald had resorted to counting pebbles on the beach and sitting idly on the porch of their dilapidated shack, an abode that resembled a hut more than a house.

This was his first experience in a room filled with books. "I sort of like this place, Cottlebone."

"Books are life, Mr. Peadlebody. They kept your father young."

Gerald pulled a book off the shelf and thumbed through it as he waited. The leather-bound manuscript was a scrapbook of sorts, with pictures. Tin plates of strangers he would never recognize, yet he knew they were probably relatives who once lived in the manor during an era when it was bright and rich and more beautiful than any home he'd ever seen.

He laughed when he spotted a fang or two on the fashion-minded folk sitting around a Thanksgiving meal, dressed to the hilt in their top hats, vests, waistcoats, and watches. Half-bloods from the turn of the century!

They couldn't be pureblood, or they wouldn't be in this photograph. Granted, there were a few empty chairs, which left him wondering as to who might occupy them, if anyone. He adjusted his own woolen scarf and fingered the button to his collar.

The back of the album had more recent photos. Many of which were houses in a lush neighborhood with what must be their owners standing in front of their garages, mailboxes, and lawns.

He paused and studied one particular photo that drew his intrigue. Perhaps it was the woman's smile that gave him pause. She looked near in her seventies. Nothing unusual about the woman's face stood out aside from her smile, as she had two very large front teeth, the tips of which rested on her lower lip. Her cheeks were rounded and dimpled and for an old woman she was attractive in a clever sort of way. Posed with one arm on a mailbox, Gerald, loving numbers, read them aloud. 3443 Lake Crest Road.

"Where is this place, Cottlebone? Lake Crest Road?

"Knobby Hill, sir. A neighborhood for the elite. Most of your father's listings were in that neighborhood."

"I wonder if he bought this woman's house."

Cottlebone didn't answer, so Gerald closed the book. "Are you about done?"

"One moment, sir. I had to shuffle things around a bit up here."

Gerald fingered a few more books. The room was getting cramped and stuffy from lingering so long and Gerald was becoming bored and impatient.

He walked to the door and stopped near his father's desk. Absorbed in the structure of a vintage lamp, he pulled its chain. A light bulb came on, casting a warm glow that illuminated a small red journal, much like the journal that had fallen out of Cottlebone's pocket the other evening. The journal had a leather cover with a strange marking, an inscription of some sort, and a ribbon that suggested someone had stopped reading in that very spot. The pages were fragile and penned in his father's handwriting.

"Here you go, sir. I found two journals side by side." Cottlebone nodded to two leather bound journals resting atop a huge hardcover that took both of his arms to hold. Under them were pamphlets of real estate listings.

"Thank you, Richard."

"Sir, that—" Cottlebone set the hardcover on the desk and pointed at the booklet that Gerald held. "Not that one. That one is mine."

"This is my father's writing, is it not?"

Cottlebone's lips trembled. "Yes, but that one—"

"And I was willed all of my father's possessions."

Suspect Hunting

At last! Nine o'clock PM! The frogging hour had come. Soon the amphibians would disturb the surface of the water and sit among the lily pads or plop into the pond. Ginger hadn't frogged since before the river flooded, but it had been a favorite pastime of hers. Now she was given an opportunity to enjoy an evening of excitement in Madison Park. She felt as though she had purpose again.

She waited on the park bench until the last pair of human lovers strolled away. She ignored them, afraid of letting lost feelings rise to the surface. She had been young and in love not all that long ago. Better she forget her own experiences and wish these people a happy ending for their romance. She certainly hadn't had one.

The sun set an hour ago, but she didn't mind waiting for the deep of night in such a peaceful environment. Water splashing from the fountain set the background harmony for the chorus of early autumn crickets and an occasional bull frog song. She fidgeted with the flashlight, slapped it across the palm of her hand occasionally to connect the wiggly batteries, tested the switch once or twice, and kept her ears keen to the humming of the marsh.

When she was certain she was alone, Ginger grabbed the wicker creel with one hand, the flashlight with the other, and tiptoed to edge of the pond. Cattails poked through the surface of the water, towering over her head as she crouched. The fuzz of their fruit glowed from the light of the streetlamp and lily pads spread like a green sheet across the shallow water.

Ginger knelt and held her breath, waiting for ripples in the water to fade and for silence to return. That's when she heard him. The rapid clicking of the leopard frog. She aimed the beam of light on the lilies, pleased that her instincts hadn't lessened since she lived on the bayou. The frog froze, stunned by the bright ray. Ginger reached to grab it but miscalculated the distance, lost her balance, and plopped into the pond.

Wet, a mouthful of mud, she came up with the wiggling slimy amphibian in her hand and quickly dropped it in the creel before shutting the lid.

She chuckled as she crawled out of the pond, set the basket on solid ground, and wrung the hem of her dress. A quick glance around the park confirmed no one had seen or heard her, so after she pinched the mud off her chin, and removed her shoes, she rolled up her sleeves.

Her escapade had just begun. No way would her clothes dry tonight, not here, not until she got home. Because of that, she might as well do the hunt justice. There was an abundance of frogs in the park pond. It made sense that the more frogs she brought home, the better the chances she had of breaking the curse.

Ginger worked well into the night, splashing along the edge of the pool, crawling in the reeds and wrestling with bramble where the sticker bushes branched out above the shore.

When the moon finally rose as a bright orange ball that lit the night sky, and a chilly breeze stiffened her face, she shivered and dropped her last frog in the now full creel. She was ready to go home. Her experiments would begin in the morning.

The Moon

"Of all the audacity. Of all the ghastly bloodsucking insolence!" Raymond kicked a stone and watched it bounce across the sidewalk into the abandoned street. "I can't believe he did that. Right when she was cooing over another man there's my uncle, acting like a loon! Right in front of the both of them!"

Raymond wasn't expecting a tear to bleed down his cheek. He doesn't cry. But there was too much frustration inside of him to contain it any longer. He blinked through the moisture and looked at the blood-red moon that was now rising over the housetops. The 'hunter's moon' some call it because it makes hunting easier, so they say.

"Hunting for what? For freedom from a lunatic uncle? From a curse? For love?" He spat on the walkway. "It doesn't matter what color the moon is. Blue, yellow! What difference does it make what kind of moon it is?" Raymond growled at his life and took another look into the heavens. That bright orange ball didn't seem to give a hoot if nothing ever happened in his favor. "It could be green for all I care. For all it cares!"

"Or no color at all."

Raymond spun around, shocked that someone had heard him muttering.

"Who said that?"

His heart thumped against his chest when he saw Amber walking down the sidewalk, her profile dark and shapely. Her hair glowed bronze as she passed under the streetlamp.

"How could the moon possibly be no color at all?" His defenses had stiffened his back and set his jaw. Why was she even talking to him? Is she alone or is this a setup? Is Tom Rutherford hiding in an alley watching and waiting to pounce on him?

When she stepped into the light of the next streetlamp, the twinkle in Amber's eye beamed livelier than the glittering stars. His heart melted though he fought each drip. Regardless of his fears, and the sick feeling in his stomach from having been humiliated by his uncle just a few hours before, he had to look into her eyes. They were mesmerizing.

"Silly, a new moon cannot be seen, therefore it is no color."

"You followed me?"

"No. But I was walking this way and saw you up ahead. I thought since you were already going in the same direction it would be pleasant for us to walk home together."

"Where is your friend Tom?"

She laughed, but her eyes examined him as if the question surprised her. "He went home."

"He wasn't gentlemanly enough to escort you to your house?"

"Well, no actually I walked him to his house and now I'm going home. He lives just around the bend."

"You walked him home? Don't you think that's kind of lame? Big guy that he is, and a sheriff's son? He should walk you to your house and then go home by himself." Amber scowled, but

Raymond didn't care. He was repulsed by the lack of courtliness. If Tom was going to steal the girl, he could at least be a gentleman. "It's dangerous for a young lady to walk alone at night. There are uncanny creatures roaming these streets." He visualized his uncle lurking in the shadows, but he wasn't going to tell Amber about Gerald. "Trust me!"

"I'm not afraid."

"You should be."

She laughed again but didn't respond and Raymond didn't press the point.

"Do you always talk to yourself like you did back there?"

"What? You mean when I was talking to the moon? No, not always. Sometimes though, when I have something to say to nature, or to myself." He wasn't sure if her laugh was mocking or not. He feared it was and his brow furrowed. "What? Why do you laugh?"

"You're just so, I don't know what the word is, peculiar, Raymond. You say the oddest things sometimes."

He had no response to that remark though heat flushed through his body. That's not the impression he wanted to make. "Peculiar?" Even though he was—even though he comes from a long line of peculiarities — that's not what he wanted Amber to think of him.

How could he blame her, though? The display that his uncle put on in the park this evening was whacky. In Amber's eyes, his outrage, and physical violence were probably worse. Why did his family's abnormal behavior have to be so evident? And in public, no less! Raymond resumed his stroll, only now was his stride wider, catching the sidewalk with his heels. He could hear her jog alongside to keep up.

"I'm sorry. I don't mean to offend you." She panted, her curls bounced on her shoulders.

He slowed. "Yes, you did. You're right too. I am unconventional, an oddity. You'll probably never find anyone as eccentric as I. Except perhaps my uncle. It's a good thing you didn't know my father." The last he added under his breath and hoped she didn't hear.

"Your father?"

The tug on his arm was slight, but so rarely had he been touched, and never by a beautiful young lady, that it stopped him in his tracks. He paled as he turned to face her, tripping on his own toes as he struggled to stop his clumsy body from falling forward.

Her hand was still there. On his sleeve. Right where his elbow bent. He stared at the long, graceful fingers, her soft flesh that cushioned her knuckles, and the shallow ridges where veins meandered over fragile bones. His gaze traveled along her coat sleeve, curly wool fabric shielding her arm, her shoulder. She smiled, her lips bowed upward, the tip of her nose shone, and her hazel eyes still sparkled.

"Is it okay that I touch you?" she asked.

Is it okay? Is it okay that birds sing or crickets chirp, that the river flows, or that the flowers bloom? How could Raymond answer that question without falling over himself? He stuttered and nodded. When she pulled her hand away, he reached for it.

"Yes. Of course," he affirmed. Her warmth immediately heated his palms. He felt her pulse, so human, so alien.

"Tell me about your father. Why wouldn't you want me to know him?"

Her voice softened and her eyes filled with sympathy. "Was he abusive?"

"No!" That came out coarser than it should have. She flinched and put her hand back in her pocket. Raymond feared he'd never get her to touch him again. "No. I can't talk about him. I mean why do you want to know?"

"Well, because you just said it was a good thing I didn't know your father and I was wondering if there was a reason."

"He wasn't a pleasant man, that's all. Maybe he was abusive. You could say that. He's not someone I want to talk about. Please don't ask about my father."

"Did he die?"

The question caught him off guard. His eyes widened, and then he looked away. "Well, actually yes, he did die." She had no way of knowing that it was his father that hit the headlines in all the newspapers across the country only a month ago. She most likely read about the crash probably over a cup of coffee and a poached egg. Who knows who she was with? Her mom? Her boss? Tom Rutherford? Maybe her whole office had a conversation about his family? Who knows? Some tabloids even showed Rockford Peadlebody's image and reported how he was a vampire and sucked blood out of the conductor just before the train derailed. Raymond wasn't going to elaborate on his father's passing.

"I'm sorry," she said.

Right! What's his reply to that? 'I'm not?' or 'You wouldn't say that if you knew him'? Raymond focused on his feet as he walked, glued to the sound of his rustling slacks and the squeak of his patent leather shoes on pavement. "It's not your fault."

She sighed. "Well, I didn't think it was."

That was the end of their conversation. Raymond was headed to his neighborhood, a good mile down into the city. Amber's house was on the cul-de-sac only two blocks from the woods on top of the hill, where the Peadlebody estate stood. She stopped at the crosswalk. He slowed, his head tucked into his collar painfully aware of messing up the night. The evening could have ended differently. Maybe she would have invited him over to her house. Maybe they could have kept walking longer. Perhaps they could have strolled into the park, where they could sit together and talk about important things, or pleasing things.

Instead, there she stood, eyeing him for only a second before she stepped into the street to cross the cul-de-sac.

"Amber!"

She stopped. He felt like a fool. He had nothing to say to her and yet he didn't want her to leave. "I hope we can walk home again together. Maybe from work. Or something."

"I don't see why not."

"It would be nice to talk to you. About things."

She stepped back onto the curb. "What kinds of things, Raymond?"

His shoulders relaxed. "Just things about ourselves, you know, so we can get to know each other?" He'd love to get to know her, but he bit his lip after he said that. How much would she want to know about him? How much would she ask?

"I have time now, Raymond. I'm not the least bit tired. Let's walk?"

"Where to?"

"I wouldn't mind sitting in the park for a little while. It's such a beautiful night and I love to hear the crickets and frogs."

To what he owed this sensational turn of events, Raymond wasn't sure. But he wasn't going to let the opportunity slip by. "That sounds pleasant. And I'll walk you all the way home afterward, too! Right up to your door." Unlike some people, he knew!

"I would like that!"

Surprisingly, Amber took his arm. He hoped she couldn't hear how fast his heart was racing. Still, he questioned her sincerity. After all, she had been on a date tonight with another man. "So, what's this about Tom?"

"I thought you'd ask. I know you saw us together today."

"You two looked pretty comfortable together. Arm in arm."

"After getting to know him better I decided he's an all right guy, but I'm not in love with him or anything. We dated. That's all. Nothing serious."

"He won't jump me if he sees us together."

"Are you scared of him?"

"What kind of question is that to ask a guy?" It was Raymond's turn to laugh. Of course, he was petrified of the sheriff's son. The man was big, three times his bulk, and he had a father that packed a gun. Why wouldn't he be afraid? But Raymond just snickered and said. "Heck no."

"He isn't going to be angry or jump you, so don't worry. He has other girlfriends."

Raymond kept his sigh internal. This wasn't the time to make waves about her boyfriend, this was time to be with Amber. They were making memories right now. The night was young. He had a beautiful lady on his arm, and the stars were out. Why think about the sheriff's son? Tonight, was a night to remember! Forever!

"You know, Amber, ever since I first saw you I hoped we could spend time together but I've always been kind of shy to ask you out."

Raymond was certain she blushed because she snuggled up closer to him.

"That's funny because I always hoped you would ask me out. Funny how that works. How two people are intrigued by each other yet neither have the guts to do anything about it."

"Really? You thought the same way about me?" He pulled her closer to him and inched his arm around her waist. Gosh, she felt good. Warm, gentle, and human.

Just as they turned the corner and stepped through the hedged archway into Madison Park a woman coming from the opposite direction bumped into them. Amber jumped back and gasped. The impact was so sudden and abrupt. The woman squawked and stumbled backwards, dropping a large creel she'd been carrying.

The wicker basket tumbled onto the path, the lid flew open and a dozen frogs hopped out. Amber jumped again when several of the amphibians bounced on her foot. She kicked them away.

The woman slapped at Amber's foot. "Don't step on them! Watch your feet!"

Seeing the frogs were getting away, and the woman scrambling to collect the slimy runaways, Raymond knelt helped. He didn't mind touching frogs. Anything to be of assistance.

The woman grabbed the frogs two at a time, opened the lid to the creel, and shoved them inside. Raymond slid his frogs into the basket as well. He couldn't see the woman's face. She was hunched over and crawling around, chasing after the other escapees. However, she looked strangely familiar.

"What on earth are you doing?" Amber asked once the frogs had been assembled and tucked away. "Did you catch those frogs here in our city park? Isn't that illegal?"

The woman held the small of her back as she unfolded her feeble and dripping wet body. Thick threads of mud hung from her hair. The whites of her eyes glittered in the moonlight, shining like round balls in a pool of oil. She looked like a monster aside from the grin and the flowers on her printed dress.

"There's no license required to catch frogs. I looked it up." Her voice changed when she saw Raymond. "Oh! I didn't see you, Raymond! What's my handsome son doing out so late on a night like this?" She winked at Amber.

Amber's mouth fell opened. Raymond tried not to look her in the eyes, and he certainly wasn't going to look his mother in the eyes, either. He pulled Amber back, away from the woman. "I'm sorry. I don't know you. You must have me mixed up with another Raymond."

"Don't be ridiculous. I know I'm a little wet." She pulled a glob of mud off her face. "Maybe a little dirty, but not that bad!"

At this moment, she was. Raymond moved toward the park exit and tugged on Amber's arm to follow him. Amber stayed her ground.

"And I'm not stupid either! I know my son when I see him!" Ginger retorted.

Amber pushed his arm away. "This is your mother?" Raymond stepped back.

"Raymond this is your mother?" Amber asked again.

"She's just a crazy old lady. I don't know this woman."

"Shame on you Raymond!" Ginger threw her hands on her hips and looked at Amber; a glance which mortified Raymond.

"If that's your mother you'd better admit it. Even if she is crazy and has a thousand frogs in that wicker basket, that's no way to treat the person who raised you."

This couldn't really be happening. His mother was dripping wet — mud caked on her face, giving her more cracks and wrinkles than she normally would have had—and already Amber was taking her side. Mum was a mess, yet he was being made the fool.

"Okay, so I admit it." He turned to Ginger and scolded her. "Mum, what are you doing here? Why are you all wet? And what's with all these frogs?" He thought twice about asking her that last question, certain he didn't want Amber to hear the answer. "Never mind. I don't want to know." He held his hand up to stop any response she might be ready to blurt out. No telling what her excuse would be, nor whether her answer would include magic potions and vampirism. Nothing she could say right now was for Amber's ears. "We'll talk later."

Amber pulled her coat around her shoulders and buttoned the top button. "Look, Raymond, I need to get home and I can make it there perfectly fine by myself. It appears your mother needs your assistance more than I do. You should get her home before she catches pneumonia." She squinted at Raymond. "You should work out your differences in the privacy of your own walls. Not here in a public park."

Amber scurried away before Raymond could protest or stop her. Her words stung, leaving him feeling much like a red ant that had been partially stepped on. He turned to his mother, a scream sweltering inside of him but what good would it do? She glared at him, oblivious to Amber walking out of his life.

"What?" she asked.

"What do you think?"

Her stare was blank. Obviously, she wasn't thinking.

"Come on. Let's go." He'd take her to the top of the hill and make sure she made it to her tree house where she belonged.

"Home?" she asked.

"Of course. Where else? Your home."

"Okay." She grabbed her creel and pulled her wet sweater over her shoulders. He tried to help her with it, but it was so laden with mud, he threw it on the ground, took off his coat, and wrapped it around her instead.

"You really disappointed me, Raymond. I can't believe you denied I was your mother!"

"I can't believe you don't know why! What did you think I'd do? That was Amber. That was the girl I care about, Mum. It took me forever to get her to even look at me and here you come, bumping into her and spewing frogs all over? How can you take that so lightly? Besides she's probably right. There's probably a law against frogging in the city park. Leave those things here. Let them go."

"What? The frogs? It took me all night to catch them. I'm not leaving a single one behind. Not one. Not on your life."

"Mother!"

"I'm doing this for you, Raymond. For both of us. This is going to save us from the curse. I swear this time it's going to work."

She had her wicker basket in one arm and slid her other arm into Raymond's. "I've been reading, Raymond. There's some powerful stuff going to come of this. You just watch."

He picked her filthy sweater off the ground and slung it over his shoulder. The mud could be cleaned up later. His heart will never mend.

"I'm going to find a cure for us, Raymond, so that you can marry your princess and live a normal life. I want that for you."

"I'm afraid by the time you find a cure, there won't be any princesses left. None that would have the likes of me, anyway."

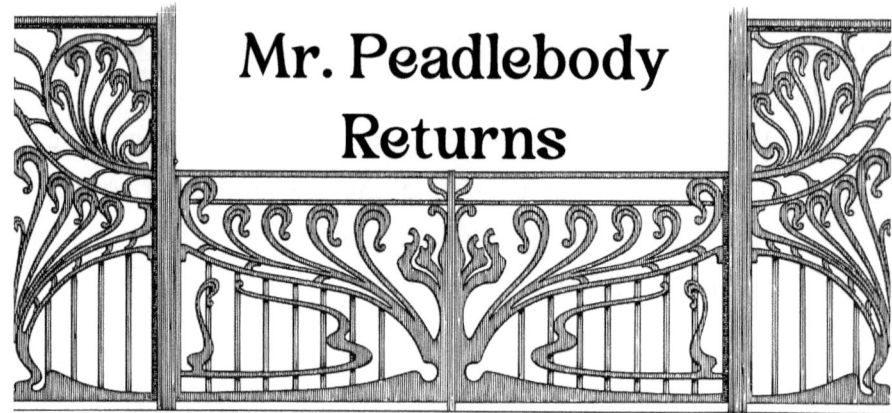

Mr. Peadlebody
Returns

Ginger waved goodbye to Raymond from the top of the stairs. He returned her wave with a simple nod. She couldn't help but feel sorry for the boy as she watched him walk toward the driveway; his head bent low, hands in his pockets. Oh, if only she could find the cure tonight. That would cheer him up!

There's no time to waste. She wrapped her muddy hair in a towel and carried the creel to the bathroom. Already an inch of water coated the tub, enough to cover the pebbles she'd collected and to moisten a few limbs and rocks that were big enough for the frogs to climb on. She spread decomposed maple leaves over the floor of the tub and added some newly picked leaves that were still brilliant green. She built up the leaves in three separate piles, in case any of the frogs wanted a soft bed.

"There! That should make you a nice cozy home." She gently lifted a frog out of the basket and held it in her hand. Its wet toes tickled her fingers. "I expect you to help me, you know? We have to find a cure for the vampire curse." The frog gave no indication of understanding, so Ginger leaned closer to grab its attention. "Hello? I say. Are you there?" Still no answer. "You're nothing like the frog in the story."

She set him back down and tried a very large fat bullfrog, which was too hefty to hold in one hand, so she slid her other under him. He blew his throat up like a piece of bubble gum and inched toward the end of her palm.

"Hey, sir, I think you and I should talk."

The bullfrog winked, but that was the only reaction he allotted to her, so she took a deep breath and did what she thought she would never do. She kissed it. He smelled like fish, his texture rough on her lips like wet sand, but kissing him wasn't as gross as she thought it would be. She waited.

Nothing happened.

"All right. I can wait a bit more. Maybe it's too soon. You don't know me that well. Maybe you're shy or maybe I'm mistaking you for your brother." Ginger had read many fairy tales, so she knew that with magic, every detail needed to be in order before a spell would work. "Or maybe the moon is in the wrong position, I don't know."

One by one, she took the amphibians out of the wicker basket, peeling them from each other's backs, and placed them in the tub. Being kind to them seemed fitting, since she had temporarily robbed them of their natural home. She spoke affectionately, softly, into what she assumed were their ears, making note to look up frog anatomy next time she was at the library.

Once her basket was empty, she shifted her weight to a more comfortable position and admired the new frog haven she'd created. Her bathtub was alive with colorful creatures, chirping, and shifting under leaves, swimming, wading in the water and hopping on the multicolored pebbles she'd collected. What a sight! She was quite proud of the little habitat. "You are all so precious.

Should I give you each a name?"

She decided against personal identification having read one

scene in a particularly morbid edition of The Frog Prince when the princess threw the frog against the wall. Giving them names would only generate additional trauma should they have to meet such an unfortunate end. That event only happened in the edition written by the Grimm brothers, but that was the only one she read so far. She hadn't touched the story revisited by Disney.

Who knows what other spells are in those books? No. Naming these critters would not be a good idea.

Once she set all the frogs neatly in their bath, Ginger covered the tub with a mosquito netting in hopes it would keep them from escaping.

She jumped when she heard the screen door in the kitchen slam. The intrusion not only interrupted the quiet time she was spending with her newfound pets, but also frightened her. The hour was late and only two people would enter her home without knocking. It could be Raymond coming back to apologize for having treated her so rudely at the park. She wiped her hands on a towel and then washed them since they smelled like fish. She expected to find Raymond sheepishly waiting for her in the kitchen. She'd accept his apology no matter what he did. Granted, denying his own mum was over the top, but he's young, probably stressed, and most likely having a bad day.

"Is it you, Raymond?" She peeked around the corner to see Gerald standing by the door wearing the sheepish look that she had expected of her son.

"No. It's not Raymond, not at all. It's me."

Ginger picked up her alarm clock on the way out of the bath and laid it on the counter next to the dirty dishes. When she read the time, she gasped and flipped on the light. Gerald recoiled from the brightness and covered his eyes.

"Good grief, Gerald, it's three thirty in the morning? What are you doing up? Why are you here?"

"Really, Ginger? You thought I was Raymond. What would Raymond be doing up? Turn that off!"

"Ginger flipped the switch again and fumbled through the drawer nearest the stove looking for a match. With success, she struck it on the edge of the counter and lit a candle. Gerald staggered to the table and grabbed the back of a chair. "I can't sleep."

"Well, I should have guessed. It's your witching hour."

"No. No, that's not it."

"You're hungry then?" She perked up, hoping to accommodate a ravenous vampire with her frozen squirrel blood. She headed for the freezer. "Did you see Dusty out there by any chance?"

"No. Why?"

"He hasn't been around for little while. It's not like him. Let me get you some food."

"No, I didn't come for food."

"Well of course you did. You haven't had anything nutritious to eat in days."

"Actually, I had some nutrients this evening. But let's not talk about that, yet. I came here for console."

Gerald's tone carried fewer pleasantries than usual. Ginger wiped her hands on her apron and pulled the towel off her head. Her hair had dried somewhat, but clumps of mud remained attached to her tresses and fell against her shoulders. "What's wrong?"

"I'm upset because of your son."

"Oh dear." She set the candle on the table and drew a chair next to Gerald. "Why is Raymond causing so much trouble?" She feared any wearisome news that might proceed out of her brother-in-law's fanged mouth. He was a whiner to say the least, and his temperament was never pleasant.

"He's mad at me."

"What did you do?"

The kitchen chair scrapped against the floor as Gerald pulled it out from under the table. He collapsed like a mummy falling out of a coffin. Pity overtook Ginger. She'd never seen Gerald display such despondent body language.

"Why on earth would Raymond be mad at you? And even if he were, since when is it in your character to be put out by it? You've never cared how he felt about you before." She untied her apron, slung it over the chair, and scooted closer to him.

Gerald told her everything about his visit with the lawyer. He told her about the long walk and the confrontation with Ferguson's secretary.

"The same woman Ferguson was with the day they came to the manor and read the Will?"

"The same."

"I didn't like her."

"Neither did Raymond."

"You say she had a gun? The secretary pulled a gun? On you?"

"She was going to. I think."

"Odd. That's very odd. Why would she pull a gun just because you asked to see Ferguson? Or was there more? What did you do?"

"Oh, stop it Ginger! Why is it always my fault? I didn't do anything. I swear. My only guess is that both she and Ferguson know we're vampires." "Correction; they know you are a vampire, not me. Not Raymond."

"That's what your son said."

"He's right."

"I told Raymond he's guilty by association. And blood. So are you." Ginger scowled, sat upright, and crossed her arms over her chest. They'd been through this argument way too many times. She'd never lost footing in her position, but neither had he. "Not blood. Not me!"

"The way she acted makes me wonder even more about my father's demise. It's rather frightening. What if they want to do away with us, too?"

"You think Ferguson killed your father? Why would he do that?"

Gerald flung off his scarf and wiped the sweat on his brow. He looked ill from worry.

"I don't know. Why would a lawyer resort to murder? He knows it's illegal," Gerald asked.

"Maybe he just doesn't like vampires."

"Is that a reason for murder?"

Ginger scoffed at Gerald. How could he be so naïve? "It's not like you vampires go around acting normal or anything. What if the murder was in self-defense? What if Benjamin attacked him?"

Gerald must have really been broken today. Instead of delivering one of his usual retorts, he simply covered his head with his hands. His whole body bent forward and he shook. Ginger waited a moment before she spoke, giving him time to do whatever it was he was doing, gurgling, whimpering, whatever it was. Finally, she patted him on the back. When he sat up, she looked him in the eye.

"I had a frightening experience yesterday, too. Maybe as frightening as your day was today."

"What happened to you?"

"I wouldn't have known about this, except the house filled up with smoke and drove me outside."

Gerald grimaced and looked around. "Someone tried burning your tree house down?"

"No. I just didn't get to my cooking pot in time, but never mind about that. The brew probably wouldn't have worked anyway. The important bit of information is if I hadn't started a fire, and hadn't been forced to go outside, I wouldn't have seen what I did."

"Seen what? Where outside?"

"The driveway. A very large, rich man's car pulled into our driveway yesterday morning. I don't know how long it had been there because I was in the house. When I ran down the stair with my burning pot and set it on the walkway to cool, I looked up and saw that big fancy car turning around as though whoever was driving had done their business and it was time to leave. Not too quickly either. Like they were spying or something. I didn't get a good feeling about them at all."

"Is that why you had Cottlebone close the gate and lock it?"

"Wouldn't you?"

Gerald shrugged. "Of course. That was a smart thing to do and it's exactly what I would have done. I think. What color was the car?"

"Cream color. Real shiny. New with windows tinted as dark as coal."

More attentive now, Gerald flung his scarf around his neck, and then twisted his mustache ends into points. "I'll keep a watch out. Locking the gate was a good idea."

"Now tell me what happened between you and Raymond." The story about the secretary was concerning, but then so was everything that happened with the Peadlebodys lately. Two fatal accidents, one that reeked of murder and no one but Gerald investigating. She listened with interest especially when Gerald talked about feeling mortal. Surprisingly, Gerald thinking he may be mortal was a pleasant thought. Perhaps there was hope for the old coot after all.

When he came to the part about sucking Raymond's blood from the hankie, she retched and jumped out of her chair. Ginger didn't usually pace, but tonight she found herself bumping into things as she covered the kitchen floor.

"I can't believe you did that! Good penance, Gerald. You did what?"

"You heard me."

"No wonder he's mad at you. So am I! You dim wit! I'm surprised Raymond didn't give you a fat lip so you could suck some of your own blood."

Gerald sat upright, indignant. "I came looking for sympathy."

"And I should give you some after attacking my son with your disgusting habits?"

"I didn't attack him. I just, well I just stopped the bleeding. But that's not the only reason he's mad. In fact, if that were all I don't think he'd still be holding a grudge against me. It was nothing, really."

"What else did you do?"

"It wasn't my fault, but I did that bit with the hankie in front of some girl he has a liking for. She showed up at the park out of nowhere. How was I to know? Raymond went berserk on me."

"Ah! The girl! Curly auburn hair? Red lips?"

"You know her?"

"I ran into them just a little while ago. Literally. Raymond acted like a fool; said he didn't know me. He insulted me right in front of her. The girl told him off though. Told him not to treat his mother like he did and then she stormed off. Sassy little thing that she is, I kind of liked her!"

"What were you doing at the park in the middle of the night?"

"Frogging."

Gerald slapped his hand on the table and sat up. The look on his face made Ginger cringe. "What?"

"I'm not eating frog blood," Gerald insisted.

"Who asked you to?" She stared at him as he gaped at her. "No one's eating these frogs. They aren't for cooking. Nor are they for your consumption. It's a spell. A new spell I'm studying."

Gerald made a face.

"You can mock me and ridicule me all you want. I'm going

to save me and my boy from this wretched curse, Gerald, whether you like it or not."

Gerald raised an eyebrow. "The magnitude of your research with this project is implausible, Ginger. Frogs? Is it really that terrible being what you are? You may regret finding a cure. Just remember, vampires live forever. Humans don't!"

Ginger spat on the floor between her stocking feet. "Forever? Seriously? If that's the case why isn't your father here? Vampires have no more guarantee of living forever than a mountain goat. What's more, you and I aren't full-blooded vampires. Something else might kill us. A gorgon or something."

"Gorgon! Pfft!" Gerald snickered. "The more I investigate my father's murder, the more certain I am that the branch through the window didn't happen. A gorgon? Why do you bring up a gorgon?"

"Raymond saw one at Rockford's funeral, that's why. They're in your family bloodline. Cousins, or distance cousins or some such nonsense."

"My great Grandmother on my mother's side, I believe. I'm not so sure a gorgon could kill us. I think our genetic structure would prevent it. Something about bone density." He inspected his fingers as he wiggled them. "Even so, my father's journals have some interesting facts about the species. Raymond saw one, did he?"

Ginger headed for the refrigerator, remembering that she had offered Gerald some brew. "The point I'm trying to make, Gerald, is that your father is dead. Vampires don't live forever. That legend is false."

Gerald didn't answer. How could he, Ginger thought. He was wrong about vampires and immortality.

"I give in." Gerald exhaled. "Our existence is no better than what yours was before you met my brother. I just don't understand, though. Why do you hate us so?" Gerald's pout was pathetic.

"Humans are fascinated with vampires, but they aren't ready

136

to embrace any of you. You're the enemy, Gerald. Why? Because you trap people into a living death. No one wants to live like I have to. Alienated from their friends, unable to smile because we don't want our teeth to show! People stare at you in the shopping mall because your eyes are all black from sleepless nights, you're thin as bone because you're hungry for wholesome food like salad and peanut butter sandwiches and— and lasagna."

She knew Gerald had no concept of good tasting food. When had he ever eaten lasagna? The silence was stiff after that. Ginger had to stop talking because thinking about lasagna made her stomach gurgle.

Gerald was obviously trying to maintain his dignity. He stood, carefully pushed the chair back under the table, and looked long and hard at Ginger. His eyes were sorrowful, as though Ginger had just abandoned him. Maybe she did. If Ginger and Raymond do find the cure for this curse, Gerald will be one lonesome half-blood vampire. She almost regretted being so hard on him. Almost.

"I'm going to find out who killed my father."

"Why?"

"It's just something I have to do." Gerald turned and walked out. The screen door bounced five times after him.

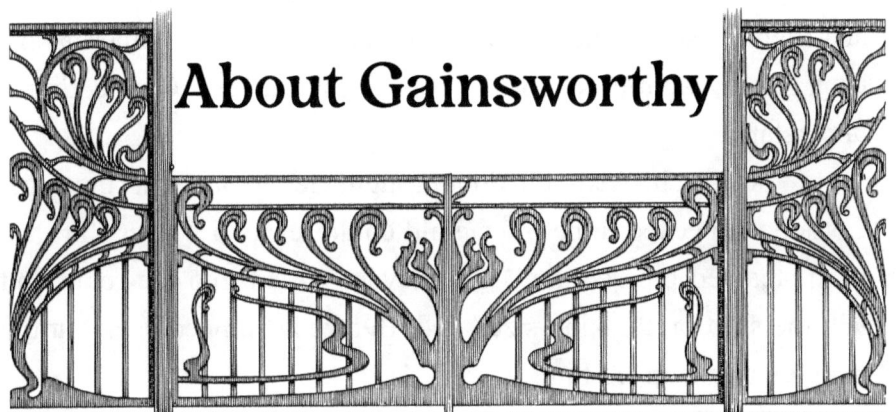

About Gainsworthy

Gerald groomed himself well the next morning, gelling his gray hair into waves and trimming his brows, spending the excess gel on his mustache twist. Today his itinerary was a visit to Mr. Simon Gainsworthy's estate in Lakeview. He'd go as a wealthy gentleman in his tailored suit with the velvet collar. He would put forth his best façade.

A stranger to Gerald, the only time he'd heard the man's name was when Ferguson's secretary mentioned him at the lawyer's office. Gerald suspected this Gainsworthy fellow had attended his father's wake and perhaps his brother's funeral. Most of what he read described the real estate agent as the wealthiest businessman in Mason County. Penned as a cunning shrew, his father wrote little in Gainsworthy's favor. After the last pages of the largest of Benjamin Peadlebody's autobiographies, Gerald gained a sincere distaste for the man.

His father must have hated him.

According to the ledgers, Benjamin Peadlebody, and Simon Gainsworthy had been friends ever since Gerald and his brother left for Louisiana. They entered the business of real estate together, buying and selling property using Benjamin's money and Gainsworthy's charisma. Gerald surmised it was this arrangement that turned sour. What else could have led to the many scratching and illegible scribbling in his father's notes? Why his father hadn't been more cautious choosing a business partner, Gerald didn't understand.

A tap at his bedroom door brought Gerald out of his musings. Cottlebone peeked in before Gerald could respond. "Your shirt has been steamed pressed, sir." The servant glided into the room and laid the shirt on the king-sized bed. Before he slipped back out the door, Gerald stopped him.

"Cottlebone, come in." Gerald eyed the servant's reflection in the mirror. "I want to talk to you, Richard."

The man tossed his head in protest and lifted his chin in resentment.

"About what, sir?"

"Gainsworthy."

"I have matters in the kitchen to tend to."

"You have matters here to tend to." Gerald turned to the servant.

Cottlebone's face was pale even though the ambient light that filtered through the crimson curtains should have cast color on him.

"What's with you, Cottlebone? What are you hiding?" This was one time that Gerald would take advantage of his position over the servant, though with Cottlebone's size and muscle tone, he wasn't sure why Cottlebone submitted to him at all.

"Nothing. I've given you access to all the information you could possibly want."

"But you haven't told me a blasted thing!" Gerald was beside himself with Cottlebone. Living with him had become unbearable.

"You have spent years with my father. Every moment of every day. You have seen every person that ever entered this house. You answered the door for them. You surely heard their conversations. And yet you have nothing to tell me?"

Cottlebone stood at attention. Not a word escaped his lips.

"Those journals I've been reading; several pages have been torn out of the book. Why? Why were some pages half torn? Where are those pages?"

Cottlebone shook his head and cleared his throat. Gerald paused, thinking perhaps he'd speak. He didn't.

"There was reference to an argument shortly before my father died."

Cottlebone lifted his head and stood stiff and unyielding but offered no information.

Gerald paced back and forth in front of the servant. "Five such sections marred the otherwise neat and orderly volume, which was a rather dry account of everyday living at this manor. All five of those scratches came toward the end of the journal and were dated very near father's death."

"Are you asking me or telling me?"

"I'm hoping you are already aware. I'm hoping you know the reason. I am hoping you will tell me what all this means!"

Cottlebone only swallowed and blinked, his eyes glazed over as though going into a trance.

"Two scratched out entries had been timidly scrawled as though my father had been unsure he should record his thoughts at all. Why? From what I remember my father was not a timid man!"

Silence.

"If you don't say anything I'm going to assume you had a hand in my father's murder!"

He caught the servant's eye. The man's face turned red. "I had nothing to do with his death. I was faithful to your father."

"Well then! Were you aware of any inner turmoil he was going through?"

"Your father talked to me, yes. I cannot tell you anything. What he told me was given in confidence."

"Good heavens, man, he's dead!"

Cottlebone cleared his throat again, covering his mouth with his fist.

"The other three unusual marks in the book were written with a heavy hand indicating he was mad," Gerald continued. "Enraged more exactly! What do you know about that?"

"I was not with your father when he wrote in his journals. He demanded solitude," Cottlebone explained.

"Very well. What about the houses he mentions? And poor elderly ladies. What do you know about them?" Cottlebone sighed heavily.

"My father describes a general lack of gratitude his associates had for all the work he did. What work? Did he confide in you about those matters?"

"Anything Benjamin Peadlebody wanted his sons to know he wrote in his journal. If he tore those pages out, perhaps he changed his mind about wanting you to know."

"Is that right? Why would he change his mind? Or did someone else tear the pages out? Did someone threaten him? Is that why he needed a bodyguard?"

"I don't know and I resent being interrogated in this manner."

"You resent this interrogation? Who are you? You're a servant. My father's servant! Tell me what you know!" Gerald pulled the red journal from his pocket and held it in the air. "Who bullied my father, Cottlebone?" Still silence. Coaxing more information from Cottlebone about Gainsworthy and his father's relationship was proving impossible. He was getting a good venting, for what that was worth. "Surely you saw much of their interaction. You had to have listened in on some of their conversations."

Cottlebone waved at the air, chasing an imaginary bug away from his face. He blinked nervously. There was nothing Gerald could do to make him talk. He whirled about one last time. "Richard Cottlebone as my servant I insist you tell me. Was Simon Gainsworthy a vampire or not?"

The silence was so stiff Gerald swore he almost heard that same bug buzzing. He walked up to Cottlebone and peered into the man's eyes, though the servant did everything he could to prevent contact.

"No," the servant replied. With that, Cottlebone's faced turned red, and he breathed deeply. His fist clenched and Gerald felt a power emitting from the man's chest. Fear swept over Gerald as he remembered being pinned to the floor by this same servant not too long ago.

"You may go." Gerald opened the door. "Go!"

Cottlebone hesitated for a terrifying moment, flexing his hands. Gerald would be mincemeat should Cottlebone attack. No longer was the servant's face pale. The red curtains behind him gave the man an aura the devil himself would have blushed at. Fortunately, the servant stepped into the hall without hitting him. Cottlebone descended the stairwell and disappeared into the kitchen.

Gerald breathed easier once he was gone, yet his heart still raced both from anger and fear of Cottlebone. Taking a moment to compose himself, he glanced at his image in the mirror again. He couldn't leave the house this angry. Not today. Not where he was going.

If only he could get on the good side of the butler. What he'd give to have the same devotion from the servant that his father had. Gerald could use a bodyguard about now.

He walked down the stairwell cautiously, hoping not to encounter the servant again before he left. When he reached the bottom of the spiral staircase, he stopped and listened. Water ran in the bathroom down the hall. Smells from the kitchen told him Cottlebone had been cooking earlier, but other than those minor disturbances, the house was quiet.

Gerald took his overcoat from the rack and slipped it on. He chose the red and black wool scarf in hopes the brighter colors would lift his spirits.

There! Now he could leave. He tapped his hat and maneuvered his derby in place. He hooked his cane onto his arm and took a deep breath. Ready for his new adventure, and hopefully clues to the mystery, Gerald Peadlebody stepped outside.

Early rays of sunlight danced in the tops of the trees. The rocky footpath to the driveway was laced with golden maple leaves freshly fallen from their hosts. Winter would be here soon enough and then the snow would come. It's been a long time since Gerald saw snow. Not since he was a little boy living here with his parents.

He shrugged off the nostalgia as he slipped on his gloves, opened the gate and swung it back around, trussing it. Courage alone would make this expedition successful. Living in the past weakened him.

***

Simon Gainsworthy was not a hard person to find. Everyone in the city knew the name. He had an office on Elm Street at the foot of Lake Crest Center, a highborn neighborhood of Ohio's elite, and the site of the last bus stop before the transporter returned to the downtown area. Once he stepped out of the bus, Gerald stretched, planted his feet on the sidewalk and held his hand over his nose as the vehicle puffed its exhaust and drove away.

Before him, acres of meadows and woodlands blanketed Knobby Hill. Rich man's property with land parcels no smaller than ten acres each, and some estates boasted a hundred, all with lush green grass and pruned hedges, rose gardens and stone fences. Walking through the parkland would be difficult, and that's why Gerald chose to stop at the real estate office and see if Mr. Gainsworthy was in. Perhaps the man would welcome him and give him a personal tour of his property.

Certain his apparel fit the venue, Gerald straightened his scarf, twisted his mustache, and opened the door, triggering a bell that hung over the doorway. Inside, a sweet-smelling room greeted him.

Maroon carpets and stark white walls, which were adorned with photographs of significant properties for sale, and some that had been recently sold. Gerald made the rounds, reading the listings. While admiring the photo of a turquoise swimming pool, white walkways, and tiled floors of one notable manor, Gerald made note of the address. 3443 Lake Crest Road. Why did that address ring familiar?

An attractive young woman dressed in a black silk suit stepped out of the back room. She had apparently noticed his interest in the flyer.

"The Bilberry estate is our newest listing. It won't last long, I assure you. One of the most handsome properties in that district, with a view of the lake to the north. You really should take a look."

"Hmm. And just exactly where is this piece of property?" In playing along, Gerald might not startle the receptionist into pulling a gun on him.

One can never be too careful after the encounter with Ferguson's secretary.

"I have a map if you like."

"Yes, please. I am actually afoot at the moment."

"We have shuttles."

"Do you? Excellent!" Dare he ask about Gainsworthy now and request a shuttle to the realtor's house? Or should he be subtler?

"I'm actually here to see someone."

"Oh, I'm sorry. I should have inquired. You had an appointment? With whom?" The woman shuffled papers on her desk and unfolded a calendar.

"Simon Gainsworthy."

She pouted. Her blue eyes enchanted him when she scowled. "There must be some mistake. Mr. Gainsworthy isn't coming into the office today."

"I see. Well, we didn't really have anything on the calendar. He just told me to stop by and see some of his listings."

"Oh, that shouldn't be too hard to do. I'll get you the map. He has three manors in the park, and then five in the surrounding neighborhoods."

"I would like to see all of them, if you please. And where might I find Mr. Gainsworthy should I develop a special interest?"

"I'm afraid he's out of town today."

"Pity!" Gerald took the map, and after glancing at it, rolled it up and tucked it under his arm. "Your shuttle?"

"I'll call the driver."

Gerald continued to browse the posters on the bulletin boards. Not because he had an interest in purchasing a piece of property, but because this investigation was so important to him, he didn't want to spoil it like he did with the lawyer.

The receptionist was lovely, and Gerald hungry, yet those were trivial details which he could overcome. He would wait for the driver of the shuttle. If Gerald ever were to do anything to please his father in his lifetime, unraveling this mystery proved a perfect opportunity. Gerald peeked over his shoulder at the receptionist.

She smiled. He grinned. His stomach growled. He turned away.

The sharp ring of a doorbell announced the driver's presence. In walked Rufus Belington, a short plump man who filled his uniform snugly. His cheeks were rosy and a bit chapped, but the condition didn't seem to bother him. The most striking feature about the man were his bright blue eyes. With a tip of his hat, he nodded to Gerald and immediately offered his hand.

"Good afternoon sir! Rufus Belington's the name! I hear you want to take the tour!"

"Yes, please! I'm excited to see what you have."

"Would you like the full route which includes some of the eastside district?"

"I'm only interested in Simon Gainsworthy's properties."

"Your wish is my command!" With a bow, the man ushered Gerald outside to a small open vehicle similar to a golf cart. The roof was gold vinyl with navy blue trim, the scats were black leather and the wheels were whitewashed and clean. There was a handlebar on the passenger side for Gerald to hold on to, and a clip for him to fasten his walking stick.

"The seats go back, just release the lever under you. Oh, and this button here," Belington touched the dashboard. "Activates a seat warmer if you get cold."

"A seat warmer? Really? That's simply amazing, Mr. Belington. What will they think of next? Thank you."

"Heck, forget the formalities and just call me Rufus, I don't mind."

"Very well! Rufus!"

The engine was astoundingly quiet, the ride smooth — though going over the speed bump into the grounds jostled his hat as Gerald bounced and hit the roof of the cart.

"Hang on there, fella," Rufus said. "Are you all right?"

Gerald dusted the felt derby and punched it from the inside to reshape the crown, forcing a smile. "Yes, yes. Nothing a little reforming can't fix.

We'll be fine."

Rufus nodded as he shifted gears. "You might want to hold your hat.

That won't be the only bump in the road."

Gerald took the man's advice and rested the derby over his knee. He wasn't used to having his hat misshapen. "They're expensive, you know!"

"I'm sure they are! Me, my uniform comes with the job so I'm not as finicky. I can imagine what it'd be like if I actually had to pay for my hat." He laughed and tapped the boxed cap that looked more like a band leader's shako. Gerald responded with a polite laugh.

The road curved and meandered among manicured lawns, gated entries and tall trimmed hedges. Sprinklers dampened the grass, triggering a refreshing fragrance of wet earth. Rufus was an excellent tour guide, showing off the grounds while giving a detailed history of every homeowner of every manor. Quite the busybody, Gerald concluded, but a friendly one. Rufus knew how many roses grew in which gardens, what pets guarded the homes, what sort of plane the residents flew, the boats they sailed, and the cars they drove.

As the rolling hills turned to a more wooded area, Rufus nodded toward a property encircled by a hedge so tall and foreboding that the only view was the end of the driveway. "That there is Gainsworthy's summer home."

"I see." Gerald took a good long look as the cart bounced over the speed bump in front of an elaborate wrought-iron gate. The regal panels topped with extravagant fleur de lis tips stretched from one brick pillar to the other.

Atop the pillars on each side were two marble statues larger than life. The statues themselves were of noticeable interest. In the shape of two gentlemen, top hats, and woolen scarves chiseled out of white marble, they had smiles on their faces. One held a newspaper,

148

the other a cane and a cat. They reached out as if greeting each other in a friendly hello, their fingertips touching to complete the arch over the driveway. Remarkable characters, every feature was cleanly sculpted down to the last button.

"Amazing artwork, "Gerald said.

"One of his best."

"Does he do the sculpting himself?"

"No, no he has an artist who works for him. But I believe he designs them or works closely with the artist. Actually, I'm not sure. The work is all done in private. Every statue he has is a tribute to a former owner. He makes a big deal of it too. Has a big unveiling at his open house, invites lots of important people. Those are good days for me, I make lots of tips."

"I see. And he's that familiar with the former owners that he can build a statue of them?"

"He goes from photographs I think."

Gerald thought long and hard over what Rufus was telling him. Some of it made little sense. Why would a real estate agent make statues of the former owners? "Tell me Rufus, would you want a statue of a former owner of the property you buy?"

Rufus thought for a moment. "You know if you put it that way, probably not. But there's so much character in these things. You know, fancy clothes, a crooked smile, an eye roll." He laughed and shook his head. "I've been told from some of the buyers it's a salute from the ghosts of the past, others say the statues are like guardian angels."

"How many statues does he have?"

"Twenty-four with this new one. He's really found a niche, you know? It's his signature. The Gainsworthy Icons, they call them. Wish I had thought of it! They're like the avatars of Knobby hill. It's what his company is known for all over the world. To purchase one of Mr. Gainsworthy's homes with a signatory statue boosts the sale price a couple million dollars."

Gerald thought about that for a moment as they drove. How would his father have played into this strange custom?

"Tell me something, Rufus," Gerald's voice died out as the cart bobbed up a hill, kicking stones in the air, and skidding on others.

"What would you like to know?"

"Are all of the former owners—the ones whom these statues are portraits of—are they all deceased?"

Rufus didn't answer right away. He busied himself with keeping the cart climbing, checking the rearview mirror, and at one point, he glanced at Gerald. "I never thought about it. But you know, you may have a point. Of course, with big estates like these, they don't change hands very often, you know. People buy these places or inherit them and they just keep them until it's the end of the line, until there aren't any more relatives to pass them on to."

"I suppose you're right." Still, it would be worth investigating and Gerald made a note to himself.

"This latest listing," Rufus said, "It's pretty impressive. We'll go there next."

Rufus steered the cart past the Gainsworthy estate up a woodsy drive. The road narrowed considerably and just as Rufus was about to switch gears to accelerate, a car appeared at the top of the hill.

"Oh drat!" Rufus grumbled when it was obvious the car was not going to stop, nor was it backing up. The guide looked behind him, and then at

Gerald. "These carts don't have reverse. We'll have to roll. Hang on."

Gerald had little time to ready himself before Rufus put the cart in neutral, turned halfway around to watch where he was going and let the open vehicle trundle down the hill. Gerald held onto his seat. The ground was not more than a foot away from the floorboard and he feared he could fly out at any moment. Rocks flew helter-skelter and even landed on his lap. His hat had already suffered several crushes on its crown, but this was not the time to fret about something so trivial. Not as long as the car in front of them charged, at what seemed to Gerald, to be increasing speed. The forest sailed by. Gerald wondered for a split second how much it would hurt if he were to jump. He glanced at Rufus, who at the moment looked more like the man of steel than a robust tour guide, steering the cart with confidence.

The car in front of them rolled closer still and curiously fit the description of the one Ginger had seen at their estate a few days before. The sedan was so shiny that not only the chrome, but the body caught rays of the sun and flashed spots in Gerald's eyes. The windows were tinted a dark gray, making it difficult to see inside. Difficult, but not impossible. The driver was a frail body, a woman wearing sunglasses and if Gerald was seeing correctly, she had a turban-style scarf on her head.

As the cart rolled down the hill, it gained speed, meandering hurriedly over bumps and turns until Rufus spun it into a pile of leaves in a flat area nearly hitting a maple tree. Rufus was an excellent driver and even though Gerald jolted forward and back again as the tour guide applied the brake, the cart stopped without mishap and the two watched their pursuer speed by.

"Well she could have at least slowed down!" Rufus grunted.

Gerald sighed, glad to still be alive. "Indeed!"

"You okay?"

"I believe so." He held up his flattened hat and pouted.

"We can put in a claim with the company if you want. We've got insurance for that kind of thing."

"No need." Gerald didn't want to make waves with Gainsworthy until his investigation had been completed. A little punch on the inside of the crown and the derby took its shape again, though there was more dust on the wool than he could wipe off with his sleeve, especially since his gloves and coat were equally dirty.

"No, really. We'll get you a new hat!" Rufus started the engine, shifted gears, and headed back up the hill.

"Who was that, do you know?"

"Yeah, I know. That was Mrs. Gainsworthy. She's a crazy driver. That's not the first time she's run me off the road. But hey, it's the boss's wife so what're you going to say? She comes up this way to check on their properties once a week. I think it's her job to make sure the servants are doing what they're supposed to, you know?"

Gerald looked over his shoulder at the sedan that was now in the valley, a trail of earth rising like a rooster tail behind it. If that's the same car Ginger saw, and there aren't too many fancy vehicles like that one around, then why had Mrs. Gainsworthy visited the Peadlebody estate without announcing her presence?

"You want to take a break for a minute? Get out and stretch your legs?"

Gerald shook his head. As upset as he was, the sun was already high in the sky. He had a long bus ride home, and he didn't feel as though he'd seen enough to satisfy his curiosity.

"No. Let's continue with the tour. Show me that home you were talking about. The newest listing."

"Yes sir!"

They wound lazily through the woods and out of the forest, cresting at the top of the northeast side of Knobby Hill. The road ended at a T, a driveway heading both to their right and to their left, two separate estates in two different directions. Rufus turned left and slowed the cart.

The drive was narrow, steep with no shoulder and a drop off was a good hundred feet onto the estate lawn. Gerald caught sight of the address on the mailbox as they passed. 3443.

"This is your latest listing? The one on the bulletin board?"

"Yes sir, it is! The Bilberry estate."

"Is the name of this road Lake Crest Drive?"

Rufus laughed! "How did you know?"

"I guessed. What do you know about this place?"

"I don't know much about the mansion except that it's a big one. I did know Mrs. Bilberry, though." Rufus kept his eyes on the road, but his demeanor softened. Gerald found him to be sincerer than anyone he'd talked to in a long time, especially as he told his story. "I knew Mrs. Bilberry since high school. She was my history teacher."

"Is that right?"

"Lots of us locals knew her. That's why it was so odd that she disappeared the way she did."

"She disappeared?"

"I'm not one to believe in horror stories, but rumor had it she got swiped."

"Swiped? What do you mean 'swiped'?"

Rufus turned to him, the oddest look on his face. "Vampires. That's what people were whispering. Funny thing, the vampire they named, the same one they held vigils against at the church, he had the same name you have. Peadlebody."

"Do tell!" Gerald kept his composure so as not to initiate suspicion, but he made certain his lips covered his teeth. "Lots of Peadlebodys in this world."

"I've heard the name before. Didn't mean to imply anything."

"No offence taken."

"Anyway, after she disappeared, Gainsworthy helped the community out and held a benefit for the old lady. Sort of a wake I guess. In lieu of flowers, everyone gave money to the school in her honor. Real big heart that Gainsworthy has." Rufus shook his head and let go of the steering wheel with one hand while he wiped a tear from his cheek. "That was a year ago. He said he'd wait a while before he sells the place to give the people time to get over their grief. She was a great lady with a big heart. She helped a lot of people out. Everyone loved her. She probably taught history to all of Mason County at one time or another."

"That's a shame. I'm sorry for your loss."

"It's time for closure. Gainsworthy is still working on the property. I think that's where the Mrs. was coming from just now."

"You mean when she almost ran us over?"

Rufus nodded and pushed his hat back off his forehead. "He's bringing out the statue in a few days and the whole town will be out for the unveiling. He's donating a percentage of the sale to local charities. The entire community is getting involved."

"I see. Why do you think Mr. Gainsworthy is making such an ordeal with this piece of property?" he asked. He also wondered if his father had killed Mrs. Bilberry.

"Says it might be the last statue for a while. I'm not sure why he's quitting. He's got a good thing going for him."

"He's giving up his signatory statue making?"

Rufus laughed and gave Gerald a wink. "Maybe he just figures he's got enough money."

Gerald didn't find humor in any of what Rufus told him, but he smiled, careful to keep his teeth disguised, in return so as not to be rude. The whole story sounded fishy—the community believing his father killed the old lady—then his father dying and now Gainsworthy ending his prosperous statue making? A chill ran up his spine and he shuddered. "Rufus, I've seen enough. I'm ready to go home."

"But you haven't seen the house."

"No. And I don't care to. But I do appreciate you telling me about Mrs. Bilberry. A very compelling story."

"I'm glad you found it interesting." When they reached the

bottom of the hill, Rufus made a U-turn and stopped the vehicle. "Maybe we'll see you at the unveiling?"

"Yes. I think you might."

Oh Not his Uncle

Why buses emit more fumes at night than they do during the day was a puzzle to Gerald, but this one was extremely foul-smelling, and it was well worth the trouble to get off at Pine and walk up the hill, than to arrive at his doorstep nauseous from carbon monoxide poisoning.

Cane in hand, Gerald waved good evening to the driver and stepped on the curb as the bus rumbled away. Once the sound of its engine could no longer be heard, nor its fumes inhaled, Gerald took a deep breath. He pulled off his derby and with a good slap against his coat, shook the dust off. He grumbled to himself as he punched back the dents in his hat.

"Used to bounce back after a hearty swat. I may have to buy another before winter. Perhaps I should offer this old derby to Raymond. The boy could use a covering for his head. Peace offering, maybe."

The sky was filled with stars, and the song of crickets chimed in his ears. A gentle breeze carried a chill as the evening set in, but Gerald was warm enough with his scarf and coat.

A full day had gone by since he had anything to eat, and now that he was so near home, he craved Ginger's brew. His stomach gurgled, but he fought it. His innards could wait a little while longer. Before he returned to his house, to Ginger, and to the irritating Mr. Cottlebone, he would take time alone to contemplate the overwhelming events of the day.

He had a lot to think about! Madison Park was a perfect place to ponder all that he learned about Gainsworthy and the man's real estate properties, the statues, and the news about Mrs. Bilberry.

The fate of Mrs. Bilberry was more troubling than anything he'd discovered to date. To think that it might have been his father that took the beloved school teacher's life. Benjamin Peadlebody? His father? How could he do such a thing? Granted, the old lady was probably easy prey, but he could have exercised some restraint, especially since the woman had been so popular. A history teacher! He didn't have to kill her, did he?

Perhaps Mrs. Bilberry's death was the reason Cottlebone was so secretive. Perhaps the servant knew more details than what Gerald even wanted to know.

How could he ever bring this news to Ginger? He dared not tell Raymond.

Gerald walked slowly up the hill. A breeze cooled his forehead and rustled the trees, grabbing hold of several leaves and sending them on their journey along the sidewalk. Clouds floated in front of the moon. A changing season, still warm during the day and pleasantly cool at night.

There were no cars on the streets, which lent to the quiet. A most pleasant nightfall for walking. The houses in this neighborhood were old. Some were brick, most had wooden porches with vines climbing up their beams, roots from the maples poked through the pavement on the streets and moss blanketed the stone fences. All the homes were two stories with pointed gables and set on small lots close to one another. No house in this neighborhood could match the magnificent mansions he had visited today.

His father's estate included a large parcel of land, largest in this district. Yet, even if the manor had been remodeled, neither the acreage nor the house would hold a torch in size or splendor to any of Gainsworthy's properties.

What happened? Benjamin Peadlebody had been one of the wealthiest figures in all of Mason County when Rockford and Gerald left. How did this partner of his, who had relied on his father's bankroll to start in business, gain so much more than Benjamin Peadlebody in so few years?

And if this man swindled his father, a pureblooded vampire, how did he get away with it?

Gerald growled at the thought of someone taking advantage of his family. It angered him even more when he thought of Mrs. Gainsworthy with her turban head and her lead foot driving poor Rufus off the road. Surely she had never taken a driver's training class in her life.

Gerald rounded the hedge and headed for the alabaster fountain, glowing in the light of the park lamp. He was disappointed to see that the wrought-iron bench was already occupied. As he neared, his disappointment turned into delight. The woman on the bench was none other than the girl that Raymond was enamored with. A hapless figure huddled alone, looking vulnerable. A smile crossed his face as he forgot all about Knobby Hill.

Being careful not to alarm her, he strolled quietly near, one hand tapping his cane to the beat of his footsteps, the other hand fidgeting in his pocket. He stopped in between the bench and the fountain, took a moment to contemplate on the ripples in the water, the goldfish that swallowed a dragonfly, and the lily that had closed its slender petals to protect itself from the nippy evening air.

On cue, he spun toward her, acting as though he were

surprised someone was sitting on the park bench. "Oh, hello! I didn't see you there."

She didn't answer, but kept her head bowed. She might be deep in thought. Perhaps she was thinking about Raymond. Who knows?

"Excuse me, do you mind?" He pointed with his cane to the open space next to her. She slid over to give him more room. Gerald sat and made himself comfortable, crossed his leg over his knee, and rested his cane against the décor of the arm. "I believe I saw you here the other night."

She looked up at him. The starlight caught her hazel eyes and Gerald understood why Raymond was so enchanted with her beauty.

"Amber? Is that correct?"

"I don't know you."

"Ah, well, perhaps you don't." He was about to announce his relationship with Raymond, and then he thought better of it. She was so pretty and his stomach so empty. Why complicate things? He licked his lips and moved closer. She moved away. He repeated the shuffle, moving near enough to catch the rose scent on her coat. She stood.

What was it his brother used to do? Rockford had been so good at catching defenseless victims with no forethought whatsoever. If he waits one more second, she'll flee. Gerald reached out, grabbed her hand, stood and pulled her close to him, his lips curling up over his fangs, his head bending toward her neck.

She screamed, slid from his grasp, shoved him against the bench, and kicked him in the shin. He squawked and doubled over, his hands caressing his leg.

"You scoundrel!" She picked up his cane and hit him once in the leg and again over the nape of his neck and then smacked him across his shoulders before tossing the walking stick on the ground and running out of the park.

Gerald sunk back onto the bench and rubbed his wounded leg, groaning. When he straightened, a spasm of pain raced across his shoulder blades. He pulled out his hankie and wiped the drool from the corner of his lips. "You're no vampire, Gerald Peadlebody," he said to himself. "You bring shame to your father's name."

Standing was difficult, and even harder when he tried to straighten. He remained bent over, grappled for his cane, and eased himself upright enough to lean on his walking stick once it was in his hand. The journey home would take more effort now than if he had never stopped in the park. Where did he get such wild ideas?

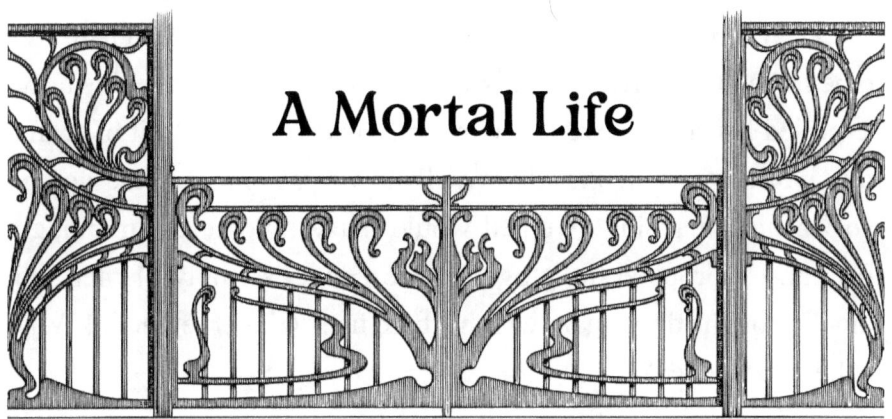

A Mortal Life

As much pain as he felt, Gerald did not go directly to his house, but instead took the mossy cobblestone pathway that meandered past the hedge, over the koi pond bridge, and onto Ginger's spiral staircase.

The way was dark, for there were no street lamps in the Peadlebody yard, and the house barred the moon from shining light over the south side of the manor. Still, it was time to see his sister-in-law, and confide in her. Perhaps she had some left-over brew from her evening meal. If anything, a bit of nourishment would be a comfort.

The quicker he limped, the more his leg hurt. Climbing the stairs would have been impossible were it not for the handrail. Gerald paused at the bottom of the rickety steps to retrieve his leather gloves from his coat pocket. As urgent as he felt this mission was, he refused to risk tainting himself by coming in contact with bird droppings. Once gloved, Gerald began the long climb upward, relying on the railing to support his weight. This was the slowest stretch of his journey, and the hardest.

One painful step at a time Gerald caught his breath, winced, and shook his glove free of filth. He surprised himself when he reached the porch and rested before trying the door, which was locked. He rattled the screen by tapping it impatiently with his cane.

Where was she? There was no reason for his sister-in-law to be in bed this early. With his walking stick tucked under his arm, he pulled his right glove off with his fingertips and held it over the rail. Worthless now, the glove will never pay him service again. No washing machine invented would make it come clean enough to wear. He dropped the glove next to Ginger's empty planter and knocked on the door again with his bare fist. "Ginger let me in! Why is the door locked?"

He heard shuffling inside, and he waited. Footsteps back and forth in the kitchen assured him she was home and awake. He knocked again. "Why are you ignoring me? I can hear you in there! Ginger! Let me in! It's your brother-in-law. Gerald!"

"Wait a cotton-picking minute!" she yelled back.

Gerald stepped out of the way when she finally pushed open the screen door.

"Get in here quick. Quick before the frogs get out! Hurry up!"

"Oh, good night, you still have the frogs?" Gerald slid inside, dragging his stiff leg behind him as he stumbled into the kitchen. After the screen door slammed, Ginger flipped the chrome hook into the eye bolt.

"What's wrong with you?" she asked, wiping her hands on her apron and staring at his leg as he fell into a chair.

"I was attacked."

"Attacked? By whom? Did you find out who the murderer is and they tried to shut you up? Thugs were they? I told you to be careful!"

Gerald rolled his eyes. Surely she didn't believe that. Ginger waddled away, her arms swinging low to the ground, grabbing frogs that hopped throughout the kitchen.

"Not hardly," he said.

"What then?"

"Do I have to tell you? It was a stupid thing, really."

She looked up, her brow furrowed into a frown. "You mean another stupid thing? Really?"

"Just forget it. Do you have anything to eat?"

She stood tall, her mouth dropped as though she couldn't believe he was asking for food. Gerald wondered if she had heard him. Suddenly, a smile stretched across her face. "Of course, I do! Let me get these varmints into the tub and I'll be with you in a minute. Sit down." She left the kitchen with a frog in each hand.

Gerald sat and positioned the other chair in front of him. He lifted his bruised leg onto it and rolled up his pant to inspect the damage. A black and blue mark had already spread over his bone, and he could only wonder what bruises were on his back."

"Good penance, Gerald what happened to you?" When Ginger returned, she pulled a waxed carton from the freezer and on her way to the sink, leaned over Gerald's leg.

"I told you I was attacked."

"By what?"

"A girl."

"Fool! When are you going to admit you don't have what it takes to be a vampire? You aren't your brother you know."

"I know." Gerald rubbed his calve and brushed Ginger's hand away when she tried to touch the bruise. She grumbled at him, so he rolled his pant leg down again. "How are you coming with that 'cure for the curse' thing?"

"Slow. I thought all I'd have to do is communicate with one of these frogs, but none of them are cooperating. It takes two to tango, you know. They don't seem to want to talk."

"Maybe they're holding out for an intelligent conversation."

Ginger shot him a daggered look.

"Did you figure out exactly what kind of communication you're supposed to have?"

"The books aren't clear on that issue. None of them say exactly the same thing. You know how you have to be specific with magic, so it's confusing."

Gerald waited for her to go on, but she was busy slamming the carton of frozen brew in the sink, breaking the ice crystals away from the wax liner. "You mind lukewarm? I don't want to scorch the pan."

Gerald shook his head. He'd be happy with a Popsicle at this point.

"One book says the princess just talked to the frog, and promised him things."

"Like what?"

"Like letting him eat at her dinner table. Reading to him. Sleeping with him."

"Good grief, Ginger!"

"In another book, the princess throws the frog across the room."

"Did you?"

"No, I was saving that for last, in case nothing else works. I think it has to be done with passion." She dropped the frozen juice into a pan and licked her fingers. "In almost all the books, the princess kisses the frog. I think that's what I have to do. Kiss them."

"And?"

"I've kissed them all. Look at me. I'm still here." She set the pan on the stove and turned the burner on. Propping her mouth open with her hands, she leaned over and showed him her fangs, pulling her lips up. "See?" she grunted, unable to talk with her mouth ajar.

Gerald could see quite well, but he preferred not to. He

looked away. She released her mouth and massaged her cheeks. "I'm just not sure what to do next."

"Maybe you have it backwards."

"What do you mean?"

"Well, you aren't trying to turn the frog into a human. You're trying to get the frog to turn you into a human. So maybe it's all backwards."

Ginger pushed his leg off the chair and sat down, studying him with a bewildered expression. She scratched her head. He waited for the light bulb to come on, but she only stared into space.

"You don't get it?"

"I'm trying." The pot lid rattled. "It's done." Holding the handle with a potholder in both hands, she poured. The bubbling juice sizzled into a swirling red brew and settled into his cup dark and steamy. A familiar potion, and regardless of how he felt about the beverage prior to tonight, the odor was pleasing. He expected the drink would help change his attitude as well as nurture his bones. He took a sip and licked the flavor from his lips.

"Perhaps a little salt?"

Ginger sat down next to him again and tossed the potholders on the table. "I don't understand what you're trying to say, Gerald. How am I working the spell backwards? Do you think I have to find someone to kiss me?"

Gerald looked up quickly. "Perhaps. Someone not related to you of course."

She pushed the salt shaker toward him.

"Where did this come from?" He held the ceramic skull in his hand.

"The other half is pepper. Over there." Ginger pointed to the ceramic crossbones.

Gerald shook a dash into his cup and carefully set the gloomy pottery piece next to his cup of broth.

"Your brother collected them. A kiss huh? I wonder who would do it. I don't know anyone out of the family. Are you sure this kiss can't come from relations?"

"Absolutely not. Neither I nor Raymond would work." Even the thought of kissing Ginger made the broth smell bad.

Ginger grunted and stared out the window for a moment before she changed the subject. "How did you fare today besides being mauled? Any clue to who murdered your father?"

"Not exactly. But I did discover a couple of interesting tidbits."

"What's that?"

"The car that came up our driveway could very well have been Mrs. Gainsworthy."

"Who's Mrs. Gainsworthy?"

"She is the wife of a man who used to be my father's business partner actually. I saw her driving around on Knobby Hill today."

"Partner in what?"

"Real Estate."

"No lie? Your father sold real estate? Ha!" she laughed. Gerald grimaced. "And this Mrs. Gainsworthy, she's in real estate too?"

"I'm not sure. She oversees the maintenance of all of her husband's properties."

Ginger laughed again, holding her belly. "So that's it! Maybe she came here to see what kind of landscaping she could do for us. Wouldn't that be nice!"

Gerald snickered. "Perhaps."

"So, was her car a cream color sedan?"

"Yes. I've never seen a car that color before. The woman nearly ran us over while we were in the tour cart, too. I'm certain it was a Jaguar MK9. If you knew your automobiles, we could be certain."

"Well, I don't. I just know the color and that it looked like a rich man's car. Tires were white walled though. Why would Mrs. Gainsworthy come here unannounced?"

"Good question, and one I'd like to know the answer to. Those journals I've been reading have leaked some information, but not enough. Of course, I haven't finished going through all of them and I plan to do so this week. Father and Gainsworthy bought and sold real estate together but they had a falling out not too long before he died."

"Over what?"

"Another good question, and if we find the answer we may have a motive."

"Maybe your father talked about it in his books."

"I've been studying. However, it seems that the important clues to that relationship are either scribbled in illegible writing across the pages or torn out of the book altogether."

"Ha! That points to Cottlebone!"

"Cottlebone!" Gerald shifted in his seat as a spasm of pain raced up his leg. He paused and closed his eyes. Thinking about the servant was painful enough without his leg aching. "Obstinate old goat, he is! I think he knows everything that happened. The why, the who, and the how. Unfortunately, he won't say a word. My father's business seems to be a pretty touchy subject with him."

"Maybe he killed your father?"

"Maybe. He's strong enough. Violent enough."

"Violent? What do you mean he's violent? How do you know that?" Oh dear, Ginger knows nothing of the day Cottlebone attacked him. Gerald refused to answer that question. Why tell Ginger that he's scared to death of Cottlebone? "Just a guess."

Ginger sighed and shook her head, staring into her cup with a melancholy expression on her face. "Seems like we're both kind of spinning our wheels."

Gerald took another sip of squirrel brew and leaned back. Already he could feel the nutrients work. His stomach settled, his attitude changed. He felt more alert and focused than before. "There's another very disturbing piece of information that was leaked today as well," he said.

"What's that?"

Though it bothered him to tell Ginger, he couldn't hide it from her. He sat up in his chair, winced again, and then let the truth come out. "A woman named Mrs. Bilberry was murdered a few years ago. Gainsworthy is just now selling her property. It seems she was a teacher and a philanthropist.

Everyone in town loved her."

"That's a shame." Ginger folded the dish towel she'd been wiping her hands with and slung it over the arm of her chair. "A lot of people have been murdered around here, it seems."

"The rumor is a vampire murdered her."

Ginger whistled low and sunk back. "Oh dear."

"That's what I said, especially when the rumor identifies the vampire as a Peadlebody."

Ginger's wide eyes met his. "You know that?"

"The tour guide told me."

He didn't put two and two together, did he? I mean, your name and Benjamin's name."

"No. He apologized for making it sound like he was implying anything."

"Well that's good. I hope he's wrong."

"I do too. I hope my father's journals will give me more of an insight."

"Do you think it was a revenge killing? An eye for an eye?"

Gerald shook his head. "With an old lady?"

She shrugged.

"Ginger, although people do that kind of thing from time

to time, vampires don't normally carry the same sort of sentiment. Vampires kill for food, not for any emotional satisfaction."

The two sat quietly for a while, Gerald lost in his thoughts. A sense of shame had been coming over him all day. He wasn't a killer. No wonder he had made so many foiled attempts to hunt. What if he quit trying to feed on humans, like Ginger and Raymond had been prodding him to do ever since Rockford died? What would be wrong with that? Better than having a reputation like Benjamin Peadlebody.

Today he saw his father in a whole different light—he saw him from a human being's viewpoint. Why had his father killed a helpless old lady? He glanced at Ginger, her eyes fixed on the curtains above the sink most likely lost in her own daydreams about being a human again. He felt for her.

Tonight, he wished she would find a cure.

He shook himself out of those thoughts. That thinking seemed unnatural and unvampiric. What was happening to him? Getting soft, he supposed.

He cleared his throat and gave Ginger a long hard look. "I presume it's going to take time to get our puzzles solved. I'm looking forward to that day when we both have a breakthrough."

Ginger woke from her stupor wide-eyed and surprised. "What? You're looking forward to me solving my problem? I hear you singing a chorus to a completely different tune! What gives with that?"

"Yes. I suppose my way of thinking is evolving."

"I can't believe it! You used to argue with me about wanting to be human. You said I should be happy living in this disgraceful state of being. Now you're encouraging me to pursue my goals?"

He had said that, yes, and it was appropriate for him to feel that way at the time. Not so much anymore.

"Times are changing, Ginger." Indeed, they were, especially

since Gerald Peadlebody was realizing he was not who he was supposed to be. Gerald was no more a vampire than Mighty Mouse. Perhaps, if Ginger was successful finding a potion that would turn her human again, she could help him out of the curse as well.

Gerald put the cup of liquid, which had cooled, to his mouth and as he inhaled and held his breath, the brew slid down his throat and filled his gut, satisfying his hunger. Something that hadn't happened in a long, long time.

The Opposite is True?

Ginger had a simple bedroom with a twin-size bed, a lamp table by its side, and an old pine armoire that Raymond had carried up the stairs and wrestled into her room the day she moved in. In that antique portable closet, she kept all her treasures—memoirs from her life before Rockford.

Raymond had framed a small glass window above her bed, which she kept open most of the time, since she hated a stuffy room. A tatted curtain hung over the opening and today a slight breeze lifted the hem and ushered in the morning sunlight.

She'd been putting off getting out of bed. Not only because she enjoyed listening to the sounds of the critters in the woods, the trees rustle, the birds sing, and the frogs in the bathtub, but because there were too many things to think about after her conversation with Gerald the night before — too many emotions to organize and slip into their proper place. Having Gerald agree with her and support her after all these years was overwhelming. He had offered an interesting concept, one which she would do well to consider since she wasn't getting much accomplished on her own.

According to Gerald, she had everything backwards. The correct way to interpret The Frog Prince was to see herself in the frog's position, since she's the one that needs to change into a human. The goal would be to find someone outside of the family to kiss her!

This interpretation opened new doors. All she needed to do now was to find someone to take a little bit of interest in her, and to give her a good smack on the lips. Ginger was certain getting a kiss was still possible. She just needed to be out in the world and to flirt a little. And to disguise her teeth.

Ginger had been an attractive woman when she was human. She had a good figure. Her hair was strawberry blond, and people told her she had beautiful blue eyes. She had a bit of Irish blood in her, so there was nothing too pronounced about any of her facial features. She had been quite popular at school and had been raised in a middle-class neighborhood. Fashion-minded, her wardrobe caused much envy in the southern parish she grew up in.

Still buried in her armoire were a few of her dresses she had salvaged during the flood. Buried, also, was the gown she had worn to a high school dance competition nineteen years ago.

Most of her old cotton sack dresses had been washed away, but the clothes bag her mother had given her, and which she found floating in the backwaters after the flood, still protected her black chiffon frock.

She jumped out of bed and threw off her covers. Finding the gown was easy, with only one suitcase to go through. A handful of mothballs fell on the floor when she unzipped the bag, filling her bedroom with a soapy fragrance, a scent that brought back memories of her youth—the smell of Mom and Dad and home in New Orleans.

She held the dress up to her shoulders and spun around, reminiscing on the last date she had as a human teenager.

In early summer, her senior year in Skyview High, there were only thirty students who graduated in her class. Because their parish was so small, they were all good friends. To celebrate graduation, she and her date,

Johnny Freemoth, and several other couples caravanned in their cars to Skyview Valley Grad Night, and a dance competition the neighborhood high schools had arranged. If Johnny Freemoth hadn't been the key instigator of the trip, Rockford Peadlebody might never have seen her.

Ginger pouted at the wrinkled image of both the dress, and her body, in the mirror. How different things could have turned out if she had stayed home instead. "I should never have gone. Look at me. If I had stayed home like my parents wanted me to, I wouldn't need to kiss a frog!"

Rockford had been a stranger to almost everyone in attendance that night—a friend of a friend of Johnny's. He shouldn't have even been at a school dance because he was a few years older than everyone else. But at the time, everyone thought it was cool.

The band had a saxophone player from out of town, so there were a lot of grads from Louisville as well. Ginger and Johnny did the Swing with everyone. Johnny didn't know the Jitterbug, so when the really crazy music started, he took Ginger's hand and led her away from the dance floor. She stood by the fireplace and watched everyone else. She must have looked a little bit perturbed because Rockford came up to her with a sympathetic smile. She had no idea who he was, but he was very polite and asked Johnny for permission to dance. Johnny nodded, much to Ginger's disappointment. She didn't have eyes for the stranger, she had eyes for Johnny.

But Rockford swept Ginger onto the dance floor and changed her life.

She'd never seen anyone dance like him before. It was as if he were a professional, some kind of celebrity. His whole body moved. His steps were in perfect beat, quick, tricky, his turns smooth and sexy. Some of the other dancers stopped to watch. He took her

175

hand and spun her. He tossed her up in the air and before she could catch her breath, he caught her and slid her across the floor. His movements were so fluid she felt like she knew the Jitterbug too! What a dance! What a night! That was the time of her life!

"I still remember those shiny shoes he wore. What a good-looking man he was! Back then."

Not only was Rockford good looking, he had a new Cadillac. One that she and Johnny and all their friends piled into, even though there wasn't enough room. They drove to the drive-in where Ginger made a big mistake. She smiled at Rockford when he bought her a chili dog. That smile was too wide and lasted too long. Oh, how she wished she hadn't smiled at him — catching the twinkle in his eye with her own.

Ginger shook her head and held her hand over her throbbing heart as she thought about what happened next.

"If a flirtatious smile can get me into this mess, a flirtatious smile will get me out!" Ginger said to the frowning woman in the mirror. "Don't you think?"

The dress still fit. In fact, it was a too big. She hadn't any dress shoes, just her Oxfords, and if she rolled down the white sock and matched it with the pale pink one, no one would notice. Who'd be looking at her feet?

Ginger didn't normally wear lipstick; however, she was convinced no gentleman would look at her, much less kiss her if her lips weren't coated with a mouthwatering red. A jeweled handbag in her drawer still held a bullet case that twisted up a stick of crimson probably as old as the prom dress.

She never had much opportunity to enjoy her youth after she met Rockford. Riveted by his wicked charm, she let him steal her away from a lot of things. He took her youth and her humanity that very night, and then he raced out of state with her. If she hadn't insisted he take her home to get her belongings, she wouldn't have her dresses, or these few simple artifacts.

Ginger pinned her hair back in a bun and dabbed make up over the horrid scar on her neck. When that disguise didn't work, she found a scarf to wrap over it and hang off her shoulder. The mirror was honest with her, but there was nothing she could do about the wrinkles. They were there to stay.

"I don't need a young man. He can be as old as the Mississippi for all I care, as long as he has some kissing' left. That's all that matters."

After she opened the door and the cool of autumn hit her, she went back inside to get her rabbit fur coat.

"Where does one go to get a kiss nowadays?" she asked herself and hesitated at the bottom of the stair. She could try Madison Park where lovers go, or she could be more social and wander to the Five and Dime at the end of Buckeye Avenue. There was enough change at the bottom of her purse, over a dollar and thirty cents, which should be plenty for a malted milk. She drank a shake once before and it didn't upset her stomach too much.

"If I could find one willing soul to lure to the park I could tell him my story. Well, some of my story. Probably not about being bitten by a vampire. That might drive him away." With her eyes fixed on the sidewalk as her mind wandered, she walked briskly down the hill, mumbling to herself. "I could work on his sympathy. Tell him how lonely I am. All I need is a little smack on the lips. Just a little affection. Nothing much. Nothing lasting." Ginger spent the entire walk rehearsing different scenarios in her head.

She passed Madison Park, turned left on Buckeye Avenue, and then walked another block to the Five and Dime on the corner; a four-story building that must be a hundred years old. Nothing in the store was under a quarter, so the name of the store proved misleading, but they had some interesting items; stationary, pot holders, aprons.

Today Ginger pushed through the rotating door and wandered

past the check stand. A neon-lit soda sign announced the fountain in the back of the building. She stepped in the sectioned off area onto the checkerboard linoleum. Behind the Formica counter were toaster ovens, shelves with glasses and cups and a malted milk machine. An assortment of pies and pastries encased in a glass tray caught her attention. Oh, if only she could eat sweets again!

The young man behind the counter wore a three-pointed cap and an apron around his waist. Clean- shaven, his eyes were brilliant blue. He must be new because Ginger had never seen him here before.

"Hi there, ma'am! What can I do for you?" He greeted her with a wide smile while he wiped the counter in front of her.

No other seats were occupied. She hadn't expected an empty store, which made flirting a little difficult. "I'm not sure. No one's here?"

"You're the only one, Ma'am. No lines, no wait. I'm at your service. Whatever you want!"

Whatever? Ginger thought and discarded the idea of asking him for a kiss. She'd have to be subtle if it were to count for magic. Although the idea was tempting.

Ginger grunted and sat down. "Are you expecting anyone in today?"

The young man laughed; his blue eyes glistened in the artificial light. "A good businessman always expects customers!"

"Are you a good businessman?" she asked. He was much better looking when he smiled.

"Order something and see for yourself."

She glanced at the menu to check the prices while he waited, still buffing the counter with his rag, and still smiling.

"I'll have a chocolate malt."

"Very well, coming right up."

"What time do you get off?"

He pulled a bottle from the fridge, turned his back to her and poured the milk into a stainless-steel shaker. "Five o clock sharp, Ma'am. Why? Want to take me out?"

He chuckled as he filled the cylinder with ice cream, chocolate syrup and two heaping teaspoons of malt, stuck the shaker onto the beater and turned it on. The mixer created such a loud grinding noise Ginger could no longer hear him. He spun around with a grin.

She offered him a return smile.

The malt machine stopped.

His beam faded.

"Just wondering," she muttered.

The soda jerk, gagging, turned back around. Guessing what might be the trouble, Ginger pulled out her compact to check her image in the mirror. Sure enough, the lipstick was so thickly coated on her canine teeth they looked blood-soaked. She peeled a handful of napkins from the holder and wiped her fangs as best she could.

The young man set the malt in front of her, head bowed. Ginger held her hand over her mouth and nodded a thank you but it didn't matter. He wasn't going to look at her again. He must be terrified. Pity. He was handsome, too.

She pushed her coins across the counter to him. The two didn't exchange words after that. Ginger only drank a few sips of the drink. Any more foreign liquid would have her stomach gurgling and she certainly didn't need any internal sounds adding to the damage that had already been done.

"Thanks," she mumbled and flipped one more nickel on the table for a tip. The terror on his face ascertained it was well earned.

Money spent, there wasn't much else to do but sit in Madison Park and hope some poor homeless person might be as desperate for affection as she was.

Ginger settled on the park bench to watch the water dribble from the fountain. She wrapped her fur coat closed and shivered;

continually running her tongue over her teeth, hoping there wasn't any remaining lipstick on her fangs.

The hour wore on, the park empty. Ginger grew bored. She thought about heading home, but before she could lift her cold and tired body from the park bench, a middle-aged man wearing a black Fedora, gray flannel shirt, and black slacks strolled through the hedged archway and wandered toward the pond.

Ginger eyed him with her head bowed so as not to be too obvious. He paced back and forth, seemingly waiting for someone. He jiggled something in his pocket—keys, or loose change maybe. Ginger couldn't tell what. He wandered aimlessly by the bushes, inspecting the foliage as though he were some sort of biologist performing scientific research. Ginger knew it was a front because no one just wanders into the park and starts looking at bushes with their hands in their pockets. He wanted something.

She stared at him, no longer being discreet. Why should she be? She was there to be noticed. Maybe he's the one. She believed in Serendipity as much as she believed in curses and cures and magic. He could have been sent to her through some kind of divination. To help.

It worked! He eyed her and nodded a greeting. After what happened at the soda fountain, Ginger knew better than to smile. No sense upsetting this fellow, too. She nodded back and then scooted over on the bench just in case he'd want to sit down. Not too far, so if he did sit down he'd have to be close.

He circled around the fountain and when he got near enough, Ginger cleared her throat and mustered up enough nerve to talk.

"Waiting for someone?" she asked.

"My business partner." He pulled a pack of cigarettes from his vest pocket and then a box of matches. His movements were smooth as he struck one of the matches on the bottom of his shoe and came up with a flame.

"Oh. What kind of business you in?"

His smile slanted a bit as he hung onto his fag with his lips. Now that he was nearer, Ginger saw that he was not a well-shaven man. He had whiskers and his teeth were yellow but at least, unlike hers, they were all the same size.

He held the match for a while, pausing before touching it to his cigarette.

"Promotion."

"Promotion?"

"Yeah. Advertising."

"Like sales?" He nodded.

"Oh. I guess that's a good business to be in," Ginger said, knowing nothing of what she was talking about.

The look he gave Ginger kept her from asking any more questions. With his hands cupped around his mouth, he lit the cigarette and sucked the smoke in with three hearty puffs. Once the end of it glowed, he threw the match on the ground and snuffed it in the dirt with his shoe. He exhaled the smoke away from her, which was a gentlemanly thing for him to do, she thought. He nodded toward the empty space next to her and she scooted over a little more, pulling her purse onto her lap.

"What's a queen like you doing in a lonely park all by yourself?"

"Well, to be honest," she started, but coughed when his smoke got in her face. "I was waiting to meet someone myself."

"Oh? Male or female?"

Ginger laughed. "Male of course."

"Is that right?" He looked at his watch and then glanced at the park entrance. "What time?"

"What time what?"

"When's he going to be here?"

"Oh, he's not real. I was just hoping a man would come and

sit by me." Ginger wanted to smile, but she resisted.

He took another hit off his cigarette and this time ushered the smoke out the side of his mouth as he inched closer and put his arm on the back of the bench. "Pretty dress," he whispered.

Ginger wasn't sure whether to be afraid or excited but her heart raced, regardless. She puckered her lips and closed her eyes. He leaned in so close she could smell his rotting teeth, but his lips never met hers. Instead, he grabbed her purse and with a yank, the bag was his.

"Hey!" She opened her eyes, but he was already halfway out of the park.

"Scream and you'll be floating face up in that pond old lady," were the last words she heard.

The man, the purse, and her potential kiss disappeared before Ginger knew what had happened. When her heart finally slowed. She sighed. "I suppose I had that coming!"

Though her stomach churned from both the robbery and the malt, she was glad she had spent the last of her coins. The "kiss theory" was history by the time she climbed up the stairs to her tree house.

The Journal

Gerald stayed in bed late on Saturday morning, reading his father's journals. A plate of cinnamon rolls which Cottlebone had baked lay on a silver tray on a table by his side. Still hot out of the oven, the rolls smelled delicious. He didn't eat them, of course, as they'd make him sick, but he could breathe in the aroma and somehow be satisfied.

Next to the plate of buns brewed a teakettle of Ginger's notorious squirrel brew, which he had asked Cottlebone to fetch from his sister-in-law and keep handy in the refrigerator ready to warm and serve on demand. He was tired of going hungry. A sprig of mint had been placed next to his cup as an added touch of breakfast elegance, and to disguise the wild odor of the tea.

Gerald was buried in the handwritten pages of his father's life story when a tap on the door announced the servant's entrance.

"Did you want another bun, sir? I have another batch coming out of the oven in a few minutes."

"No, this is plenty."

Vampires were conditioned to devour blood, but there were

no rules as to what they could savor with their other senses. Gerald had a theory that being around human food might change him into a human, or at least make him feel more akin to Homo sapiens; erroneous concept, but refreshing scents.

"Very well, sir." Cottlebone stepped into the room and pulled open the lace curtains that covered the tall narrow windows. Sunlight invaded the space and Gerald, who had been perfectly happy in the dark, winced at the intrusion.

"No! Close those!" When Cottlebone turned to face him, Gerald lowered his voice. "Please?"

"It's morning."

"Close the curtains."

"As you wish, sir." The servant was slow to return the curtains the way they were. He stared out the window first, awakening Gerald's curiosity.

"What are you looking at? Is something wrong?"

"Wrong?"

"Outside? Is something outside that shouldn't be there?"

"No. I was just making certain we were alone, that's all."

Once the drapes were pulled together and the room dimmed again, Cottlebone slowly approached Gerald, and leaned over his bed to retrieve the tray.

Gerald sat up, afraid of Cottlebone's intentions, and though he wore his nightclothes, he pulled the covers over his chest. Why was he making sure they were alone? Gerald cleared his throat. "You're right," he agreed. "If I get any visitors today, would you turn them away please? I feel I should stay here and read these journals. I need to concentrate. It behooves me to uncover the mystery behind my father's death."

He said that last sentence in order that he might provoke a reaction out of Cottlebone. He had not ruled out the servant as a suspect in his father's demise. How often in murder mystery novels did the culprit turn out to be the butler? And if he were a murderer, would Gerald be the next victim?

"Sir?" Cottlebone cleared his throat as well.

Gerald rested his book on the bed. "What?"

"Not to be rude, but who would visit you?"

"Probably no one, except maybe my nephew. By the way, if Raymond does come by, he will probably be ill in temper. I don't need to see him. I don't want to see him!"

"He does have an attitude, doesn't he?"

"You could call it that. A little rash, sometimes. He's young though, so I grant him exception."

"Young is no excuse for angry."

Gerald glanced at the stiff lipped man standing at his bedside. He never guessed Cottlebone held judgment against his nephew.

"He's not all that bad considering the hard knocks life has thrown at him."

"No more than you, sir. He's twenty-one years old. He should grow up."

"He will."

Silence pervaded. Morning glow filtered through the curtains into the room and cast a soft shadow on Cottlebone's hardened guise. What had the man experienced that caused him to be so cold?

"Have you time to talk?"

The servant hesitated, not too eager to answer. "About what, sir?"

"Just some things. About my family."

He raised an eyebrow. "We've been through this before."

"I have different questions this time."

"Then perhaps."

A safe answer. The man is not stupid. Gerald pointed to the chair next to the bed. "Please sit down and talk to me. I haven't found anything in these writings about my mother being an elf, but

185

that was what I was led to believe all my life. My mother's name was Sandra, but in these journals my father keeps referring to Elisa as his wife. I don't understand. Did he remarry?"

Richard Cottlebone did not sit as Gerald had invited. Instead, while still holding the tray he glanced out the window. His silence was as an ice pick stabbing at Gerald's heart.

"Good heavens, Richard you can answer that! You knew my father. Speak up, fellow. Did my father remarry?"

"Yes, sir. Your father remarried shortly after your mother died. I told him time and again to correspond with Rockford, so you boys would know, but the new missus would not have it."

Then something happened that Gerald would not have suspected. Cottlebone, the brawny servant, still staring out the window, trembled. His hands shook so fiercely that the cup on the tray rattled. This struck Gerald as odd. A big healthy man like Cottlebone shaking at the mention of Gerald's new wife?

"You told my father to correspond with Rockford? Not me?"

"Your father insisted that your name not be mentioned in this house. Ever."

"What? Why not? I knew he was ashamed of me, but I didn't know to what extent. What did I do?"

"Nothing, sir. It wasn't anything that you did." Cottlebone set the tray on the table. He tucked his coat even and fixed his collar. "It's just that the new Mrs. Peadlebody knew of one son only. Your father didn't want her to know about you. I'm not sure why. Rest assured it had more to do with her than you. I suspect that your father didn't trust her. In fact, I know he didn't."

"No? He'd marry a woman he didn't trust? That doesn't sound like my father."

"There were extenuating circumstances at the time. Your father felt he had to marry."

Gerald sat up, alerted by Cottlebone's statement. "What

kind of circumstances? Why would my father feel he had to marry anyone? That's way out of character."

"Elisa Peadlebody was a wicked woman. I'm not at liberty to say anything else, sir. Please don't ask."

"Perhaps there's an explanation in these writings?"

"Perhaps. I'm sure if there is, sir you will discover it. You just need to keep reading."

Gerald opened his mouth to argue, but the servant spoke quickly and before Gerald could stop him, he turned to go. "If you'll excuse me I have cinnamon rolls in the oven."

Gerald's temper had flared. "Richard! Someday you will tell me everything you know. Someday soon!"

Cottlebone turned to look at him, his tattoos beaming in the morning light. "No, I will not. Sir."

The breath on which Cottlebone spoke was both hot and absolute, and made Gerald's stomach turn. The butler's refusal to cooperate was as much a mystery as Benjamin Peadlebody's death. However, Gerald's prior run-in with the tattooed man was fresh in his memory. He had no intentions of wrestling with him again. "Go on. Get your rolls."

After Cottlebone left, Gerald set the larger journal on his lap and skimmed through the pages, looking for Elisa Peadlebody's name. She was mentioned throughout his father's book, but not in ways a man would talk about a loving wife.

One passage mentioned Elisa's sister, Ellen just before the first scribbling. Why? Who was this Elisa that lured Benjamin into wedlock? And why was her sister's name crossed with marks so vehemently lain that the writing tool had torn a hole in the parchment?

Gerald, still in his pajamas, retrieved the smaller, red pocket-sized diary. After fluffing his pillow, he snuggled under the covers, and leaned against the padding in preparation for another journey into his father's documented life. Four hundred sixty-six thin pages were penned. Gerald skimmed the contents, handling the fragile book as though it were a delicate piece of porcelain. Instinct told him that if any of these manuscripts had a clue to his father's death, this would be the one.

The diary was divided by dates and subdivided by months. Sandra's name was mentioned in an endearing eulogy. He sniveled as he read his father's tribute to his mother, and reached for the tissue on his bedstand, blew his nose, and wiped his eyes.

Gerald flipped backward and then forward again. Surely his father had recorded data concerning his second wife! Where they met, how they had been attracted to each other, some sort of courtship. But nothing of significance. He found a mysterious poem, the single passage alone written in finely applied calligraphy.

Great alabaster form that once held life.
Your spirit frozen, embalmed inside.
Give me your dust, your powder, and pride
To mix with my blood as mortal I die.

If there were more to the poem, it was unavailable. The end of the page had been ripped out. Gerald thumbed through the journal hoping to find the remnant, but he found nothing that would fit, nor were there any scraps of paper wedged in between the pages.

He sat against his pillow and read the words over again, yet he couldn't make sense of the verse. Still pondering, he flipped the pages until he came to the fourteenth chapter. The penmanship had changed, as if the writer had entered this chapter more cautiously than the others. Indeed, it drew Gerald's interest immediately and he read aloud to himself.

A year to the day that my wife and mother of my sons died, I had a vision. From the other side of the planet Neptune, I looked in the mirror until the sun was so bright I could no longer see. It was then that a woman appeared more beautiful than I had ever laid eyes on. More beautiful than my beloved Sandra though that is difficult to admit.

She told me her name, Elisa, and beckoned me to join her. She and her sister Ellen had been forbidden to walk on earth and so she asked me to stay on the planet she inhabited. I could not. I have my own calling and I left her grieving for me.

I soon found out that our encounter had been real, and not a vision. I had indeed traveled in my spirit and when I came upon her again, it was much closer to earth. I asked her how she came to leave her home, and she told me that she had fought the gods that kept her away from me. She confessed that her passion was so great for me that her mortality no longer mattered.

Of course, my manly instinct gave in and I embraced her with open arms. I had no fear of feasting on her blood the way I had feasted on human beings, for she was not of bodily form and there was no blood to be had. Yet when we reached this meager estate where I now write this account, the woman changed. I hated to see the transformation she went through when she entered the door. Flesh peeled off of her face, her hair coiled into serpents. I watched, helpless. I thought she would die from entering this world, but Elisa did not lose strength. Instead, she became powerful, energized. She insisted that we wed, that matrimony would rescue her from her predators and restore her beauty. I obliged the woman as I felt great pity on her, for she had gone through this trauma because of her love for me. How could I know that the moment we sealed our bond nothing in my life would be the same?

Though I am immune to her powers because of my breed, no human could withstand her spell. That's why I trained my faithful and beloved servant Richard Cottlebone to avoid laying eyes on her, and why we have one room where the walls are made of mirrors.

For her to enter that room would be the death of her, but a haven for anyone else. Elisa cannot withstand her own curse. In the parlor, Cottlebone is safe.

Elisa has the ability to hide her ugliness. When she does, her beauty is incomparable, yet her heart is black, as is her sister's. I had no idea that from the moment we were married I would hate her. She manipulates me daily. There is nothing in this world that makes her happy, and she seems to thrive on contempt. Her distaste for humans has become so vile that I feed only at night and have fallen away from all conversation with humans aside from Cottlebone and the man married to her sister. If Elisa were to read this book, as she had forced me to remove passages from some of the other journals, she would tear its leaves to shreds. Were it not for the size of this pocket diary I am certain this record would be lost.

Gerald shut the diary. His heart raced as he pondered his father's words and the circumstances that prompted them. What horrendous powers did this woman possess that left Benjamin Peadlebody, a full-blooded vampire, defenseless and hating her?

Where is she? And why is his father dead?

Remorse

After that terrible night in Madison Park, Raymond's job as a vacuum cleaner repairman lacked the same luster it used to. There was a time when walking to his job was a joy. He would tingle with excitement on his way to work, expecting a glimpse at Amber. Now he only smoldered with regret. Now he dreaded seeing even her shadow. His chances of having any kind of normal relationship with Amber were totally ruined all because of his mother and her ridiculous obsession with frogs.

He was careful not to say anything to Beverly when he walked in the repair shop that morning, lest he be another one of her melodrama victims, like her daughters, grappling in the mud of an imaginary pity pool.

"Good morning Raymond!" she called.

He returned her greeting with a grunt. "I hope there's a lot of work today."

"You will be pleasantly surprised then." Her rosy cheeks radiated way too much joy. "Bowers Department Store brought in their old machines. They all need repair of some kind, and none of them are clean."

"Good!" That was all he had for her. He pushed through the double doors, hung his coat on the coat rack and loosened his collar, expecting not to come up for a break until lunch. Burying his head in a filthy vacuum cleaner should provide all the therapy he needs.

Canister after canister, dust bowl after dust cloud, Raymond peeled clumps of grime, dust, rubber bands, and paperclips from around the belts, hair, and crud off rollers, and copper pennies from wheels. He coughed often and sneezed even more. Whenever his mind wandered, he'd find a string to unravel off a roller, or a gear to lubricate.

The lunch tone sounded, but it made no difference to him. He had a thermos of his Mum's brew in the fridge, but he didn't stop to drink any. Better his stomach churn than to be distracted from his job.

Hours passed. Vacuum cleaners began to mass by the 'done' bin, shiny and restored. So intent on cleaning the vacuum in hand, Raymond didn't notice the time until the whistle blew.

"Maybe I'll work late," he said to himself as he screwed in the last screw, looking up to see how many more jobs still waited. There were none. However, standing next to the bin was Amber, hair tucked into a fur collar on a wool coat that fitted temptingly to her figure. Her legs were smoothed by the nylons she wore, and her patent leather shoes reflected his image, a gawking dunce who couldn't believe his eyes.

He stood and dusted the cloud of vacuum residue off of his clothes, stopping when he saw the particles landing on her. "Oh, I'm sorry." He brushed her coat and stepped back. Maybe he shouldn't have done that either. "What are you doing here?"

"Will you walk me home?"

He hesitated and gave her a puzzled look. "What's this? I thought you were mad at me."

"I was. But I'm over it. I thought about what happened in the park, and really, if my mother acted like yours did last night, I would have disowned her too." She smiled that sweet dimpled smile that melted his heart.

"Well, no I was wrong to shun her. She's my Mum, after all."

"Never mind about last night anyway. You aren't responsible for your mother's actions. It was wrong for me to judge you."

Raymond would like to believe that he's not responsible for his mother's insanity. "Well, thanks. That's kind of you." He buttoned his collar and knotted his tie.

"Anyway, something happened last night that scared me and I remembered what you said about creepy things in the night. You said you thought a gentleman should walk a lady home, so I'm asking you to be a gentleman for me."

Raymond grabbed his coat and shuffled his arms into it as she spoke. "What happened last night that frightened you?"

"I'll tell you on the way."

Raymond smiled to himself. Whatever ghosts had scared Amber; they were his friends!

"Anytime you need me to walk you home I will, Amber. And I promise I will protect you from the ghosts and goblins and anything creepy that lurks in the dark!" Before switching the lights out, Raymond grabbed a vacuum handle from the parts bin, tossed it lightly in the air and caught it again with a confident grip. "This should work to ward off the monsters just fine!"

She hooked her arm into his and they strolled out of the Charles Mueller Building together. Raymond tucked the vacuum grip over his other arm, ready for battle if need be. Never in his whole life had he felt so good!

When they stepped into the cold night air, Amber began her story.

"Last night I walked Tom home."

"You walked Tom home?"

"Yes. And I think it was the last time I'm going out with him."

"Really? Well, not to gossip or anything but why did you decide not to date him anymore?"

"He's just not my kind of guy. I mean, I have to walk him home, right?"

Raymond chuckled to himself. "So, is this going to be a common practice between you two?"

"It seems like he'd like me to walk him home on a regular basis. He's big on the outside but he's kind of a wimp on the inside. Don't tell him I said that."

"Oh! No, don't worry. I won't."

"And then instead of going straight home, which I probably should have done, I went to the park. It was a beautiful night last night and I had some things to sort out."

Dare he get even more personal by asking her what she needed to sort out? He peered at her from the corner of his eye. She nestled closer and slipped her hand into his pocket, clasping his fingers. The touch not only gave him chills, but made him comfortable enough to ask.

"What kind of things did you need to sort out?"

"Well, I was trying to sort out my feelings. You know I went out to dinner with Tom. We ate at a really fine restaurant. Did you know Gillian's has lobster on the menu now?"

A feverish feeling flowed through his blood at that moment. Jealousy?

"No. I didn't know about lobster at Gillian's."

"Almost no one in Mason County serves lobster. But there it was with steak and Tom said I could order anything I wanted, so I ordered lobster."

Raymond swallowed. How nice of Tom! "So, did you like it?"

"It was okay but I didn't eat a lot of it."

"Well that was probably wasteful."

"I took it home. No waste."

"So that's what you had to sort out? Lobster?"

"No, Raymond. The reason I didn't finish is because I didn't feel well."

"You were sick?"

"No. I didn't feel well because I had to sort out my feelings."

"Your sick feelings?"

"Raymond, I was thinking about you."

"I made you sick?"

"No!" She stopped, but kept her hand in his pocket, so he pulled it out and turned to face her. There they stood under a street lamp holding hands. Raymond had started out that morning certain he would never hold her hand again, and here he was. Good fortune was on his side.

"I felt bad that I turned against you. You could have used my help last night when we met up with your Mum. But I bailed on you instead. Friends shouldn't do that to each other. And I want to be your friend."

All of Raymond's jealousy disappeared. The only thing he could do was gaze into her eyes. If that was his cue to say something, he was speechless. She smiled and tugged at his hand gently, piloting him along the shady sidewalk. "Your mother's kind of gooney."

Raymond laughed and pulled her closer to him again, this time locking his fingers around hers. "Yeah, she's not all that bad. She's doing her best to make things right."

They turned onto First Ave. Oak and maple trees shadowed the sidewalk, and leaves that swayed in the breeze played hide and seek with the moon. So old were the trees that the asphalt under their feet rose in gentle mounds, swelling from roots that demanded the return of their natural habitat.

"What do you mean make things right?" she asked.

Oh phooey! Slip of the tongue. He sighed a half laugh and looked at her. Why is he so careless with his tongue? She stopped again.

"Nothing, really. She just does her best to help me out."

"There's something different about you, Raymond." Amber took his hands as if to say he's safe to tell her. "I want to know. I need to know what you're hiding. If we're ever going to have a relationship, we have to be honest with each other."

Raymond's head suddenly felt hot. He brushed his tongue over his sandpapered fangs, hoping they hadn't shown or grown when he wasn't paying attention. He looked away at leaves that had fallen from the trees, dancing in haunting circles as the breeze played with them.

"Raymond!"

"What?"

"Listen to me."

"I hear you Amber, I'm not ignoring you. It's just that, well it's something I'm really ashamed of so it's not easy for me to talk about."

His answer ruined the mood, but what was he going to do? Blurt the truth out and risk losing her when he wasn't even sure he had her?

She sighed, clearly dissatisfied that he didn't tell her what she wanted to hear. Her discontent bothered him. Another wall of silence and secrecy had been erected.

"Amber." Should he? No. Not now. Their relationship was too new, too fragile. "What scared you last night?"

"I was in the park just minding my own business. You know our housing district was always a really safe neighborhood. Despite rumors in this city about vampires and haunted houses and other creepy things, which I've never been one to believe, I was stunned

196

by what happened. Simply shocked. More like horrified."

"What happened?"

"And I'm a pretty tough girl. I can hold my own. I've done some Karate, a little blade work in high school. I'm not opposed to defending myself."

"No, I suppose you're tough on the battlefield."

"And I did. I got him good, actually."

"Someone attacked you in the park? Did he hurt you?" Raymond raged. "Did you see who it was?"

"All he did was grab my hand but then he opened his mouth and with the stars shining the way they did."

"What? What did he do to you?"

"Nothing! He was going to—well he had these great big sharp pointed teeth that glistened in the starlight. The most horrendous things I've ever seen. Worse than the movies. Worse than Dracula! I swear, he was going to bite me. If I hadn't kicked him in the shin, I might not be standing here today."

Her words rang sharp as a fire alarm. "A vampire?" Raymond asked.

"I didn't believe in vampires either, but I swear! Do you believe that vampires exist?"

"Well yes, I do. I think."

"What happens when a vampire bites you? Do you die? Do you know?

"No! I'm not sure. I mean I think you either turn into a vampire or you die. I guess. It's worse than you can imagine though. It's not like the movies, Amber. This is serious." The compulsion to hug her was overwhelming, yet he wasn't sure if she would be receptive. He stopped her and searched her eyes. "Who was it? Had you ever seen him before?"

She shook her head. "No, but." Her eyes pierced his like she was acquainting Raymond to her attacker. Raymond couldn't stand the stare.

"What?"

"Well he was kind of dressed like the guy that you were with the other day. The one you rushed out of the park. You know, tailored suit, wool scarf."

"My uncle?" Oh, no! He shouldn't have said anything.

"That was your uncle?" She stepped back.

They'd been through this before with his mother. Now it was too late to deny his relationship with Gerald Peadlebody.

"Raymond, who is your uncle?"

"Amber, don't do this. You said it wasn't my fault what my relatives are like."

"It's not."

"Then please, don't ask."

"Who is your uncle, Raymond? I'm just asking a simple question."

He risked losing her if he told her, and losing her if he didn't. How did he get himself into messes like this? And did his uncle attack her? Because if Gerald Peadlebody attacked Amber, Raymond would pay the Peadlebody Estate a visit! Raymond tightened the tuck on the vacuum handle hanging on his arm, shifted his weight and looked at the warm light of the streetlamp. "My uncle is Gerald Peadlebody."

The silence could have cut fudge, and Raymond wished there were some to cut. He could do with a taste of sweet at this moment. He refused to make eye contact with Amber, though she seemed to beg for it the way she stood on her toes to see his face.

"Is that the same Peadlebody family that was involved in the train wreck?"

"It is."

"You're related?"

"Not by choice."

"You live in that old, haunted house up on the hill?"

"No. I have my own house in a different neighborhood. Far away."

"Who lives up there?"

"My uncle. And my mother. But she doesn't live in the house. She lives around back. In a tree house."

"Your mother lives in a tree house?"

"Yes."

"With a bunch of frogs?" She giggled and he cast a glance at her. "You poor boy!" Amber, still laughing, poked at his chest. "Raymond do you know what kind of things they say about that house?"

"I can imagine. It belonged to my grandfather, and he was, well, worse than my mum and uncle."

"And you refuse to talk about your father." "Yes."

"Fair enough. I can probably guess why."

Raymond scowled. "You can?"

"The name Peadlebody has always been the talk of the town ever since I was a little girl. And that house is the Halloween icon, if you don't mind me saying so."

"It could be worth a lot of money."

"Not hardly. It's haunted. No one in their right mind would live there."

A tinge of resentment buzzed through him. That was, after all his family she was talking about, though he had to agree they weren't in their right minds. "There are plenty of people not in their right minds."

"True."

"Let's not argue about my family. I care deeply for you. I would like to keep it that way. If you could just like me for who I am and pretend I am —say—an orphan, then I would be honored."

She laughed and then nodded. They resumed their walk.

"That's fair! As long as you don't tell me you're one of those vampire guys." Her laugh was a flaming torch scorching his insides.

Once the pain subsided, he swallowed. "Okay. I won't. But if it was my uncle who attacked you, I will kill him."

She stopped again and squinted at him. "So, wait a minute. Your uncle actually is a vampire?"

"Did I say that?"

She stepped away, but he followed, holding onto her arm. "Don't! Don't move away from me. Don't let that information change your mind about me. Even if my uncle is a vampire, I'm not. I swear. Or at least I control that part of me. I do! And I will make certain Gerald Peadlebody never, never comes near you again. I promise."

Whether the look on her face was one of panic or amazement, he didn't know. And why she stood so still, Raymond didn't care. He wanted to kiss her, to kiss her and tell her he loved her. He wanted to let her feel his mouth so she'd know he didn't have fangs, would never have fangs. He'd make sure of it. He'd grind all his teeth away and get dentures if he had to. He wanted her to trust him.

He leaned closer and hesitated, checking her eyes to make certain she wasn't going to flinch or back away. She didn't. She just stood there, looking at him. He touched her lips with his. When he felt how warm and luscious they were, he pressed against them, licked them, and held her tighter so he wouldn't knock her over.

She kissed him back.

Something happened at that moment. His heart raced. He felt warm, and a tingling sensation passed through his entire body. The phenomenon was so great he thought he'd faint. He released his kiss for want of air, panting.

"What's happening to you?" Amber touched his face. "You're burning up."

The fever subsided as quickly as it had come, leaving his

gums tingling. "You kissed me," he said.

"I did."

He rolled his tongue over his teeth. The abrasive edge where he had filed his fangs was now smooth. Where once his fangs had been, there were teeth now, smooth and rounded just like his other ones. A grin spread across his face. "Come with me."

Raymond took Amber by the arm and hurried her up the hill to the park. They laughed as they ran and gasped for breath as they dashed under the hedge and hurried to the bench. Raymond pulled Amber next to him and they kissed again, embracing one another well into the night.

You Didn't!

Raymond bought a box of crackers after he walked Amber home. As an experiment, he ate the entire contents on the way to his neighborhood, to see what human food would do to his stomach, if he'd be sick or not. Nothing. The food satisfied him. He stopped at the corner deli before turning the corner to his house, and bought a brick of cheese, and a lemonade, and devoured both.

When he got home—and after a good long burp — he brushed his teeth and examined his mouth in the mirror. Sure enough, his fangs had morphed into regular human choppers. Not only that, but his face glowed with color, no longer that pale, morbid vampire-blue. In fact, his eyes glistened with life the same way Amber's eyes sparkled.

"I'm normal!" He couldn't hold his excitement in. He leapt through the house, dancing a jig. "I'm normal, living in a human neighborhood. As a human! It's happened! I'm alive!"

After he tired of celebrating, Raymond fell asleep making plans to marry Amber and raise a family that he will support by working at the Gypsum Vacuum Cleaner Repair Shop.

"Maybe I'll buy a car and take vacations and go to soccer games with our sons. I'll eat human food that Amber will cook, watch TV or go to the movies. Maybe I'll even get to meet Mum's family in Florida."

Yes, Raymond Peadlebody could now live like he ought to be living.

***

Morning came. The sun shone through his window, yet dreams of the princess that kissed him and made him whole still lingered in his heart. He felt his teeth with his tongue, checking again. "It's true. My dream came true. I'm human. I'm in love. No dark closets. No more hiding. Mum's spell worked!"

What a wonderful Saturday to wake up to!

Raymond would pay Mum a visit today and bring her the good news!

Perhaps she, too, was released from the curse.

Then he remembered the conversation prior, and his stomach turned sour. Even though the night ended with a miracle, there was the unsettling dialogue he'd had with Amber. She'd been assaulted by a vampire. There was no mistaking who. If Amber hadn't been so strong, she'd be a living curse as well.

Raymond felt responsible for what had happened, and for her safety. He could not predict his uncle's predatory instincts, but he would confront him, nonetheless. Gerald Peadlebody must learn how to control himself! Before Raymond visited his mother, or met with Amber that afternoon, he'd pay his uncle a much-needed visit.

Within the hour, he was out of his bed, in the shower, dressed and on the bus headed to the Peadlebody Manor.

"You are dead, Uncle," Raymond grumbled as he jumped from the transit and stomped up Pine Street. "You will be begging for mercy when I get done with you. I'll yank those fangs out of your head bare handed!" The closer he came to the estate, the stronger his rage. Once on the porch, Raymond beat the clapper against the wooden door several times, pacing as he waited for the butler to answer.

Too long of an interval passed before Cottlebone appeared. When the servant cracked open the entryway, the gap was so marginal that only his nose and beady eyes showed in the crevice.

"Let me in!" Raymond demanded. He was not particularly fond of his grandfather's servant. Cottlebone was stuffy and cold and took no interest in being friends with anyone aside from his master. He looked like a thug, had a bland personality and a repulsive disposition. Raymond had purposefully avoided his uncle's house ever since the reading of the Will. Cottlebone was one of the reasons.

The door closed quietly.

Raymond knocked again, this time with his fist.

If he were Gerald, he'd pack Cottlebone's bags and send the servant back to the ship he came on. Employment of housemaids was old-fashioned. The manor was way too big to keep up. There was too much cleaning and sorting and gardening to do for one person, yet to pay servants was absurd. Better to live in a smaller house. Gerald should sell the place, find a more suitable home, and do his own housework.

His fist hurt from knocking so hard. Raymond's argument wasn't with Cottlebone this morning, so when the servant peeked out from behind the door again, Raymond changed his tone and smiled politely. "Is my uncle here?"

Cottlebone examined him from head to foot, contempt folded over his lips. "He is."

"Well, I'd like to see him, please."

"He's not accepting visitors."

"I'm not a visitor. I'm his nephew."

The servant said nothing, but opened the door and stood in the way.

Raymond's eyes narrowed as the two stared at each other. The tattoos on Cottlebone's neck pulsated; attesting that he had a heartbeat, but not until the man lifted his chin could Raymond acknowledge he was a living being. "He said not to let anyone in. He mentioned you, specifically!" Cottlebone folded his arms over his chest.

"Good gargoyles, fellow! What do you mean? I'm his relation. He can't exclude me. He's my uncle."

"So he is." Cottlebone stepped back to slam the door, but when it swung closed in Raymond's face, Raymond stopped it with his toe and inched it open with his foot. The servant backed, and Raymond pushed his way into the house.

"Tell my uncle I'm here."

There was indignation in the servant's stance. Cottlebone's face reddened. When Raymond saw the butler's fist clench, he opened his eyes wide. Cottlebone did not scare him.

"What?" Raymond asked.

"You need to leave."

"Get my uncle and let him speak for himself."

"Very well. Wait here." He gave Raymond a spine-tingling glare and then walked up the stairs, stopping once to look over his shoulder.

Raymond paced throughout the manor as he waited. A disgusting excuse for tidiness. The living room reeked of filth and clutter. If Cottlebone were a real servant, he'd at least dust the mantle, sweep cobwebs off the walls, or polish the mirrors. What does the man do all day?

He moved from the entry to the stairwell and into the parlor. When his uncle didn't, he tried to quiet his mind by watching the grandfather clock count the seconds with a silent and mighty sweep.

What was taking so long?

Five minutes passed. Finally, Cottlebone descended the

flight of steps. He came without Gerald. "He's ill."

"Oh? That's a lame excuse!"

"I'm sorry?"

Raymond dashed toward the servant who stood at the foot of the stairwell. Cottlebone stepped in front of him, big as he was, but Raymond wiggled around the servant's body mass.

"Don't go up there." Cottlebone grabbed at him but what Raymond didn't have in size he had in speed. He jumped the stairs two at a time. "My uncle is ill, all right, but bed rest is not the cure to his ailment!"

At the upper level hallway, which he'd never seen before, Raymond banged on doors until he found one ajar. He pushed it open.

His uncle lay on a bed in that room, books on his lap, tea set at his side. Raymond charged at him. Gerald sat up in surprise, and recoiled, folding his hands over his head to protect it. Raymond grabbed him by his flannel nightshirt, sending the teapot and cup against the bedpost, tea splashing on the sheets. Books fell on the floor, papers sailed across the room and cinnamon rolls flew into the air as Raymond pulled Gerald from under his covers and pushed him past the dresser. Gerald's shirt ripped open as Raymond lifted him by the collar off the floor and pressed him against the wall.

"I swear I'll drive a stake through your heart if you ever touch Amber again. If you ever even look at her."

Gerald's Adams-apple rolled. Beads of sweat popped from the pores on his forehead and his eyes burst so wide they nearly exploded out of their sockets. Raymond could feel him trembling and was glad of it. Anything to get his point across!

"Let him go!"

Both Raymond and Gerald turned their head to the bedroom door where Cottlebone stood. Aimed at Raymond's back was the barrel of a .44 Magnum. Raymond glanced at his uncle, tightening his grip, and then looked over his shoulder at Cottlebone again. He was too angry to fear a bullet.

"Richard put it down," Gerald ordered with a trembling voice.

"He's hurting you, sir. I'll not have anything happen to another master of mine. I have a duty to you."

"No, he's not hurting me."

"He's threatening you."

"He's my nephew, Cottlebone. Put the gun down."

Raymond gave Gerald a puzzled look. Here he was roughing his uncle up, pinning him against a wall and threatening his life, while his uncle defended him. Perhaps the man was less vampire than he thought. Raymond released his hold on Gerald and stepped back.

"Raymond, I swear I'm not going to touch your girl again." Gerald's lips quivered when he landed on his feet, though his knees buckled and he would have fallen if Raymond hadn't caught him.

"Your words are not good enough for me, Uncle. You've lied to me before. I don't believe your promises."

"Richard! Would you leave us alone please?" Gerald said as he gathered his composure and his balance.

The servant wavered.

"Go!" Gerald insisted.

With an audible sigh, Cottlebone lowered his gun, stepped into the hall and shut the door. Raymond presumed he still lingered on the other side of the entry, eavesdropping.

"Give me another chance." Gerald's request was meek. His hands went to his throat where Raymond had clung. Raymond wasn't touching him any longer, but he still had him trapped against the wall.

The initial fury had passed. Raymond had vented. The anger that brewed on his walk along Pine Street was now diminishing. "I mean every word I said." Raymond stepped back and allowed his uncle some breathing space.

"I know you do."

"If you hurt her I will kill you. I don't care if you have a bodyguard or not. You won't escape."

"I believe you."

"I love her. You shamed me, and you scared the daylights out of her. What was worse is that you had the audacity to think you could possess her like that. You're rotten. Your whole family is rotten."

"I know."

"You know?" Raymond spat at his uncle's feet before he turned away from him. "What do you know?"

"We come from some bad blood. I'm not proud of our heritage either."

"We? No, Mr. Peadlebody. Your blood, your relatives, your legacy, not mine. You come from some bad blood. Mum's blood is pure and wholesome and neither you nor your brother can take that away from us. The curse is broken. I'm no longer your flesh and blood nephew and if you keep stalking Amber, who is going to be my wife someday, you can consider me your enemy."

"I'm sorry you feel that way."

"Well, I'm not sorry."

Gerald wiped his brow with his sleeve and walked to the mirror, inspecting his torn nightshirt. "You didn't have to rip my clothes."

"You're lucky I didn't rip out your heart."

Raymond paced, wondering if it was time to leave, if there was something more he could drive home to his uncle before he departed. There wouldn't be another confrontation like this, he was sure. With Cottlebone as a sentry, Raymond might never have access to his uncle again. At least not at the manor.

No other words came to mind, so Raymond took three long strides toward the door when Gerald, who was still brooding in front of the mirror, broke the silence.

"What do you mean the curse is broken?"

Raymond glimpsed his uncle's eyes in the looking glass. Gerald's lips quivered over his glistening teeth and for a moment Raymond froze.

Why had he told Gerald the curse had been broken? He should have waited until he and Amber were far out of the county on a train back to New Orleans. Or somewhere. Anywhere. If ever! More vulnerable now than he had ever been, nothing stood in the way of his uncle from attacking him and shattering his dream of living a human life. If Cottlebone waited in the hall behind the door, Raymond was utterly defenseless.

His only hope was to run. And run fast.

He tripped over a leather-bound journal on his way out and rather than kicking it aside, he, reached down, grabbed it and tucked it in his pocket before Gerald could stop him. Raymond slammed the door open, not looking back to see if he had hit Cottlebone with it, and flew down the stairs two steps at a time. Once out the front door, he glanced over his shoulder. No one followed.

Inhaling a breath of fresh air, he felt safer outside. Despite the panic, the day was going along exactly as he had planned. His uncle succumbed to his demand for an apology and he succeeded in defending the woman he loved all in the same breath. Now he would bring Mum the exciting news of his transformation.

Stepping onto the driveway, Raymond tripped again, this time over a piece of yard art, one he had never seen before. A stone chipmunk.

"Odd," Raymond mumbled to himself. "What's a stone chipmunk doing in the middle of the driveway where it could get run over?" He picked up the statue and instead of setting it in the garden, he decided his mother would appreciate it more. He carried it with him to Ginger's house.

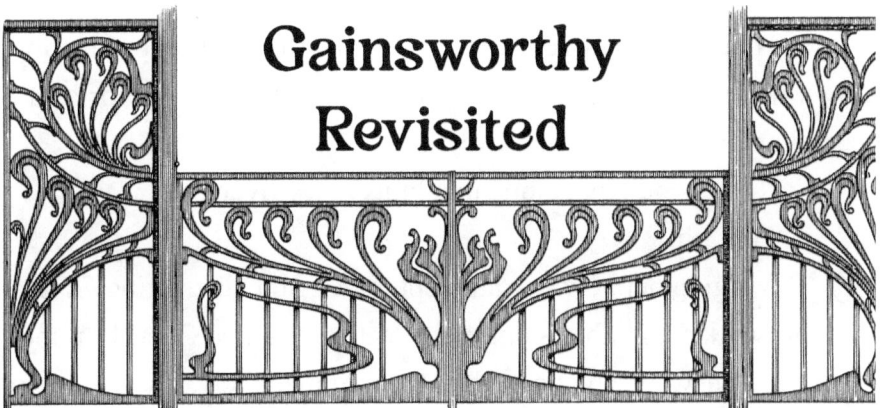

Gainsworthy
Revisited

Cottlebone had stopped the door from slamming into his face by pushing his shoe up against it as it swung. Now that Raymond was gone, the servant stepped inside Gerald's room, flipped his linen hankie from his pocket and wiped the scuff mark off his toe. Gerald remained in front of the mirror, eyeing Cottlebone but listening to his heart beat in hopes it would calm before his servant would have to do CPR on him. His fingers tapped the dresser nervously.

"Are you all right, sir?" Cottlebone inquired.

"I'm fine. Give it no more thought, Cottlebone! I'm fine. Raymond is just a hot air balloon when he's riled. Harmless, really."

Raymond had certainly upset him that morning, but the boy's cause was understandable. Gerald regretted having attacked Amber and he could think of no other way to make up for his mistake other than letting his nephew take his aggressions out on him. "It's done. Over, now. Nothing more will be said of the matter ever again," so he hoped. He had paid his penance.

"Your nephew didn't appear harmless to me."

"Well he is. Leave him alone. And leave me alone. You may go. Please."

The servant bowed slightly and fumbled with the gun that had become an awkward prop in his hand.

"And for pity sake, Richard, unload that thing."

"Sir, it was never loaded."

That was more of a surprise to Gerald than Cottlebone having drawn the gun in the first place. He gaped at the servant for a full second and then waved him away.

"Don't you have cinnamon buns in the oven?"

"Yes, sir."

A raging nephew and an inept butler were distracting Gerald from his work. His father's untimely death tormented Gerald's mind. He needed answers, and he needed them immediately. It was time to talk to the people that shared his father's last days.

Gerald unbuttoned the torn pajama top, pulled the rag off his shoulders, and rolled it in a ball before he tossed it on the bed.

A cunning real estate partner and his insane wife would be the first people to interrogate. He stalked to his closet and pushed aside hangers in search of the appropriate shirt to wear. A white one freshly starched. He wouldn't play games this time. No beating about the hedge. He would knock on Simon Gainsworthy's door and confront him.

He found a pair of wool trousers and pulled them from their hanger. He'd take a shower first to calm his nerves and then he'd travel the thirteen-mile bus trip to Knobby Hill and confront the man, much like Raymond confronted him this morning. He'd use more tact and maturity than his nephew, but he'd apply equivalent boldness. How else would he discover the truth?

***

Thanks to Rufus, Gerald knew where Gainsworthy lived. When the time came to give the realtor a visit, he'd dodge through the fancy wrought-iron gate and under the two happy alabaster gentlemen. Entry would be easy.

Even on the bus he primped himself, twisting his mustache and brushing the wrinkles out of his sleeves. His thoughts wandered. Time flew. Even the woman with the two unruly children that boarded the bus a mile down the road didn't bother him. Neither did the man with the dog tucked in his sleeve. Gerald nodded a greeting.

He disembarked at the real estate office. Once the bus drove away, the whole earth seemed to stand still. No one stirred. The building where Gerald met Rufus was locked and the lights inside were off.

A closed sign hung on the door. The sun had not risen high enough to warm the pavement much less awaken any white-collar workers for the day. Rufus' cart was parked across the street; dew clung to its bumper and glistened brightly, reflecting the colors of the dawn on its hood and on its roof. Gerald gave no mind to the solitude. He enjoyed it. A brisk walk would do him good and besides, he knew the way.

Gerald hadn't reached his destination as early as he had expected. He'd forgotten how steep the hill was and the climb slowed him down. As hard as it had been to travel up that winding road in the cart, walking was much more difficult. He panted. Every few steps, he stopped to rest. The heat of the day became unbearable by the time he arrived at the flat where Mrs. Gainsworthy had run them off the road.

Gerald peeled off his coat and folded the fleece over his arm. He pulled the woolen scarf from around his neck and tucked one end into his pocket while the rest of the red and blue stole hung as a tail past his knees. Sweat seeped out of his pores and he could smell himself, which was concerning. Should he be invited into Gainsworthy's home he would make an undesirable guest.

Finally, when the sun was well into the ten o'clock hour, he found himself on the shady part of the drive and thereafter at the gate in the presence of those two remarkable stone figures. The cheerful statues seemed much larger than they had been the day he was here with Rufus. He paused to admire the artwork before he slithered between the iron bars of the gate.

Their suits were well fitted, and they wore scarves, like his, intricately chiseled so the plaid was visible along with strands of fringe. One of the men had a top hat tucked under his arm, an indication of the era when he must have lived. His lips were full, his eyes smiling over robust cheeks. Gerald would have enjoyed knowing this man, even if he were a human.

The other statue, the one reaching the furthest over the gate, was older and less cheerful. The man had a curly beard, his hands were gloved and he held his index finger out toward the other statue. A pose that reminded Gerald of Michelangelo's The Creation of Adam. Such a sacred pose seemed out of character here in Gainsworthy-land.

Gerald stared at the figures until the sun topped the trees and shone on them so brilliantly the glare was unbearable to his naked eye. It was time to move on.

He pulled his own scarf from his pocket, brushed the creases out of it, then wrapped it around his neck and tucked the ends in his vest like an ascot. He put his coat back on, brushed his eyebrows, and hooked his cane over his arm. He'd be as prim and proper as these men in their alabaster coats. Regardless of what he had to say to Gainsworthy or his wife, he'd be tactful. Surely his refinement would make an impression.

Gerald spat on his fingers and twisted his mustache as he walked down the asphalt drive past the cream-colored car. The walkway divided the freshly mowed lawn in two large sections each of which rolled up and over Knobby Hill into stone walled gardens and bright green meadows. In front of him, a brick turnaround circled a fountain and ended at a porch, the roof of which was supported by marble columns. Huge pots atop ornate carved pedestals lined the portico, all with vines and blossoms pouring over their rims.

Gerald walked slowly to the entry and was about to use the brass knocker when the double doors rolled apart. A short pear-shaped woman with a weathered face, wearing a black dress and white apron appeared. Gray locks streaked her hair and came together on top of her head, fastened tightly to her head by a hairnet. She wore red lipstick and rouge. Though her wrinkles suggested age, Gerald counted no more than forty-five years of hardship in her past.

"Who are you?" she asked, none too politely.

Gerald felt his normally pale face flush red. He stuttered, adjusted the top button on his coat, and cleared his throat.

"I am Gerald Peadlebody."

Evidently, his voice had been amplified by a speaker, for he heard an echo inside the house. He peered over the maid's shoulder, but he could see nothing except a long hallway made of black tile both on the walls and floor behind her. The woman touched a button by the door.

Gerald jumped when he heard a man's voice laughing. "Gerald Peadlebody, is it? Well what do you know? Hi there, Gerry ole boy! I remember you from your brother's funeral. Come in, Gerald Peadlebody!" The nickname struck a sour note in his gut. Gerald cleared his throat to talk, but the woman released the button and interrupted his thoughts.

"Try using the speaker by the gate next time," she scolded in his ear as she stepped away and let him enter.

"My apologies," Gerald said. Already his hands were shaking. He was not prepared for humiliation.

Gerald's footsteps sent a mysterious echo down the hall. He'd worn his best shoes this morning, his cordovan wingtips that had a special clink to them when hitting hard surfaces such as ceramic tile. Now he wished he had worn a softer sole because the click of his heels sounded like an audio track from a Hitchcock film. The maid followed silently behind. Gerald hesitated once and looked back at her. Her expression never changed. She nodded for him to continue, so he did.

At the end of the foyer to his right was an arched entryway and a step down, opening into a brightly lit room with leather chairs and an L-shaped couch. The walls here were lined with mirrors just like the parlor in the Peadlebody Manor, and it gave Gerald pause. His father's journal entry immediately came to mind.

That's why I trained my faithful and beloved seafaring servant Richard Cottlebone to avoid laying eyes on her, and why we have one room where the walls are made of mirrors. For her, to enter that room would be the death of her.

A chill raced up Gerald's back and he once again turned to the maid.

"Is this a special room?"

"It's the parlor. Sit down," she answered curtly.

The coffee table was meant to be the focus decor, as all the furniture surrounded and faced this piece of art. The table armature was an alabaster statue in the shape of a collie laying on his back, whose nose and tail supported a thick layer of glass. The detail of the sculpture was as lifelike as the men at the gate.

"Wait here." The maid left him alone in the room with the white dog, glass tabletop, and thirty-six mirrors. At first, he tried ignoring his reflection, but the image wouldn't let him escape, so he resigned himself.

Even though Gerald had become accustomed to the mirrors on the Peadlebody parlor walls, this room was completely different. Instead of ambient light which only showed soft pleasing images, these mirrors lined a northern wall and faced a large south window.

Bright sunlight lit the entire parlor so that Gainsworthy's looking-glass told no lies.

Gerald saw exactly what he looked like to human beings, and if he were a human, he'd be repulsed. How ghastly were the huge bags under his eyes, his skin tone gray, not even vampire blue? His cheekbones had risen to such a height that the valley of his eye sockets resembled a skeleton. If appearances alone were why his nephew despised him, he understood.

While scrutinizing his form, he eyed another image in the mirror. In an alcove behind him, partially shielded by a curtain, stood a life-sized form covered with a cloth.

Resisting temptation was never one of Gerald's strong points and in this instance, he failed again. He eased out of the parlor and lifted the cloth, discovering an unfinished sculpture, a figure almost as tall as he. Several chisels lay at the base and stone chips covered the floor, suggesting the artist was still working on the piece. Gerald pulled the cloth off the head and cringed. In front of him stood a statue, still in the process of being sculpted. All but the head was finished. One side of the face had been chiseled into a lovely young lady with smooth skin and deep-set eyes. The other half of the face was the exact likeness of an older woman he had seen before, smiling eyes, two bucked teeth and dimples. He knew who she was. Mrs. Bilberry.

Gerald quickly covered the statue and stepped into the parlor again.

"Mr. Gerald Peadlebody!"

Mr. Gainsworthy held out his hand and when Gerald took it, he was pulled away from the entrance to the alcove and guided to the couch.

"What a pleasure meeting you! What brings you up this way?"

Ah yes! Niceties? Gerald remembered his father's description of the man. A true sales person. Gerald straightened his back and lifted his chin. He shook the man's hand as he would have been rude not to, but he kept his guard.

"I have some questions about my father I think you can answer for me." Gerald said, coldly.

"Of course, lad. Come into my den where we can talk privately. These mirrors make me nervous!"

The mirrors made Gerald nervous, too. Being in the same room with thirty-six Gainsworthy would curdle even the grisliest vampire's blood.

Gerald followed the heavyset fellow, noting his overconfident stride, the white hair that was a bit too long and curled past his ear, the pink complexion of his skin, and the cream-colored suit that matched the car in his driveway. Already Gerald's stomach soured. The musk of his aftershave didn't help anything.

The hall opened to a living space—one huge chamber with a spiral staircase in the center. Atop the staircase, an elaborately decorated loft circled above them. Several closed doors faced the aisle, and a wrought iron banister lined the walkway and flight of steps. The main floor was dimly lit as shutters on the picture window blocked the sunlight from entering the room. The den where Gainsworthy led Gerald was furnished with a Cherrywood desk, an old rocking chair and a plush easy chair. On the wall behind the desk were topographical maps with push pins stuck into it, signifying properties, Gerald assumed, that they were either Gainsworthy's real estate listings or potential listings.

"What sort of questions do you have for me, Gerry?" Gainsworthy opened a drawer to a small buffet and pulled out a pipe and a package of tobacco. As a second thought, he took out a small box as well and opened it, offering its contents to Gerald. "Cigar?"

"I don't smoke," Gerald said. He would have liked if Gainsworthy addressed him more formerly. This was not a good ole friendship, as the man's manner of speech would suggest.

"How can I help you?" Gainsworthy pinched some tobacco from the package and worked the wad into the hollow of his pipe with his finger. Shavings dropped onto the floor, but the man didn't seem to mind. He motioned for Gerald to sit down.

"Well!" Gerald cleared his throat. His questions seemed to have dissolved and his mind was suddenly blank. What did he want to know, besides the obvious? Did you kill my father? No. That wouldn't work. He tried again. "I didn't know my father in his later years and since you two were friends I thought it would be advantageous for me to have a conversation with you. Concerning him, of course."

Gainsworthy raised an eyebrow. "Oh? What do you know about our friendsh—?" He hesitated and strolled to his easy chair.

Indeed, Mr. Gainsworthy, your what? Gerald thought.

"—our friendship?" Gainsworthy seated himself and continued playing with the contents of his pipe, avoiding Gerald's eyes. "Did someone tell you we were friends?" Gainsworthy's eyes narrowed.

Gainsworthy's reaction was not a good sign, and Gerald immediately realized his tongue had slipped. His father's diaries were supposed to be secret. Benjamin Peadlebody made it quite clear that none of his writings, nor their content, should ever leave the estate. Were it not for the journals, there would be no indication that Benjamin and Simon Gainsworthy had been friends.

"Yes, well I just assumed that you two had been friends."

"Why would you assume that?" He laughed, but it was a forced laugh and didn't fool Gerald.

Gerald smiled politely. "Okay, well your assumptions are correct. We were friends. We were quite close, actually. We did some business transactions together. Ate at some fancy restaurants, had a few beers. Have you been reading some of your father's books?"

Gerald did not show his surprise at that question. He was not always smart, or quick-witted, but he played enough chess to know that a win remains with the offensive. "Books?" he asked.

"Oh, come on, Gerry. Everyone knows your father was a journalist."

"Everyone like who?"

Simon lit his pipe and puffed out a huge cloud of smoke. His beady eyes rested on Gerald. "You got me there."

"How did your friendship end?"

Silence. Mr. Gainsworthy grimaced. Perhaps Gerald was moving too fast, but if he stopped asking his questions, he may learn nothing.

Movement in the loft above the staircase grabbed Gainsworthy's eye. Gerald followed the man's focus to a woman looking over the rail. Mrs. Gainsworthy? Was that the woman at Rockford's funeral? The same woman who ran him and Rufus off the road and into the woods? The woman in the loft wore a scarf turban and pointed sunglasses, the same attire Gerald had seen through the tinted windshield. She disappeared into a room and Gainsworthy interrupted his thoughts.

"Did I say that our friendship ended?" Gainsworthy chuckled, a poor attempt at making light of things as he leaned back in the easy chair. "If it ended, death was the gavel." He looked at his pipe again and pushed the smoldering tobacco around with his little finger.

Gerald's focus turned sharply from the retreating figure atop the stairs, to the pinkish rogue who was seated comfortably across from him.

"Well, no you didn't say your friendship with my father ended, but I assumed it had."

"Why?"

"There wasn't a word about any business left to my brother and I after my father died." Nice save, Gerald, he thought to himself.

The man puffed on his pipe and then licked his lips before he replied. "Oh. No, you're right. Your father bowed out of our partnership several years ago. Whatever he earned is in your share of the Will. But just because we parted as partners, doesn't mean our friendship ended."

With a forceful strike against his boot heel, Gainsworthy lit another match and touched it to the bowl. He puffed several times until the tobacco glowed red and then he shook the match until sulfur smoke streamed from its head. He dropped the burned head into an ashtray and leaned forward. "I always admired your father. A man with a purpose. Pity he sunk away into the shadows. I suppose guilt will do that to a man." He cleared his throat and looked up at Gerald. "If you're seeking money, there's enough in that estate of yours. If you want cash out, I left an offer with your attorney."

Gerald's eyes widened. So Gainsworthy had been the cash offer!

"Why do you want the manor?"

Gainsworthy grunted. "I deal in real estate. Remember? I take it you came here today to sell?"

"Not at all. I merely want to know what kind of disposition my father was in when he died."

"How would I know that? I would have had to have been there." Gainsworthy leaned back in his chair, again, and smoked, his demeanor calm and confident. His stare, piercing.

Gerald's nose twitched. He scratched it. "Did he have enemies? Someone who didn't like what he was doing?"

"You don't know?"

"How would I know? I'm asking you?"

Gainsworthy laughed. "If you haven't figured it out by now, I'll tell you. Not everyone in Mason County loved your father. Especially after the death of that dear sweet schoolteacher. Of course, he had enemies. But I don't know who they are or if they confronted your father. Benjamin was a writer, among other things. I would think he might have mentioned his adversaries in his journals."

Gainsworthy was prodding. That was the second time he inquired about Benjamin's journals. "Again, how do you know he was a writer?"

Gainsworthy chuckled and looked at his pipe, dusted a piece of tobacco off his shirt, and then squinted at Gerald, scrutinizing him as if he could see right through him. "We were friends, remember? The man had a pen in his hand almost every time I visited him. He loved his journals. He even had a red one. I'm surprised you haven't come across it."

Gerald coughed, checked the buttons on his coat, and retied his scarf. "I know there's a library down in the basement but I haven't spent much time going through its inventory."

"Well, perhaps you should do some studying in your own backyard before you go asking strangers for answers."

"Perhaps."

"Of course, a long-lost son of Old Ben's is a friend of mine. I'd be willing to help you go through that library of yours. If you want. I could explain things a little better for you if I had the books right here in front of me, again."

"Again?" It was daring to ask, but Gerald couldn't help calling him on his comment.

"I've had a peek or two. It's hard to avoid when you're in a car next to someone scribbling notes the whole while."

"I see."

"So?" Gainsworthy asked.

"So, what?"

"Are you going to accept my offer?"

"No. I'm fine. I think I can read my father's journals without assistance." Perhaps Gerald's voice was too sharp, but he was stressed and could barely contain his emotions.

"Well if you don't need my help, why did you come here?"

Why did he come? Gerald glanced around the room. The discomfort was becoming difficult to bear. "I just wanted to know if you were aware of any conflicts my father might have had with anyone. That's all."

Gainsworthy laughed long and hard, but Gerald found no amusement.

"I get it! Benjamin Peadlebody's son is playing detective. You think maybe your old dad was murdered, don't you?"

Gerald wrung his hands. "Well, I have to admit; it has crossed my mind."

"So, you're knocking on his only friend's door with not much more than an assumption." He pointed his pipe in Gerald's direction. His voice sent a chill down Gerald's spine. "If you are accusing me of foul play I own half this town and a few more towns down the road."

Gerald felt the blood drain from his face.

Gainsworthy changed his tone and sat back again. "Now, I'll tell you. That lightning storm took us all by surprise. Dry lightning, they call it. Comes out of the clouds sharp as a knife. No rain. You don't need rain for lightning to strike a tree. To think—" Gainsworthy leaned well over into Gerald's space. So near, Gerald smelled scotch on his breath. "You tell me. What are the chances of a branch falling through a roof and stabbing someone in the heart? Especially someone like your father?"

Gainsworthy spent too long on that last phrase. Gerald froze. Their eyes locked. Gainsworthy smiled, but Gerald understood his grin to be a threat.

"Just keep that in mind, Mr. Peadlebody. We all knew who and what your father was."

Gerald took a deep breath to compensate for his racing heart. He needed out. Fresh air. He was considering a gracious way to excuse himself. Still, if he left now, he'd never find out what he wanted to know. The motive. There had to be a motive.

"What exactly didn't you like about my father?" The words came out broken and raspy. Gerald was brave though, and didn't peel his focus from Gainsworthy's eyes. Not once.

"His breed," the man replied, wiping drool that had seeped from the corner of his mouth. He nodded as if agreeing with himself. "Didn't like his bloodline."

"Then I don't suppose you care for mine either?"

Gainsworthy shrugged. His blue eyes pierced a hole into Gerald. "Your father gave me a reason not to like him. Don't you follow his example! In fact, I know one way you can get on my good side right now."

"How's that?"

"Accept my offer on that house of yours. You, your idiot sister-in-law, and her son. All of you high tail it out of town. Leave everything there. Don't touch a lamp, a clock, or a book. Not one book. Leave things as they are with the estate and we'll be the best friends you could ever hope to have."

"And if I don't?"

"Let's just say if you don't, you might find out what happened to your father. The hard way."

"Are you threatening me?"

"Do you feel threatened?"

Gerald should have guessed something like this would happen. "Why do you want the Peadlebody Manor?"

"I don't." Gainsworthy leaned back in his chair and looked up at the top of the stairs again. His wife was at the banister. Gerald glanced at her, and then did a double take. She was taking the scarf off her head.

"Not now, Ellen." He said. "Wait!"

Ellen! Not the wicked Ellen his father despised? His second

wife's sister? Gerald's eyes darted between the two and he jumped up. Time to leave and to leave swiftly.

"I'll consider your offer."

"You do that."

"There's a bus I need to catch now if I want to get home in a timely fashion."

Gainsworthy laughed. "Yes. You had better run. I'll make an appointment with Ferguson. We can close escrow in a matter of days."

Before Gerald could step outside, Gainsworthy called after him.

"Peadlebody!"

Gerald turned around. The pipe was still in his hand, but Gainsworthy's jovial grin was gone. He pointed his other stubby finger at Gerald when he gave his last command. "Don't you take anything from that house when you leave, Gerald. Don't take a single written word. I want it all or the deal is off."

Frogs Abound

"Mum!" Raymond felt young again, bounding up the stairs to his mother's tree house, scaring the birds on the porch into the trees and scattering the squirrels that sat on the windowsill. With the statue clutched tight against his chest, he banged on the door with his other hand.

"Mum!"

He could see his mother through the screen, racing around the kitchen chasing frogs and carrying them out of the room. "Just a minute. Wait a minute," she called.

"Mum it worked!" Raymond's knuckles were red from knocking on the metal frame so fiercely. "Mum, let me in. I have something to tell you.

Good news!"

"All right, all right! Just a minute." She made one more trip to the back and then raced to the door. Wiping her hands on her apron, she unlatched the screen.

Raymond burst over the threshold, panting. "It worked!"

"What worked?"

He set the yard art on the table. "The spell. Whatever you did. It worked. Look!" He opened his mouth and with his free hand pulled back his lips to show her that his fangs weren't there.

"What? I don't see anything."

"That's because they're gone. I'm no longer a vampire. I swear! Your spell worked. My fangs have disappeared, replaced by normal human teeth. I know it's true because I bought a whole box of crackers last night and ate them all. And cheese and lemonade. I'm fine! You've made me the happiest man in the world!" He hugged her and lifted her off the ground.

When he set her back down, she gasped. "Oh! It's true?" Her eyes widened and she covered her mouth. "Oh!" she repeated.

"Did it work for you?"

She felt her teeth and shook her head. "I don't feel any different. What do you think? What do you see?" She opened her mouth and breathed into Raymond's face. Her canine teeth were long and pointed, and a bit yellow.

"What do you see? Any different?"

"No. I'm sorry, Mum. If it worked for me it should have worked for you, don't you think? What did you do?"

"I'm not sure."

"What spell did you use?"

"I kissed a few frogs but I don't think that was the curse breaker. Your uncle had a different opinion about kissing frogs." Ginger pointed to the statue. "What's that?"

Raymond picked up the statue and offered it to her. "Garden art that I found in front of the manor. It's supposed to be a chipmunk I guess. It was in the driveway about to get run over so I picked it up. I thought it was yours, but if it's not, it should be. You've never seen it before?" The look on his mother's face subdued him. She had grown pale in a matter of minutes and circles around her eyes darkened. "What, Mum? Are you okay?" She certainly didn't look well. The color had drained from her temples and her eyes were glazed over.

"Raymond, that's Dusty!"

"What? No Mum, don't be silly. This is just garden art. Look, it's stone." He tapped on it with his fist.

"It's Dusty. I know my pet. He's been missing ever since that morning the house filled up with smoke."

"Mum, no it isn't. This is an inanimate object. Clay, stone, whatever it's made from, it isn't real." Has she gone off the deep end? She'd been rational up until her episode with the frogs. If she keeps having these sorts of fits, he might need to get her some professional help soon—if there is such a thing for vampires.

Her face reddened. She grimaced at Raymond and her voice hardened. "Don't look at me like I'm crazy. Don't you think I know my pet when I see it? Look," She took the statue from him and held his leg. "His left nail is missing. He caught it in the screen door when the house filled up with smoke. I know because I freed his foot so he could get out."

Raymond looked closely. Indeed, one toe was missing a nail.

"I swear this is Dusty." She held the stone chipmunk against her breast. Tears seeped from her eyes. The look she gave Raymond was pathetic. "What happened to him?"

Ginger turned her back to her son and walked to the table where she made a nest with a towel, fluffing one end on which to lay its head. Raymond had never seen his mother so distressed with her shoulders drooping, her head bowed, and a pout on her face. Once Dusty was settled in his towel, she buried her head in her hands and collapsed into the chair.

"Everything is falling apart, Raymond. Everything."

This was not the reaction he expected. He'd been upstaged by a varmint! Did she really think more of her stone chipmunk than of him? "Look, Mum, I'm sorry about Dusty, if that even is

231

Dusty. It's a shame really, but the forest is filled with squirrels and chipmunks and all sorts of critters."

She grimaced at him.

"Just like Madison Park is filled with frogs. There are more."

"You just don't get it. I loved Dusty!"

"Okay. You loved him. I'm sorry about what happened. Can we change the subject for a moment because I'd really like to drive this other matter home? I brought good news. Don't you want to celebrate with me?" Raymond straddled the other chair. "Mum, look at me."

She slowly pulled her sorrowful gaze away from the chipmunk.

"Your son is no longer a vampire!"

She wiped her eyes with the back of her hands, tore a paper towel from the roll that was lying on the floor by the chair, and blew her nose. "I'm sorry Raymond. I'm happy for you. Don't think that I'm not. It's just that seeing Dusty in this condition is heart wrenching. I don't understand what happened to him. But yes, you are more important." After another snivel, she looked him in the eyes, hers wet and red. "I don't know what happened to you either. I'm thrilled though. You know I am. I'm so happy you're human." She touched his cheek and finally Raymond felt a surge of gladness come from her. "It's wonderful. Don't pay tribute to me for your good fortune. I would love to know if it were one of the spells that I was working on, but honestly, I don't think I had anything to do with it. If any of these spells worked, it should have worked for me too. I wish it had!"

"Aw, Mum."

Then the tears gushed. "I'm so tired of this!"

"I know Mum. All that you've been through it's not fair, is it? I wish I could change things for you." Raymond was at a loss. He had never seen his mother cry so fiercely.

"I know you do." She patted him on the knee. "Ever since your father died, all I've wanted to do is get us back to being human. Even before he died, but I couldn't admit it openly then. Well, now you're free and that's good. At least one of us was successful."

"It'd be best if we were both free." He scooted next to her and held her hand as she cried.

"It's been so long. So very long. I have tried and tried."

"I know Mum."

She blew her nose again. "You know, when I first met your dad I fell in love with him. He was so good-looking, like you. He wooed me, dined me. We did such fun things together. He'd take me to the drive in, we'd go fishing, though I was always the one to clean the fish, and he never ate. I should have had my suspicions then. But love is blind, son. Remember that."

"That's what they say."

"He wanted children. I loved that about him. Without my son, I don't know where I'd be." She squeezed his cheek.

"I love you too, Mum."

"There were no warning signs. Nothing. He dressed well, he had good manners. How was I supposed to know things would turn out the way they did? He was handsome. Strong. Sexy!"

"Mum!"

"Well he was. I fell head over heels for your dad. I really did. And then we got married. He bit me on my neck and I turned into a vampire. How rotten is that?"

Raymond squeezed her hands. "It's pretty rotten."

"He wasn't nice to me after that. He wasn't nice to you either. I've been doing nothing but hating my life ever since. Well, at least you don't have to hate yours anymore. That's one good thing. I'm glad you're happy now."

"I am too, Mum and what's even better is that I'm going to ask Amber to be my wife."

She stopped her crying long enough to look at him. "Are you sure about that? Because last time I saw your Amber girl she was mad at you."

"We made up, Mum. Not only that, but we made out."

Her eyes widened.

"Well, just a little. We kissed."

"You kissed her?"

Raymond nodded excitedly. "And she told me she loved me. I'm supposed to meet her at ten at the end of the driveway. She wants to meet you properly." He glanced at his watch. Here it is, nine-thirty already.

His mother's mouth hung open, her eyes wide with curiosity. "Wait a minute. You kissed?"

"Yes. In the park. I love her."

"Is that when you noticed you weren't a vampire any longer?"

"Yes. Right after she kissed me back I could feel my gums tingle. I literally felt my fangs disappear and when I rolled my tongue over where they should be, they were gone. Amber noticed a change too. She said I looked flushed like I had a fever."

"Raymond, don't you see what happened?"

"What?"

"It wasn't me that freed you from the curse, it was Amber. It was the kiss."

"Are you sure?"

"Yes! All the books I've been reading validate what you just told me. When you're under a curse, being kissed by someone that loves you can break the spell. Look here."

She rummaged through the piles of newspapers, shopping bags, birdseed packages, and books. One by one, she brushed off the hardbacks she had borrowed from the library and piled them on his lap. "The Frog Prince, Snow White, Sleeping Beauty, Beauty and the Beast. The Daughter of Hippocrates, Same thing in all those books!

My concoction was all cock-eyed though. I got the dynamics wrong. Me kissing a frog wouldn't help me, or you. It might help the frog were he under some kind of spell, but none of mine were, I guess." She pouted and looked over her shoulder toward the bathroom. "I quit kissing them after number fourteen."

"You still have all those frogs?"

"I'm not sure what to do with them."

"Take them back to the pond in the park."

"I could I guess. Anyway, that's what happened. Amber kissed you." Ginger's grin returned and she squeezed his cheeks tighter this time. "And when she did, you turned into her prince. That's such a sweet story. I'm so proud of my boy!"

"Gee, Mum."

"And now what's that red thing in your pocket? Is that a present for me, too?"

"This? If you want it. I picked it up off Gerald's floor."

"You were inside your uncle's house? What for?"

"I had some things to talk to him about."

"What?"

"Personal business."

"What personal business?" When Raymond looked away, she added, "You aren't going to tell me?"

"I wasn't going to, no."

"Why not?"

"Because I don't want you mad at me. Let's put it this way, I wasn't nice to Uncle Gerald."

"Why not?"

"I wasn't going to tell you."

"Tell me."

"If you must know, Uncle Gerald attacked Amber the other night. He terrified her out of her mind, which made me furious. I can't stand what he is, Mum! I confronted him this morning."

"I know about what he did to Amber."

"You do?"

"He told me. I scolded him as well."

"I wanted to kill him."

"You didn't though, right?"

"No, of course not. Though Cottlebone almost killed me."

"What did you do to your uncle that riled the servant?"

"I didn't kill him."

"Did you start a fight?"

"No. There was no fight." Raymond was not lying. Cottlebone pulling a gun on him can't be considered a fight.

"You should respect your uncle."

"Respect? You're kidding me, right?"

"He's not himself. He's having issues."

"I'll say he is. I can't believe you're defending him!"

"I'm not defending him. I'm just saying go easy on him. You're younger than he is and you're stronger."

"He's still alive."

"He's still your uncle."

"And he's a vampire Mum, and he attacked the girl I love."

Ginger shrugged and reached for the red leather book tucked in the pocket of his coat, fingering it timidly. "That's one of your grandfather's journals isn't it?"

"I don't know. I haven't read it. Maybe."

"Let me see it?"

"Go ahead."

She pulled the journal from his pocket and thumbed through it, carefully turning the fragile pages. "Look what it says. It says she manipulates me daily and were she to read this book she would tear it to shreds. Who is he talking about?"

"How should I know? Ask Uncle Gerald."

The pages were so fragile Ginger turned them with great care, using her finger to keep place as she followed the writing. "I think your uncle is getting in over his head. This is not good, suspecting people of murder and all. It's not healthy." She looked up at him, a dark scowl on her face. "He could get in trouble."

Raymond kicked at his chair as he stood. "Let him reap his harvest.

What do I care?"

"Raymond!"

"He's filth, Mother. He's a half-blood vampire that can't be a decent blood-sucker or a civilized human being. He fails miserably at both!"

"I'm also a half-blood vampire."

"No, you're not. At least you aren't going to be. At least your heart isn't in it like Uncle Gerald's. He wants to drain innocent people of their life source. He cares for no one. No one, mother. Not even you."

"Give him time. He's coming around. I think that's all going to change someday soon."

"Coming around? Do you think?"

A knock on the screen door interrupted their conversation, and it was just as well. Raymond's blood boiled again and it wasn't his intent to be angry with his mother.

She looked at him inquisitively. "Who's that?"

"There's only one way to find out."

Ginger set the red journal on top of the other books on the table and before she covered the chipmunk statue with a towel, she stroked its head affectionately. Raymond eyed the stone figure as his mum welcomed the guest.

"Oh! Well hello honey. How are you?"

"I'm fine Mrs. Peadlebody. Is Raymond here?"

Amber! Raymond's heart bumped against his ribcage. He stumbled over Ginger's chair and bee-lined for the door. "Amber!

How did you find us?"

"Well, you did give me the address, Raymond." She grabbed his hand and pecked him on the cheek with a bright red kiss, leaving a smudge of lipstick. Raymond's face welled with warmth and he kissed her back. "Introduce me to your mum. I didn't really get a chance to say hello the other night."

Ginger quickly patted her hair, twisting the flyaway ends behind her ear. She reached out to shake Amber's hand. "Pardon the mess, and my hair."

"You're beautiful, Mrs. Peadlebody. Don't worry about how you look."

"Aren't you a dear?" Ginger ushered Amber into the house.

"Raymond says such wonderful things about you. I am so happy you two are getting together. This has been a very trying period for him, what with his father dying and all. I want to thank you personally."

"Thank me?"

Raymond's eyes popped open. "Mum."

"Yes, thank you so much for freeing my son of the curse. I am just thrilled about it."

Amber grimaced and looked at Raymond. "Curse?"

"Mum!" What was she doing? Amber stared in bewilderment at him, so he twirled his finger at his head and nodded at his mother, mouthing the word, "senile."

Amber's brow furrowed even deeper. She studied Raymond, and then she grimaced at Ginger. "I'm not quite following you."

"Raymond was under a curse, a vampire curse. It's okay, Raymond, I won't tell her the details."

Raymond rolled his eyes.

"That's okay, Mrs. Peadlebody. I'm glad I could be of help. I don't need to know any details. Yet."

The 'yet' was for Raymond and it took hold of his heart. He

would have to tell her everything. He would. Alone. In private.

"So, how is your frog hunting going, Mrs. Peadlebody?"

Ginger flushed, her fingers fiddled nervously with her skirt. "I was about to take them back to the park. I decided I don't really need them anymore. It isn't working out for me."

Before she said another word about frogs working out for her, before she might get into too many details and reveal to Amber how she's been kissing them, Raymond interrupted, pushing the kitchen chair aside and racing for the bathroom.

"Good idea, Mum, let's do that. Amber can help us. Let's take your frogs to the park! Where is the creel?"

"I'd be glad to help," Amber offered cheerfully.

Dusty

Ginger probably should have paid more attention to Raymond when he first told her the good news about being human again, but the initial shock of seeing Dusty hard as rock was devastating. All she could think about was that poor frozen chipmunk who never did any harm to anyone. Even now while in the park with her son and his girlfriend Dusty's predicament haunted her.

The three knelt at the poolside and released the frogs one by one.

Amber's willingness to help was honorable, and Ginger knew she'd make Raymond a wonderful wife. Good for him, she thought as she watched the two swoon over each other. She felt separated from them. Not only was she losing a son to this lovely young lady, she was also losing a son to humanity.

Even though Raymond would never abandon her willingly, he would be taking a different road from now on, one that led to an entirely different world. A world she used to know. She wiped a tear from her eye, her thoughts returning to the only other friend she had; Dusty, who was now a piece of clay sitting on her table. What else could possibly go wrong?

As soon as the creel was empty of frogs, Ginger excused herself.

"You're leaving, Mum?" Raymond asked.

"I am. I have things to do and you two need to be alone."

They walked her to the hedge archway and said goodbye. From there, Ginger hurried up the hill to the estate and rushed along the cobblestone trail that led to the treehouse behind the manor and jogged up the steps. Once inside the house, she slammed the screen door and locked it, immediately mumbling to herself, or rather to her pet.

"What have I done to you? Was it one of those frogs that I kissed that made you freeze? Was it the smell of the smoke from that concoction that I made the other day? What did I do?"

She fell into the chair, took the chipmunk in her arms, towel and all, and cradled it against her breast. Maybe her body heat will help. Maybe if it knows how much she really cares, it will come back to life. Maybe kissing all those frogs made it jealous. "I didn't mean anything by it," she assured the statue.

Dusty didn't respond. He was hard rock, unmoving, inanimate. There was no life in him, and Ginger wondered if there ever had been. Maybe the piece of clay was only garden art like Raymond had suggested.

Or maybe this chipmunk-turned-statuette could very well be an outcome of all the magic spells she'd concocted. Or maybe she was going crazy. Perhaps Rockford the Vampire had caused her to go genuinely insane.

"Oh, how stupid! What an idiot I am!"

Ginger set the squirrel back down on the table and sighed. "I suppose it's possible that you are a piece of garden art and Dusty is out there in the trees somewhere." She wiped her eyes with her hands and grabbed a paper towel to blow her nose. In doing so, she uncovered the red journal that Raymond had given her.

Curiosity, and the taste for reading prompted her to pick it up. "I should at least skim through it before Raymond asks for it back, or before Gerald discovers it's missing. I might not get another chance." She held the journal up, admiring the antiquity that belonged to an infamous vampire. "Herein lies the mysterious heart of a genuine vampire." That is, indeed, what Benjamin Peadlebody had been, unlike his half-blood sons.

Ginger leaned back in the chair with the journal and opened the pages, carefully reading every word as though it were one of those enchanting fairy tale stories from the library. Soon she became absorbed in its pages.

Benjamin Peadlebody wasn't all that bad of a person. He married and loved his wife who was an elf. "My mother-in-law," Ginger whispered. "Whatever was she thinking, marrying a Peadlebody? What were her parents thinking? Or had they eloped? I guess elves can make dumb mistakes when they're young and foolish, too." She skimmed the pages looking for some heated vampire-elf romance chapters, but found none. Perhaps this Sandra elf lady was as elusive as Benjamin, floating around as a spirit and only becoming a body long enough to feed. "But that wouldn't make any sense. How would they have created two sons?"

A tear rolled down her cheek when she read about Sandra's death.

Further into the journal, Ginger found the unfortunate and terrifying story of Benjamin's marriage to his second wife and the effect that Elisa and her wicked sister had on him.

"What a pity. That poor man," she said to herself.

Here was Benjamin, a full fledge vampire, horrifying in every way with a list of 'clients' that he fed on regularly. How could he be so powerless against the woman he married and her sister? Why?

Benjamin didn't say, not outright unless some of the passages far back as Medusa and her sisters, gorgons were beautiful beings that had been cursed by the gods. So hideous did they become that whosoever looked upon one would instantly turn to stone.

Did Dusty see a Gorgon? Where?

"Oh, leaping lizards! Dusty raced out of here that morning and headed straight for the manor. Raymond found him lying in the driveway. Had he been there when that cream-colored sedan drove by? Was a gorgon in the sedan? Is Gainsworthy's wife a gorgon?"

Her heart beat wildly. As terrifying as it was, having been visited by a gorgon, what was written on these pages could be the secret of breaking the spell. She read aloud.

"Give me your dust, your powder and pride? Dare I?" It wouldn't hurt to try. Even if Dusty doesn't turn back into a chipmunk, or if this is only a common nursery rhyme from the nursery, a little chip off the old rock won't be too damaging.

She took a butter knife from the drawer and paused for a moment, anxious that this might hurt the chipmunk.

"I'm sorry," she whispered under her breath. With the blunt end of the knife, she banged on the tip of the statue's tail. Bird seed flew into the air, the books bounced, junk mail fell on the floor, but nothing happened to the statuette.

Ginger grumbled and after another try, set the chipmunk on the floor. "I know I have a hammer in here somewhere."

She couldn't find it. "Maybe Cottlebone has one." She'd seen him hang cast-iron pots in the kitchen once. And she'd seen him in his apron breaking ice on the back porch. She wasn't one to visit the manor often, but to borrow a hammer was a legitimate excuse.

Ginger grabbed her wool shawl, since the sky was turning gold and the air getting chilly, and left her tree house.

Lightbulbs

After rapping on the thick manor door, Ginger's knuckles hurt. She shivered as she waited and watched the sunset colors settle on the tops of the faux boxwood lining the driveway. A golden glow touched the flower garden. The sky illuminated the roses and heather in a cool evening light.

The door opened to a slight crack, and Mr. Cottlebone peeked out.

"Oh. Mrs. Peadlebody. Forgive me for the delay. It's just that, well Mr. Peadlebody thought you were his nephew and I was instructed not to answer the door. Raymond's not invited here. Ever again."

Cottlebone opened the door wider and Ginger walked inside. A delicious aroma seeped from the kitchen. Prime rib? Ginger breathed in deeply and immediately her mouth watered. "Richard that smells so good."

"Thank you, ma'am. You're welcome to stay for dinner, although—."

"Oh, I wish. I recognize that smell. So savory. So delicious.

You must be a wonderful cook!"

"There's a roast in the oven. Potatoes, carrots..."

He needn't say anything else. The image of the dinner formed in her mind. Tantalizing. How she longed for a hot cooked meal. Something stable, tasty. Mouthwatering. If only she could eat the foods, she used to love. "That aroma is overwhelming. Did you put bell peppers with it?"

"Yes, ma'am I did."

"And marinated the roast too, didn't you?"

"Yes ma'am, overnight."

She licked her lips, fearing that the drool would escape her mouth. "You've made me hungry."

"I'm sorry."

"Who're you cooking for?"

"Only myself. I prepare food one day a week, usually when Mr. Peadlebody is out so he isn't bothered by the aroma, and then I freeze it and warm individual portions later."

"That's wise of you. You know, my mother used to do the exact same thing. Back in the day when I was human. Before I married Rockford." Why was she telling the servant about her past? She shook her head as she looked at him. She mustn't tell him that she's a vampire. However, his eyes were sympathetic, like he already knew.

"Is something wrong?" he asked.

"No." The smell of real food made her dizzy. The longer she lingered in the hall, the stronger the aroma. "Did you use onions, Richard?"

"Yes, ma'am, and garlic."

"Garlic? Oh, I miss garlic." Another deep breath and Ginger saw stars. She shook her head to wake up. She must be famished, or perhaps it's the garlic. "Richard, I came to borrow a hammer."

"A hammer, ma'am?"

that had been scribbled out mentioned the cause.

One particular verse, somewhere around page seventy-four, captured her attention and she read it over a few times.

There is a spell my grandmother told me that will cure a curse for any mortal. Herein recorded if indeed these pages make it beyond the sisters' wicked eyes.

> Great alabaster form
> Once holding life
> Your spirit and frozen heart inside
> Give me your dust
> Your powder and pride
> To mix with my blood until mortal..."

Mortal what? The page was ripped after that, as though there were more to the spell. Was this a coincidence that she happened upon this incantation now? The very hour her beloved chipmunk lay on the table as hard as stone?

"Gorgons," she whispered. "The sisters are gorgons and they turn things to stone! No wonder Benjamin had mirrors in the house. No full fledge vampire would have mirrors, unless it were to keep his servant from looking head on at a gorgon!" Ginger set the diary down and shuffled through the pile of garbage on her table. "I had a book on gorgons. Where is it?"

There had been one book that Ginger had checked out from the library. In it was a brief description of unusual and fantastic creatures. That's where Ginger first read about gorgons. The book was on the bottom of the pile, being so large. Litter fell on the floor when she pulled it out from under the heap and set it on her lap.

Full colored images graced the pages, and the creatures were listed in alphabetical order. Gargoyles, here! Gorgons. Dating as

"Yes, there's something I need to—" she thought for a moment. Should she tell Cottlebone about her chipmunk? "To pound."

"Is it a nail? I could hammer a nail for you."

"No. It's not a nail. I need to, well to break something."

The tattoos on Cottlebone's neck seemed to pop out as the light from the back window shone on him. He had a thick neck and his veins pulsated visibly even under the Celtic cross. All the while her stomach growled.

Hadn't she eaten?

"Mrs. Peadlebody?" He leaned over too near for Ginger to ignore.

He must have gargled with mouthwash because his breath had a minty smell to it. This was too much. Food, aroma, a strong and delicious man hovering over her. She wanted him. This can't be happening. How could she be that hungry? She'd been busy all day, what with Raymond and Amber coming over, and taking the frogs back to the park. She hadn't consumed any squirrel brew since early this morning. Maybe he tasted as good as that roast he was cooking.

"I'm sorry. I just feel faint." She fanned herself and fought the desire to latch on to Richard Cottlebone with her teeth. "Do you have a hammer?"

Ginger reached for him and grabbed his shirt, stretching her head toward his collar with her mouth open. Before she could reach his neck, she collapsed, losing her balance completely.

Cottlebone caught her before she hit the floor. Ginger knew her teeth were out, but she never contacted his flesh. The tattoos were in the way.

"Ginger!" Gerald appeared at the bottom of the stairwell and hurried to the entry. "Good gargoyles what is wrong with her, Richard?"

Cottlebone hung onto Ginger, his mouth opened in

astonishment. "I don't know, sir," he muttered.

"This is ridiculous!" Gerald pulled her away from Cottlebone and carried her into the living room where he laid her on the couch. Ginger could hear him talking to Cottlebone, but she lay motionless.

"Go to her house and get a carton out of the freezer. She needs some nourishment."

"Was she going to—? I mean she was—?" Cottlebone's voice trembled and he rubbed his neck.

"Yes. I'm afraid she was very near to biting you. You're safe now. She wouldn't have gone all the way, I don't think. Now hurry!"

Ginger woke to the aroma that seeped from a cup of brew on the end table next to her. Plush pillows held her in an upright position, and a soft blanket had been tossed on top of her. Gerald sat in the chair by her head, reading. She eyed the cup.

"How long did I sleep?"

"Only a short while. Drink, so you don't pass out again."

Ginger caressed the mug with both hands before she took a sip. The warmth was comforting to her cold body and the brew was life flowing through her veins. Soon she sat up, alert and strong. "I haven't been that susceptible to my condition in a very long time."

"It's fruitless to prey on Cottlebone, you know."

She caught the look that he gave her, almost condescending, with a tad of jealousy.

"How do you know? Did you try? And while we're on the subject, it's fruitless to prey on Raymond's girlfriend."

Gerald drew in a breath and shut his book. Ginger could see immediately that it was one of his father's journals. "Why must you bring that up again?"

"Because I talked to Raymond."

"Did he tell you what he did to me?"

"He said he confronted you."

"He threatened me."

Ginger placed the cup on the table and swung the blanket back so that she could sit and face him. "You did more than threaten the girl he wants to marry."

"He can't marry her without making her a vampire, and he won't do that. I was merely helping him along."

"On the contrary, Gerald. Amber doesn't need to be a vampire for them to marry. Raymond is cured of the curse."

"So he told me. I wasn't sure whether to believe him."

"It's true."

"Was it your doing?"

"I don't think so. I think it had to do with love, or something. Raymond wants nothing more than to be rid of us."

"He's your son. He's my nephew. How can he be rid of us?"

"We can leave him alone," she said. "Let him live his life the way he wants to."

Gerald set the book down and stood. He paced so furiously she got seasick watching him. "Why are you angry?"

"Because he was one of us. That's why! And now he disowned us."

"Raymond was never one of us. He didn't have near as much vampire blood as either you or I."

"He's family." Gerald's voice was raised so loud that Cottlebone peeked in the room.

"Oh, get over it. You never liked Raymond. The two of you always squabbled. Just forget your differences and let him go about his business."

"I love the boy."

"What?" Ginger gaped at her brother-in-law. "Love?"

When Gerald stopped wearing a hole in the rug, he paused in front of her. His shoulders drooped and he had a pout on his face. "I do. I'm sorry for what I did. I told him I would never attack Amber again, but he didn't believe me."

"How can he believe you? You live by your instincts. Look at us! We lust after human blood no matter how hard we try not to. Look at me! Look what I almost did to Cottlebone, poor dear. Are you all right, Richard?" she shouted.

"I'm fine, Mrs. Peadlebody," Cottlebone answered.

"I can't help myself either if I let myself get hungry. And you starve yourself half the time so there's no trusting you at all! Leave Amber and Raymond alone. There are other matters we need to take care of."

He sighed, sat down, and stared out the window. "You're right. Pressing matters that need tending to. I discovered something distressing the other day when I went to visit Gainsworthy. I've been trying to find a way to tell you about it."

"What did you find out?"

"His wife Ellen is a gorgon."

Ginger gasped. She had guessed a gorgon was in the picture somehow, but involved with Benjamin's death? "No!"

"I'm certain of it. I'm certain that they had a hand in the murder of my father."

Last week, Ginger might have argued with Gerald over that statement, or at least challenged him. Today, she was certain he was correct. She let her brother-in-law ramble as she tried to piece what she read in the journal to what he was saying.

"Everything points to it. The sunglasses, the turban scarf, the statues at the properties I visited."

"There was a gorgon at the funeral. Raymond saw her."

"Did he?"

"I had no idea how significant that sighting had been."

"She's had a prominent role in the disappearance of some of the citizens of this county."

"You think?"

"I'm almost certain."

"Then that explains what happened to Dusty."

"Who?"

"Dusty, the chipmunk. Raymond found him in your driveway hard as rock. Is this Ellen the same woman in your father's journal? Could she be the one that froze Dusty?"

"You read one of my journals?"

"Raymond gave it to me. The red one."

"The one with the chant? Where is it?"

"Why? What do you know about the chant?" Ginger was not ready to give the journal up yet. She still had a chipmunk to save.

"Keep it safe. Don't tell anyone where it is."

"Who would want to know besides you?"

"Gainsworthy! He wants these journals along with all the other books my father wrote. They're extremely incriminating. It's the reason he wants to buy our estate. If anyone knew about his schemes, he and his wife would be in serious trouble. My father recorded everything. Fifteen volumes of scandal, plus what he journalised."

"You mean because Ellen Gainsworthy turns people into stone? I can see where that would be criminal."

"That and the reason why they turned those people to stone. It all has to do with the real estate business. My father was partnered with them but once he saw their tactics, he protested, they fought, and then my father bowed out of the relationship. I think that's why they killed him."

"What tactics?"

"Gainsworthy is in collaboration with Ferguson. Their victims are usually elderly people with a huge estate and no heirs. Ellen stalks them for a while, makes sure they don't have any distant relatives who'd make a claim on their property, and then she reveals her true colors. They turn to stone. Gainsworthy comes along and hauls the statue to his place, keeps it hidden until he can declare death in absentia. Ferguson petitions the state for a declaration of death, and then starts the probate process. The property goes up for sale cheap in a private auction, probably one that only Gainsworthy is invited to, and voila, the malefactors have themselves a new listing. Once Gainsworthy owns the estate, and his sculptor modifies the stonework, Gainsworthy slaps a bonus on the property, his signatory artwork, upping the price to millions."

"Oh my!" The story was difficult for her to follow, but it ran together so smoothly she sat with her mouth open. "You figured this all out?"

"It makes sense now, all of it!"

"So where does your father fit in?" she asked.

"He became the scapegoat."

"No!"

"The Peadlebody estate was always a spook house. Gainsworthy had it all figured out. He wanted Benjamin Peadlebody in on the deal to point the finger at in case someone contested them. Benjamin was the accused. The murderer. I don't think my father knew about that part of the deal until too late."

"That dirty dealer. How did you figure that out?"

Gerald held up his father's journal. "It's all in here. And I saw their latest victim still being worked on at Gainsworthy's house."

"That's horrifying. That is just so horrible." No longer was vampirism the ultimate evil, but this conspiracy made blood-sucking look like a tea party. They sat quiet for a moment, wondering what might happen next. How vulnerable were they? "How did they kill your father?"

"I haven't figured that out yet. Vampires are impervious to a gorgon curse so I'm sure he's not stone."

"Maybe he didn't even die."

"Perhaps, but something happened to him or else Ferguson

wouldn't have been so assertive with the wake and the Will. Gainsworthy had no idea I existed. He thought that Rockford was the only heir and nothing had ever been mentioned about you or Raymond."

"They'll be coming here, won't they?" Ginger looked out the parlor window and wondered if Gerald was smart enough to keep trouble away.

"I'm certain of it."

"Poor Dusty, an innocent victim to all of this."

"Sorry about your varmint."

"Speaking of Dusty, I came here to get a hammer and break off a chip and then I'll mix it with my blood—"

"It won't work. There's more to the spell," Gerald said.

Ginger inched her feet into her shoes. "It's worth a try, isn't it?"

"Half a spell? The rest had been torn out of the journal." He shook his head.

"Why? By who? Gainsworthy?"

Gerald exhaled and closed his eyes for a moment. "I don't believe Gainsworthy has seen the red journal. I believe it's the book he's looking for."

Ginger heard footsteps from the other side of the door, and through the crack she saw Cottlebone slip away. She flinched, and Gerald lurched to the hall. "Cottlebone!"

The servant's footsteps stopped, but he didn't answer.

"Richard were you eavesdropping?"

Ginger could hear Cottlebone's heavy breathing.

"Come here and answer me, Richard Cottlebone."

Cottlebone's lips trembled as he stepped into the room. His chest heaved, his face was red. "I couldn't help but overhear your conversation, sir."

"Of course not, your head was too close to the wall. What

did you find so interesting?"

"Nothing, sir."

"Nothing? That's why your ear is flattened from pressing against the door?"

Cottlebone's hand flew to his ear. He threw an apologetic look toward Ginger.

"Don't lie to me, Richard!"

"You were talking about Benjamin. I was fond of your father. I'm concerned about the estate, sir, it's my home."

"Then why don't you tell us what you know?"

Cottlebone's face turned red as his gaze darted between the two. "I don't know any more than you do. Honestly."

"I find that difficult to believe. Given the reach of your ears, I'm going to assume you know more than what my father wrote in his journals. You heard Gainsworthy and my father talk. Perhaps you even heard their arguments."

Cottlebone swallowed, either ashamed of what Gerald accused him of, or afraid of something. Ginger felt a wave of pity for the man. "Gerald, don't be so hard on him."

"Why not? He's deliberately withholding critical information from us.

It could cost us our lives!"

"Gerald!"

"Well?"

"The man is not going to tell you anything if you keep yelling at him." Ginger said. "You should know better. You're such a bully sometimes!"

Gerald sighed, walked to the window, and clasped his hands behind his back.

Ginger turned to the butler and smiled, hoping to calm him. She spoke in a much more diplomatic voice. "Cottlebone, we're all in this together. There seems to be a real threat from Gainsworthy and his wife. They're freaks and we can't trust them. If we don't stick together, and pool our resources, who knows what will happen? If you have any clues about anything, please tell us."

The ticking of clocks from the den filled the silence in the room. Ginger sighed heavily, and hoping to touch a soft spot added, "Besides. That chant could bring my beloved chipmunk back to life." Gerald remained by the window, no longer pressing his servant for information. Cottlebone sat down on the lounge with his head in his hands.

Ginger finished her brew, glancing at Cottlebone occasionally, hoping he'd cave.

"All right." Cottlebone finally broke as Ginger set her tea down. She and Gerald turned their heads his way.

"I'm the one that tore the last verse from the chant."

Ginger couldn't believe her ears. She clapped her hands and sat up, a smile spread across her face, but Gerald interrupted her pleasure by scolding the servant.

"Why?"

"Because I had hopes that one day I could release my pet from Ellen's spell. I wanted to make certain that prospect was never taken from me if Gainsworthy ever got hold of the journal."

"Your pet?" Ginger asked.

"I had a collie. She was my pride and joy. When Gainsworthy caught me listening in on a conversation that he and Benjamin were having the man threatened me, and to demonstrate the severity of his warning, he had Ellen turn my Bella into stone."

"I've seen your collie." Gerald said. "Gainsworthy is using him as a table armature in his parlor. Quite an impressive piece of art, if I do say so. Nice dog."

Richard's face turned red. Gerald would do well not to make the man angry, Ginger thought. Cottlebone is twice his size and Gerald has no backbone. Ginger folded her hands and leaned forward, speaking low. "You have the missing verse, then?"

Cottlebone merely nodded.

"Why did you only tear out a portion of it?"

"For your sakes, sir. So, you would know there is a spell that can reverse the curse."

"And you kept the final verse for your collie?" Gerald asked.

Cottlebone looked at him squarely. "And for my safety! If I have the final stanza to the chant, I stand to live. You forget, I contend with monsters of your kind daily, and have for years. I didn't know if Gainsworthy would get this house."

"Tell me, Cottlebone. We now know who Gainsworthy is, and who is wife is but there's still someone missing out of this equation."

"Who, sir?"

"What happened to Elisa?"

"She left."

"Left to where?"

"It's not clear. Your father said something about another world, another space where she came from. Somewhere out there."

"Well that's a good thing. She wasn't a nice woman!" Ginger said. "Not from what I read."

"What happened? Do you know?" Gerald asked.

"Your father didn't include me in his dealings with the woman. Nor did he allow me to even be in the same room with her. However—," His voice trailed and Gerald waited.

"The evening she left I was in my room and I heard her and another woman talking outside."

"Her sister, perhaps?"

"Most likely. It was a heated argument. Very much so. I stepped into the hall to see if I could be of assistance. Your father stopped me dead in my tracks. He told me to go back into my room and not come out until morning."

Stone and Blood

Gerald switched on the flashlight and waited for Ginger and Cottlebone to catch up. The cobblestone trail was shadowed from the moonlight, the ground damp from evening dew and droplets fell on Gerald's shoulder as he brushed past the overgrown hydrangeas. "This way. Come quickly."

Ginger hurried, but Cottlebone trailed behind. "What's the rush, Gerald? We have all night."

Gerald didn't answer. He'd just as soon this was over with. When he reached the staircase that spiraled up sixteen rungs to the treehouse, Gerald halted the party, allowing Ginger to ascend first. When Cottlebone stepped onto the first rung, Gerald cautioned the servant. "Don't touch that rail, it's covered in bird poop."

Cottlebone rolled his eyes, pulled his hand away and stuck it in his coat pocket. "Disgusting!" he whispered.

"That's what I told her."

"Are you boys coming or not?" Ginger had already topped the stairs, unlocked the door, and waited on the porch with her hands on her hips.

"Don't you have a porch light, Ginger? Mr. Cottlebone might need to see the stairs."

Gerald had second thoughts about bringing Cottlebone to Ginger's little abode in the maples. He didn't trust Cottlebone, not even when he pulled the empty gun on Raymond. Everyone he'd been running into lately had their own agendas, and Gerald doubted that freeing a dog from a curse was Cottlebone's priority. There was more that the butler was not telling. More about the journals, Elisa, and maybe even about his father.

Ginger busied herself on the porch. She pulled a card table outside and pushed open the screen door with her foot carrying two folding chairs and a tablecloth over her shoulder. Cottlebone stepped up to her, an unmitigated expression on his face.

Gerald came from behind. "Ginger, what on earth are you doing?"

"I thought we'd light some candles and chant the spell out here in the open air. You didn't forget to bring that verse, did you, Cottlebone?"

The man looked at her expressionless. "I have the verse memorized,

Mrs. Peadlebody. You don't need the paper." The tone was cold.

"Have a seat, Mr. Cottlebone," she retorted as she went back inside, letting the screen door slam three times before stopping it with her heel.

Cottlebone pulled the chair away from the table and sat down, keeping his hands in his pockets. Whether he resented being here, or if he were hesitant to perform magic, Gerald wasn't sure, but it was clear he was not happy. Ginger lit a candle, but the breeze was too forceful for it to stay lit, so she went inside one more time and brought a kerosene lantern, which she set in the middle of the table. After assessing the set-up, she went back inside, leaving the two men alone.

Cottlebone's strong features glowed eerily in the light of the flickering wick. He met Gerald's stare with a glower of his own, his lips stern, his massive body, though concealed under his coat, threatening. Observing Cottlebone's menacing gaze, Gerald's lips tighten back over his fangs, though he hadn't purposed for them to do so. He immediately licked his lips and looked away.

When Ginger came back a third time, she carried a bundle wrapped in cloth and carefully laid it on the table, pulling the red journal out of her pocket. If Gerald hadn't been watching so intently, he may have missed the covetous look on Cottlebone's face when he saw Benjamin Peadlebody's diary. That was the same look he had when Gerald first took the journal from Cottlebone's desk in the basement library.

What was in that book that Cottlebone was so possessive of? Gerald had read it from cover to cover and aside from the chant, he couldn't imagine what Cottlebone wanted.

"There he is, boys." Ginger wiped her hands on her apron and stepped back away from the table.

Cottlebone cleared his throat. "Before we go any further I must ask you to stop referring to me as a boy and to address me as Mr. Cottlebone. We are not friends, nor are we familiar with each other enough to use first names."

Ginger glared at him, stunned. "Very well. Here is Dusty. Mr. Cottlebone!" She opened the journal and thumbed through the pages.

"I will do the reading." Cottlebone reached out for the red diary. Gerald shifted in his chair in protest. Was it a good idea to let him handle that book?

Ginger did not release the chronicle all too freely either, but looked to Gerald for approval.

"I think anyone of us can read the words," Gerald said.

"No. Sir. Excuse me but I was at Mr. Peadlebody's side when he wrote this. I know how it needs to be spoken."

Cottlebone laid his hands on the book and gently removed it from Ginger. He thumbed through the pages. Once he found the chant, he stood and positioned the light nearer to the chipmunk. He coughed once, holding his fist over his mouth, and then loosened his collar and scanned the page. With one hand on the statue's head, he read.

"Great alabaster form
Once holding life."

Cottlebone took a deep breath and looked at the stars. He continued the spell from memory.

Your spirit and frozen heart inside

"Mrs. Peadlebody, bring me a pitcher of clean water. Hurry!"

Ginger raced into the house. The sound of tap water pouring into a cup broke the silent evening air as Gerald and Cottlebone waited. When she returned, Cottlebone nodded for her to set the cup on the table, waited another moment, and then closed his eyes as he continued.

Give me your dust
Your powder and pride
To mix with my blood until mortal I die.

Cottlebone held out his hand to Ginger and she took it. He took hold of her index finger, pulled her closer, and then scrapped her finger along the edge of the statue's tail.

"Ouch!" She pulled back, but he fought her.

"Do you want this to work? Do you care enough about this creature to make a small sacrifice?"

She didn't argue. Of course, she wanted Dusty back. Gerald quickly rose from the table and turned his back to them. The sight not only made him sick to his stomach, but Cottlebone hurting Ginger also made him angry. Curiosity won and he peeked over his shoulder in time to see the butler forcing Ginger's finger onto a sharp edge of the statue. Gerald looked away from the torn flesh and into Cottlebone's eyes. They were wide, wild. As soon as blood oozed out of Ginger's finger, she pulled it to her mouth.

"Suck on it," Cottlebone instructed, although that's what she was already doing.

Tears formed in the corner of Ginger's eyes. Gerald looked at the chipmunk, now tainted red on the tail but still stone.

"Now hold your hand over the chipmunk's face."

He guided her hand in place and then lifted the cup over her cut finger and poured slowly, letting the water splash onto the open wound, rinsing the blood into the chipmunk's nose and mouth. He guided Ginger's hand so that it hovered over Dusty's eyes. All the while he chanted.

Washing away with water the curse.
When warm again, I will sing you this verse.

Cottlebone stepped back. Gerald gawked and Ginger gasped as the white stone cracked, and hair appeared. The more hair, the greater the splits in the plaster grew. Soon every bit of stone had turned to shards, flakes, and dust. The chipmunk emerged. He blinked, breathed, moved his feet, and as life filled its entire body, he rolled onto all fours. Dusty sat up and shook itself dry, licking its hands and face clean, concentrating on wiping Ginger's blood from its nose with its paws. Ginger reached to grab the beast, but

Cottlebone stopped her.

"Don't touch it until morning. You're to sing the verse to it when you see it again."

She nodded and then raced into the house. Gerald would have followed, but his curiosity concerning Cottlebone compelled him to stay.

"How did you know what to do?"

"It was written in your father's book. It's on the section I tore out. Am I excused, sir?"

Gerald was about to say no. He wanted some answers, but at that very moment, headlights appeared in the driveway at the manor.

"Didn't you lock the gate, Ginger?" Gerald asked. Ginger appeared at the door, wiping her eyes with a paper towel.

"Raymond may have left it open."

"Raymond was on foot. Why would he even go through the gate when he can take the footpath?"

"I have no idea, Gerald. Go see who it is. Maybe Ferguson has a key."

Gerald panicked. He never thought about the lawyer having keys to locks on his estate. He raced down the rickety stairs so quickly that he tripped, caught himself before he fell face first, and nursed his ankle as he limped to his house.

Ransom

The streetlight guided Raymond and Amber to her small rambler home burrowed in among a stand of alders at the end of a cul-de-sac. Fall chrysanthemums lined the walkway to her front door which glowed faintly from the moon's rays falling on them. A neatly manicured lawn, a water fountain that babbled happily, and a porch swing that overlooked the yard; such a common and human environment. How could Raymond not be lured into staying a while longer? Amber took his hand and led him to the porch.

"Let's spend another gorgeous evening under the autumn stars together!" she said as she sat on the wooden swing. There was enough room for two, so she scooted over and tugged his hand.

"That's exactly what I was thinking. Another and another. It won't end, ever." He didn't need to be asked twice. Raymond sat down and put his arm around her. They'd been spending time together ever since their first kiss, but the newness of their affection was tantalizing as ever. His whole body tingled from her warmth. Ever since he became human, he was more sensitive to those sensations, and he enjoyed them.

"What won't end?"

"Our time together. It's going to be forever, Amber. You and me. I'm going to make sure of it."

"We have a long way to go with our relationship before we can make that claim. I barely know you."

Raymond curled a lock of her hair around his finger and looked past the lights in the houses across the street, past the street lamp on the corner at the thousands of stars that shimmered in the night sky. How magical was the evening? His life had been wondrous these last few days. He had never felt so content, so fulfilled. "That will change. I'll tell you everything about myself. I won't keep anything secret even if it hurts to talk about my childhood, or my family. I want you to trust me."

"Why wouldn't I trust you?"

"You have no reason not to trust me. I want you to know that. Otherwise, I have no business asking you to be my wife."

"You're asking me to be your wife?" She let out a faint laugh.

The request was sudden; he knew, but he was determined to be transparent. Letting her know his intentions was the first step. "I will. Soon. Yes."

"I don't know what to say."

"You don't have to say anything. Not now. It's too soon. But by the time I ask you, you'll know what to say. I mean, if there is anything about our relationship that would hold you back we'll have worked it out. I hope."

"I'm looking forward to that day."

"Are you?" His insides tickled, and it was all he could do to keep from laughing for joy. "If you'll let me, I'll start tonight, right here under these stars. Right here on your front porch. Tonight. I'll tell you my whole life history."

Amber laughed more earnestly and leaned her head on his shoulder. "If that's what you feel you need to do. I'm all ears."

"I don't want us to end up in the same situation as my parents." Raymond stroked her hair, thankful for everything—that Amber cared for him, and that he was no longer a vampire.

"What situation did your parents end up in?"

"It was tragic. They hated each other after they married."

"That's terrible! Why did they even marry?"

"It's a long story. Mum was human before she met my father, you know."

"No. I didn't know. I thought she was human now." She lifted her head off his shoulder. The look in her eyes was of grave concern. This was going to be difficult. Whether Amber would accept him after she knows his story, he wasn't sure, but he had to tell her.

"No. Not now unfortunately. Back then she was a genuine person, just like you." He inhaled and stared into Amber's eyes. What he was about to say sent a pang of despair through him. This could be the end. But he had to tell her. "Amber, my father was a vampire." He waited.

She blinked and tilted her head. "We've been through this," she said.

"Not all of it. You haven't heard it all. As soon as they married, my father accosted Mum and she fell under the curse. She's a vampire now, also."

Amber was quiet for a few moments. She didn't fidget. She just sat there, looking at him. He sighed inwardly. "Okay. So..." she started.

"Mum's not dangerous."

"Your mother never gave me the impression that she was dangerous. Of course, I had no idea she was a vampire. I didn't know there are non-dangerous vampires."

"Oh yes, there are, if they work at it. Mum's not dangerous because she has a brew she makes that keeps her fed well enough so that she doesn't have to prey on people. Some half-bloods, like my father and my uncle can be very dangerous."

"Okay, so when you say half-blood you mean half human and half vampire?"

"Or half elf, like my father and Uncle Gerald."

"Half elf." A statement. To convince herself. After that, she clammed up. Raymond watched her from the corner of his eye. Let her digest this piece by piece, he thought.

"You talk about half-bloods. What about pure-blooded vampires? What do you know about them?" She spoke softly and slowly as if choosing her words carefully.

"I don't know a lot of pure vampires. My father kept us hidden away in the back country so I really didn't grow up with much of a social life at all."

"Did you go to school?"

"Mum homeschooled me. She was intelligent. She's still smart. She studies all the time. Reads a lot. She was an honor student before she met my dad. I read too. I'm not dumb."

"No, Raymond, you're not. I didn't mean to insinuate that you were unintelligent, I was just curious about your social life."

The magic was gone. She no longer had that glint in her eye, and he'd become self-conscious.

They sat and listened to the night sounds, a motorcycle on the road somewhere, a bullfrog near Amber's pond, a neighbor's television across the cul-de-sac. Sounds that normal people listen to in their very human neighborhoods. Each one was a comforting melody to Raymond.

"Amber, my father was not a nice man. He caused people a lot of pain. I was not happy growing up."

"I'm sorry. Not having a good relationship with your father is much the same as growing up without one, I suppose."

"After talking to my mother today I dislike him even more, even though he's dead. He deceived my mum. He told her lies so that she believed he was a normal human being when he wasn't."

"Isn't that what vampires do, though?"

"I suppose."

"I'm just guessing. I don't know anything about vampires, just what I see in the movies," she said.

"The movies are all wrong."

"All of them?"

"Unless the screenwriters are vampires themselves, yes. How would any of those people know what it's like to live in the spirit world? To be undead? To roam this earth hungry, always looking for someone to prey on?"

Amber shuddered. "You seem to know."

Their eyes caught. Raymond bit his lip. It was just a matter of time before she asked, and here it comes so he might as well initiate it. "I hated my family. I didn't want to be what I was.

"And what were you?"

They looked at each other long and hard. Raymond hoped there was love in her eyes because without love she's going to hate him.

"My father's son."

"And your father was a vampire."

Raymond swallowed. He couldn't bring himself to say it.

"Roaming the earth, hungry, looking for prey. Lying to humans to lure them in?" she asked.

"No!" He took his arm from around her and sat up straight. "That's why I'm telling you this. That's my point. All my life I've forced myself not to follow my instincts. Granted I wasn't a full-blooded vampire so the spirit travel was out, I think. Maybe. As far as I know. Never did I eat human blood. Never! Mum wouldn't let me when I was young, and I grew up despising the thought of it."

"Okay, Raymond, settle down. I believe you."

Raymond sighed heavily. She took his hand and squeezed it.

"You must have someone in your family who is full blooded. Who?"

"My grandfather. Benjamin Peadlebody. He's the vampire that terrorized your town. He married an elf. That's why my father and Uncle Gerald are considered half-bloods. Uncle Gerald has a terrible time controlling himself though. He sits on the fence. He doesn't want to hunt, is rather cowardly, but he's right there if it looks like he can get something."

"Your Uncle is creepy. I don't like being around him. He scared me that night, Raymond. Which is why I'm not sure we can marry. Even though you're determined to be kind and gracious, you will always have your relatives." She squinted at him. The moon shone on her silky cheeks.

"Vampires live forever don't they?"

"Yes, they do. Unless a stake is driven through their heart."

She shook her head and looked away. "I do like you Raymond, but I don't think I could handle being around your uncle."

"He won't bother you again I promise. I had a talk with him. I wasn't very nice in my approach, either, and I'm pretty sure I made an impression."

Raymond leaned back and pushed the swing with his legs so that the swing swayed gently. "It's hard telling you all of this because you mean so much to me. I would hope you could overlook the relatives. Trust me to keep them away from you. They have a minimal role in my life except for Mum. I can't reject them entirely, nor hurt them. I had many of the same physical traits as the rest of my family. I had fangs."

He looked at her from the corner of his eye, curious as to her reaction. She looked away. He turned to her and gave her a smile when their eyes met. "I filed them down to match my other teeth."

"You filed your fangs?"

"Every day. Twice a day after I met you."

She laughed. "You were that serious about not being a

vampire?"

"Dead serious!"

"And now?"

"It's like Mum told you. The curse is broken. I'm human now."

"I want to believe that," she said.

"I swear. Look." He gestured to himself. "I'm bona fide reversed! No more fangs, and these aren't filed." He smiled and kissed her tenderly.

"You said your father lied to your mother before he bit her."

Raymond froze. There was a tear in her eye when she looked up, and it puzzled him. He wiped it with his thumb. "I'm not my father. I hate my father for all he did. If I could shed his influence on my life, I'd crawl out of it like a June bug shedding its shell. I am not lying. I swear to the heavens. I would never lie to you. Please believe me."

She didn't answer him, but she let him kiss her again. He touched her lips lightly with his. He licked the salt that the tear had left in her eyes.

"I love you Amber. That's all I can say."

She breathed heavily, closed her eyes, and leaned back on the swing. They rocked again. The temperature dipped and Raymond felt Amber shiver, so he pulled off his coat and wrapped it around her.

"You know all those frogs we let loose in Madison Park? Mum used them to relieve us of the curse, somehow."

"Is that what she was doing? She's so funny. I'll never forget seeing her all muddy that first day I ran into her. How she scooted around trying to catch all those frogs. Did your mum kiss some of them? Was that her magic?" Amber giggled.

"I told you I'd tell you my secrets, but I never promised I would tell you my mother's." He laughed with her. "I'll let her tell you hers. I know it sounds crazy, but she was passionate about the both of us living a normal life. When my father died, she swore she would free us no matter what sort of sacrifice she had to go through. She's been through a lot, too. I just wish it would have worked out for her."

"She's a wonderful mother. Which spell worked for her?"

"None. That's the sad thing. None of them worked. Mum is still a vampire."

"Oh, Raymond I'm so sorry. What curse worked for you?"

"Remember our first kiss?"

She gasped. "Seriously? You're kidding me."

"The truth. The curse was quashed in the same way spells are broken in fairy tales. It was rather magical. That's why the first thing Mum did when she saw you was to thank you."

"This is so hard to believe." Amber placed her warm hand in his. A thousand stars glittered in the sky. Aside from a dog barking occasionally, only the hoot of an owl could be heard.

"And so, with a kiss, you turned into a prince," she whispered.

Raymond's face flushed so suddenly he thought he had a fever. He never would have used those words to describe his transformation. A prince? She wasn't laughing, or mocking him. She was perfectly sincere, as though she were the princess who had been waiting for a prince. She snuggled next to him and he wrapped his arms even tighter around her. He leaned over and kissed her again. Their lips sealed onto one another so tightly that the rest of the world was cut off. There was no cold air, no stars, no sounds in the neighborhood, only Amber in his arms. He even ignored the bright light that shone on them.

That is, for a moment.

Then Raymond realized that the light was a beam from a headlamp on a car. And that beam wasn't moving, but idle and aimed at them.

Amber flinched and sat up when the horn honked. Raymond squinted and shaded his eyes.

"Who is that?" she asked.

The high beams lowered to fog lights, but the motor remained running. A car door slammed, and then another. Two people stepped out from either side of the vehicle.

"Raymond Peadlebody?" a man's voice called out.

"Stay here," Raymond whispered and then stood, his heart taking a leap.

Amber reached for his arm. "Raymond, who is it? Do you know them?"

"I don't think so." Raymond turned to the figures approaching. "Who are you?"

"You don't recognize us?" A man laughed, but the light was still too bright to identify anyone. The figures were dark shapes, backlit with a glare that left spots in his eyes. Not until the silhouettes crossed in front of the headlamps did Raymond guess who they were. He had seen the man and his wife, the lady with the scarf turban and sunglasses at the funeral. The woman who had turned the earwig to stone.

"Vaguely," he answered.

"Well let me introduce myself to you! I'm Simon Gainsworthy and this is my wife, Ellen." He moved quickly toward Raymond, traipsing through the garden, ignoring the walkway. Amber jumped from the swing and came to Raymond's side.

"I used to do business with your grandfather." He offered his hand in greeting.

"Okay." Raymond's inner alarm sounded. He didn't accept the handshake. Anyone who did business with a vampire had to be evil.

"Amber, I suggest you get in the house."

"I'm not leaving you here alone."

"Amber, please just go inside!"

"No need for her to leave, Raymond, dear." The woman had taken the footpath and now stood between Amber and the front door. "We think it might be nice to have a talk with the both of you."

"What about?" Raymond grabbed Amber's arm and pulled her to him, stepping in front of her. "Amber don't look at her," he whispered.

"What?" Amber asked.

The man approached them. Raymond could see his face. He wasn't a vampire, he was human, or at least it seemed so. His hair was thin and white, his cheeks pudgy, and he had a sinister smile on his face. Raymond remembered seeing him at his father's funeral.

"Don't be afraid, there boy. We just need to have you take a ride with us over to the Peadlebody Manor."

"Raymond, don't go!" Amber grabbed his arm, her hands trembled and rightly so. If Raymond didn't feel the need to be courageous for her sake, he'd be equally terrified.

"Why don't you come with us too, little lady." Mr. Gainsworthy suggested, nodding cordially to her.

"Neither of us are getting in that car and going anywhere with you." Raymond's temper clicked into high gear. If this were an abduction, he would fight. There must be a weapon somewhere. A rock, maybe. He perused the yard. Surely, between him and Amber they could take this guy on, although the gorgon was a different story. He knew how dangerous she was. He again shielded Amber from her view.

"Don't be afraid of me. I'm just an old man. All I'm asking is that you come to the estate and have a discussion with your family. Your input will be greatly appreciated."

"Input concerning what?"

"Remember when you said you wanted to sell the manor?"

"How do you know I said that? You weren't there."

The man snickered. "No, but I know someone who was and he paid close attention to you. He said you're a wise young man and that your family should listen to what you have to say."

"The estate is not mine to sell. I have no influence over my uncle."

"Ah! But someday that estate may be yours to sell. Someday soon."

"Are you threatening my family?" Raymond asked. His heart beat against his rib cage. He backed up a step. If he could help Amber to her front door and get her inside the house, at least she'd be safe. "My family will be around for a very long time. They chose to live there. I'm not going to try and convince them to leave."

"Selling might be to their best interest, Raymond. I would hate to see anything happen to them."

"Like what? What would happen to them?" Raymond took Amber's arm and moved her toward the house. The man followed.

"Nothing is going to happen to your uncle if you convince him to see things our way. It shouldn't be hard. We'll even coach you. Your uncle seems to be a bit stubborn at times."

They were close enough now to make a dash for the house. Still holding Amber's hand, he broke into a run, pulling her along. The woman stepped in front of him and stuck out her foot. He tripped. Amber screamed. Ellen laughed, "Watch your step, mortal!" The woman grabbed Amber's arm as Raymond fell.

"Let go of me!" Amber swung at the woman's face but missed. She kicked at her knees. Ellen only chuckled and held Amber at bay.

Raymond jumped to his feet and vaulted at the woman, tearing her hand off Amber.

"Run Amber!" he called.

Amber did run. Gainsworthy grabbed Raymond from behind and held him as Ellen sprung in front of him, leaned over and slid her sunglasses off. With a shake of her head, she pulled her turban from her head, grabbed his chin, and forced him to look at her.

He froze. He had come face to face with the most horrendous looking creature he had ever seen. Huge black snakes slithered out from her head, their quick tongues spitting at the air in all directions, and at him.

Raymond struggled to get away, but he couldn't move, neither could he speak, or hear.

He turned cold.

He had no sense of time and his eyesight diminished. Shapes moved around him. Lights flashed. The world grew dim and he knew he was no longer in Amber's yard. A low humming sound trembled through his body. He sensed Amber next to him. Her face appeared in front of him momentarily and he saw her lips move but he heard nothing. Then she was gone and darkness sealed his mind.

The Conspiracy

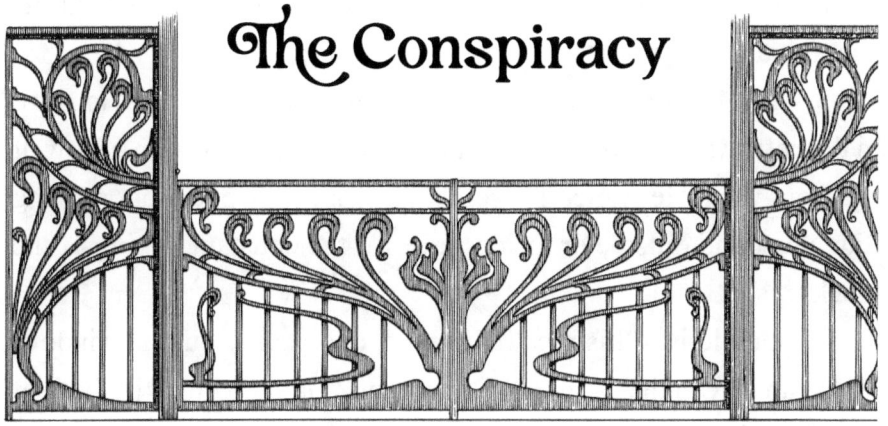

Even though Gerald couldn't see much of the driveway from Ginger's stairs, and the manor's porch was completely out of view, the glow was that of headlamps. Someone was at his house in a vehicle, and at this hour of the night, he could imagine who it might be. Though Gerald limped quickly down the footpath, by the time he came to the manor the car's engine was off and the lights had been dimmed. No one was around, but his front door hung open.

"What's going on in here?" he asked as he stepped up to the threshold and called into the house. Gerald's voice echoed down the hallway, but there was no answer. The house was dark and empty. Gerald looked back at the car once more before he stepped inside the house. The limousine glowed under the moonlight, its elegant body an intrusion to the quiet drive, glistening like a spaceship in the forest.

The windows of the vehicle were dark and foreboding, preventing Gerald from seeing inside. He could step closer, but he feared doing so. He'd heard stories about people being abducted when they got too near to a car. If he were kidnapped, who would pay his ransom?

Gerald turned his attention to the mansion and stepped inside the manor without flipping the light switch. He slowly edged his way toward the parlor.

The flash he saw in the mirror happened suddenly. He froze in the entryway. The window shades were open, giving him a view of the front yard. He waited for something else to happen, but nothing did. No sound outside or inside, save for the constant ticking of the clocks.

Gerald held his breath, listened, and peered out the window. Who had driven the car here? The gorgon? Gainsworthy? Or both of them? And, where were they?

Should he go back outside and simply knock on the window of the car? Why should he be afraid of Ellen? He was a vampire and her powers were futile against him.

He swallowed his fear and pulled his scarf from around his neck, dabbing the drops of cold sweat that had accumulated on his temple — gathering his courage to confront the trespassers should the lights come on.

He jumped in terror when he heard footsteps. He spun around and gasped when a shadow crept along the floorboards behind him. Ever so slowly, it inched. Had he not been so petrified, he would have reached for his cane that hung over the coat rack. His heart galloped like a herd of horses.

"Gerald?"

Gerald exhaled in relief as Ginger peeked around the corner into the parlor.

"Good apparitions, Ginger! What are you doing sneaking around like that? I about had a heart attack."

"Me sneaking? You're the one in here with the lights off." She flipped the lights on. The empty parlor lit up.

"Turn them off again!"

"Why?"

"Someone is in the house and I don't know where. Be quiet."

Ginger obeyed. In the dark once more, Ginger walked to the window and stood by his side. "Who's in the house?"

"I don't know. The door was open when I got here, that's all I know." "Who's in the car?" she asked.

Gerald flinched when Ginger touched his arm. "No one that I know of."

"Someone's in the car. I saw a head in the back seat."

"Just a head?"

"Well no, I think it was on a neck and shoulders and probably a body too." Ginger said and then slapped his arm gently. "It was a whole person, dummy."

"In the back seat? What about the front seat? Who was driving? Was someone in the front seat?"

"I didn't see anyone in the front. I saw someone in the back. White as a ghost, that's how I saw them. They were so white they shone through the tint on the window."

Gerald pushed his head against the window and looked out. Steam from his breath immediately fogged his view. "Now that you mention it, I think I do see someone or something in the back seat. They aren't moving."

"A decoy maybe?"

"Why would there be a decoy in the car?" Ginger asked.

"To lure us there?"

"I don't know. That sounds dumb. Why wouldn't they just call us over if they wanted us at the car?"

"You're right." Gerald pivoted around. "I think someone is in the house. Either that or they went around back but there would be no reason for anyone to go to the back of the house. Is Cottlebone coming?"

"I don't know. He was behind me, but I don't know if he followed.

Did you lock the door when you left to go to the treehouse this evening?"

"I didn't lock it but I closed it. Perhaps the door didn't latch all the way. That happens sometimes." Still, he was certain he didn't leave it wide open, and there was no wind. Besides, where was the driver of the car if not in the house?

"We should see who's in the car." Ginger leaned over his shoulder as they both looked out the window again.

"No! Don't go near the car. It could be a trap. People get murdered that way."

"Gerald, we're vampires. We won't get murdered."

"Shh. I hear something."

That was it. Something was stirring and it sounded like it was under the house.

"Clocks."

"No. Something else. Footsteps. The basement. Oh, Ginger of course! Why didn't I think of that? They are in the library." He rushed out of the parlor into the entry again, turning from the hall to the front door and then to Ginger. "Why isn't Cottlebone here yet?"

"I told you I don't know if he followed. He might still be up on my porch."

Gerald wanted to run, or attack, but more likely run. "Let's get out of here." He took her arm, but she pushed him away.

"It's your house. Don't you want to see who's here?"

"I know who's here. Gainsworthy. He's after the books. He's looking for the red journal. Come on. Let's go get Cottlebone."

Cottlebone had been his father's bodyguard. He could protect them. With the servant at their side, Gerald would feel much safer. However, there was no time to run. The lights in the stairwell to the basement switched on. Ginger's fear kicked in and she grabbed his arm so tightly he had to brush her away. The footsteps in the basement grew louder.

"Do something!" Ginger said. Gerald straightened his back and took a deep breath. He'd be strong for Ginger. He put his hands in his pocket, so he didn't have to watch them shake. He looked around for a weapon.

Gainsworthy appeared. "There you are!" His voice was loud and boisterous. The intruder turned on the parlor lamp which lit the house as bright as day.

Gerald cleared his throat and raised his chin. "What are you doing here? Why have you broken into my home at this hour of night?"

"Your home?" the man laughed. He had in his hands several books, which he now tossed on the easy chair. "You might want to rephrase that question."

"I didn't stutter. My question was worded perfectly. Why are you in my home?" Gerald didn't have to pretend indignation, Gainsworthy's presence violated his privacy. "You're trespassing. I could call the police and have you arrested for breaking and entering."

Gainsworthy laughed. "Could you now? Come on, Gerry boy, you and I both know it's only a matter of time before my name is on the deed."

"I beg your pardon? The only deed you'll have is the deed to a jail cell."

"For what?" Gainsworthy face swelled and his smile turned into a snicker.

"Breaking and entering."

"How does one break and enter when the door was wide open?"

Ginger slapped Gerald on the arm. "I told you!"

"It was not! Simon Gainsworthy, get out of my house."

Gainsworthy's focus lifted over Gerald's shoulder to the entry. Gerald felt a presence behind him.

"You hear that, Ellen? He wants us to get out of our house."

Ginger clasped onto his arm tighter as she looked over her shoulder. She mumbled his name in terror.

He patted her hand as comfort. "It's okay," he whispered to her. "This is my house! Our house. The Peadlebody Manor. The name hasn't changed nor will it." Gerald insisted.

It was then that he saw Ellen remove her sunglasses. The woman sauntered around the two, the tortoiseshell frames touched her lips. Her hair may have been in a turban, but her body moved like a snake.

"Oh, my dear, my dear, what is it going to take to get through to you. This is my house." Her voice was a raspy whisper, filled with self-confidence and cunning.

Gerald managed a cough, and then a sense of strength surged through him. He knew what Ellen was. She stood powerless against him. If Ginger and Gerald hadn't been vampires, the sight of a gorgon would have turned them to stone. But it didn't. Gerald could handle this. They both could.

"Excuse me?"

"You heard me. My house," she repeated, less of a smile this time.

"This is the Peadlebody estate and I don't believe that you are related to any of us. And even if you were, the entire household was willed to me. You've already stolen a good portion of my father's property. Leave us be."

Gainsworthy chuckled. "Face it, Gerry. You're going to sell the Peadlebody estate to me. You're going to sign the papers tonight. In so doing I will have all the book your father wrote, and not a word will have passed on. Not after the fire."

Gerald snickered. "You're going to burn the manor?"

"How else will I keep my name clean?"

"Well I'm not selling, so you'll have to burn it down with us in it."

Gainsworthy frowned. "Why that would bring the police in on this. Not a good plan."

Ellen came up to Gerald and stood an arms distance away. She reached out to touch his cheek, but Ginger slapped her hand.

"Oh, my, a feisty one!"

"Leave us alone, freak!" Ginger said with a growl. "You can't bully us around."

Ginger's tenacity surprised Gerald, but he didn't let on.

"On the contrary, little lady. Something tells me you're going to recant those words in a few minutes."

"Never!"

"Really? I have something you want." The woman grinned at Ginger and ruffled her hair.

Ginger held her nose. "You stink."

Ellen laughed and stepped away. It was true, she had an unpleasant stench to her. A smell comparable to fish mixed with rotten mushrooms, Gerald thought.

"Never mind about me. When you see what I have, you'll give me everything you own."

Gerald interrupted the two with a laugh. He tried to make it as convincing as Gainsworthy's chuckle, but fell short. "What do you have that I could possibly want?" He looked at Ginger, who was not nearly as amused as he was. In fact, her face was pale and her eyes bulged.

"Your sister-in-law knows." Ellen winked at Ginger.

"What?" Ginger asked. When Ellen nodded toward the car parked in the driveway, Ginger let go of Gerald's arm and covered her mouth with her hands.

"What's missing in this picture here?" Ellen asked, waving

at the two of them. "Seems something is missing. Someone one, that is."

"No! You didn't!"

Gerald had no idea what the two were talking about. Ellen nodded and put her glasses back on. "Yes. You're extremely intelligent for a half-blood. Good guess, Ginger dear!"

Ginger flew out of the parlor and down the hall. In seconds, Gerald saw her through the window running toward the car. He felt the wind on his face from her wake, leaving him lost for understanding.

Gainsworthy watched out the window from the parlor with his hands in his pockets and the evilest grin Gerald had ever seen on his face. Ginger yanked on the car's back door. Unable to open it she moaned. She screamed and kicked at the door. Ellen chuckled and winked at him. "You're in for a little surprise," she said.

The gorgon strolled out of the parlor toward the front door. Keys flew at Ginger and skated to her feet. Ginger dove for them and raced back to the car. She tried several keys before unlocking the door. Gerald refused to watch this madness any longer. He ran out of the parlor, down the hall, and out the front door.

By the time he got to the porch, something large had already fallen out of the car and lay motionless on the ground. Ginger fell to her knees and bent over it, weeping and screaming.

Gerald gawked in disbelief. He dashed from the porch to the driveway, slowing as he approached Ginger and the motionless form in front of her. Never had he felt such despair. His nephew lay on the ground as cold and white as alabaster, his silky hair molded in prefect waves over his ear, the side burns etched against his cheek. His sculpted Peadlebody nose and high cheekbones could not be mistaken. Even the clothes he wore were recognizable, the sweater that Ginger had knitted for him, the turtleneck, all molded into a smooth stone statue.

Most disturbing was the expression on his face and the terror Raymond had experienced in his last moment. Gerald's heart broke to see his nephew lying there, and to hear Ginger wail over him. A knot formed in his stomach. The despair soon turned to rage.

Tears welled in his eyes.

"What did you do?" He didn't address his question to Ellen. What did a gorgon care for human life? He turned to Gainsworthy who was supposed to be a human being. The man stood under the porch light with his hands on his hips and a smile on his face. "He never did anything to you! Why did you do this?" Gerald shouted.

Ellen snickered at his outburst. "Oh now, now, calm down. Your nephew had a mild taste of ill fortune. He still has blood running through him."

She walked toward Gerald with a wicked grin on her face. "His fate is in your hands, but I assure you, he won't last long. Ten minutes perhaps. Twenty at the most before his system shuts down altogether. Your call, Mr. Peadlebody. Save him or not. I don't care which choice you make but she might." Ellen pointed at Ginger.

Gerald was at a loss. Of course, he would do what needed to be done to save his nephew's life, but to be so manipulated by his father's Archenemy boiled his blood. Before he could give an answer, he heard a muffled cry come from inside the car and when he looked, he noticed Amber, gagged and with her hands tied behind her back.

"Don't touch her." Ellen warned when Gerald moved toward the girl. "Or she'll be just as pale as that nephew of yours."

"What do you want from us?"

"Everything you have." Ellen replied, her tongue rolling across her lips.

"Do it, Gerald!" Ginger sobbed. "Just do it. Give them what they want. Nothing in that house is worth my son's life. Save him, Gerald! Hurry!"

The sight of Ginger weeping over Raymond lying stiff as a corpse was unbearable. Gerald's lips tightened over his fangs. He couldn't control himself any longer. Fury brewed inside of him like a tornado forming, readying itself to tear a city to shreds. He glared at Gainsworthy. One leap and he'll have him. He'll jump on the man's neck and torture him before he drains him dry. The man will scream in pain. Gerald tore off his coat and threw it to the ground. The energy spun like a tidal wave inside of him.

Ellen stepped between him and Gainsworthy.

"I'm warning you, Mr. Peadlebody. Don't do anything foolish. You'll lose your nephew and the girl." She pulled her sunglasses off again, shoving Gerald aside as she advanced toward Ginger, Raymond, and the back seat of the car.

"No!" Ginger jumped up. "Gerald what are you doing? Give them what they want!" Ginger threw her body in front of the open door, blocking Ellen's access to Amber.

And then Gerald remembered Dusty the chipmunk and the chant that brought him back to life. "Your curse can't last! You can do what you want now, but it won't last," he said to Ellen.

Ellen raised an eyebrow.

"We have the verse that breaks this affliction. We know the lyrics that will turn every one of your statues to life again," he said.

"I'm afraid you're mistaken, Gerald dear. Once our artist touches the stone, these poor frozen people are no longer human. I must say, Raymond will make such a handsome monument guarding the gate. A fine tribute for our new manor."

Gerald had no time to process what she was saying. A sudden scream drew everyone's eyes to the mansion.

Gainsworthy lay sprawled out on the porch, face up, half in the house, and half out. Richard Cottlebone knelt beside him, wiping his mouth clean with a napkin that had been clearly stained in blood. In his other hand, he held a large mirror aimed at Ellen, her image captured. When Cottlebone rose, Gerald swore he saw a fang under the servant's lips. Before he could get a closer look, a cloud formed around the servant and another figure vaporized into being. That figure took a position behind Cottlebone. Gerald's mouth flew open.

"Shut your mouth, Gerald. You'll catch a fly." The voice that came from the mist was faintly recognizable. And then a man appeared fully formed.

He had not aged.

Benjamin Peadlebody was the epitome of beauty and everything Gerald remembered of him as a child. His long, dark cloak rippled gracefully as he stepped over Gainsworthy's body into the moonlight. His strong jaw, high cheekbones, and large eyes, mesmerizing. His pale skin glowed like sapphire. Only the very tips of his fangs were visible and they glistened like stars against his flesh. His voice resonated as though echoing through the galaxy.

"Neither of these creatures are a threat to you, Gerald." He smiled, his gestures fluid and confident. "I had hoped you could settle the matter to its end, but since you're so inept, I guess it's up to me to take it from here."

Was Gerald really seeing his father, or was he imagining all of this? He looked at Ellen. Her sunglasses had fallen on the ground and lay at her feet. No longer was she smiling. Her mouth hung ajar, as wide as her eyes, hypnotized by her reflection in the mirror. Cottlebone moved closer to her ahead of Benjamin, holding the looking glass steadfastly.

Gerald eyed his sister-in-law still weeping over Raymond. "Ginger," he whispered and touched her shoulder. In her anguish, she had failed to see that Raymond's color had returned to him. With Ellen's power waning, his nephew gained his strength again.

"Oh, my baby!" She cried when he rolled over on his back and blinked the dust out of his eyes. "Oh Raymond!" She threw her arms around him and wept on his chest.

"Mum?" Raymond patted her on the back, lifted himself up with her still clinging to him, and looked around. "What happened? Where am I? Where is Amber?"

"She's in the car," Gerald said when his nephew locked eyes with his. Raymond gently moved his mother away. "It's okay Mum, I'm okay. Stop crying." He reached in his pocket and pulled out a hankie. "Here." Once she had blown her nose, she nodded. Raymond rose and scurried to the car.

"Well!" Benjamin Peadlebody broke the silence. His sharp smile sparkled in the moonlight. "Now that you see these two freaks for who and what they really are, you can tell the authorities and I'll go on with my travels. I release Cottlebone from his servitude. Yes, he's been working for me temporarily but only to expose these scoundrels. Don't hold any of his previous behaviors against him, not even that last little bite he just finished." Benjamin nodded toward the body lying on the doorstep. The realtor's stomach bulged like a balloon under the porch light. "Cottlebone had no control over what he did. He was possessed. By me. In return for his loyalty, I'd like him to have a room at the estate free of charge. Forever. Or whatever forever means for you mortals. And Gerald?"

"Yes, Father."

"I really wanted you to solve the mystery, for your own sake as well as mine. You have disappointed me in the past and I thought it only proper to give you one last chance. It's a pity you never took those hunting lessons with your brother. You could have been to so much more. Alas, I can't be here to fang-feed you for the rest of your life and I doubt that Ginger will be making her brew once she returns to humanity. Something needs to be done about you."

"I'm sorry."

Benjamin waved the apology away. "Sorry means nothing. You're a coward and I don't see much of a future for you as a vampire. You don't cut the mustard, or in your case should we say jugular?" He laughed a haunting, wicked laugh. Gerald shifted his weight; despondent that after all these years, he still hadn't pleased his father.

"Whichever term you'd like to use. You're right." Gerald swallowed the humiliation. He wished his father hadn't embarrassed him in front of everyone.

"Very well. Maybe when Ginger casts that final spell you should just ask her to include you. You might make a better human than you do a vampire. Here's hoping."

"Yes, sir."

"See to it that the hooligan Gainsworthy gets what's coming to him. A cold cell and some bread and water. A diet would do him well. And as for that gorgon, I've arranged with Cottlebone to have her locked in a room full of mirrors in the basement next to the library. She won't be causing any more trouble. Gorgons have Narcissistic personality disorders. She'll never want to leave her reflection."

"Yes Father."

"As for Ginger, that same spell we used on the chipmunk can be used to reverse vampirism for her species. As I said before you'll do best to join her. Just, not so much blood on the fingers this time, please. It makes me queasy to see good food being wasted. Use a needle. Less messy."

"Yes Father."

"While you two are at it, see that Cottlebone's collie is released. My servant really did love that dog."

"I'll see to it."

"Would you please defrost your sister-in-law's refrigerator? Those popsicles of squirrel brew should be removed from the cartons, the boxes recycled, and the frozen brew buried by the hydrangeas. That will lower the pH level and give the flowers a nice blue color.

Blue's my favorite, you know."

"Yes, Father, I know."

"Gerald."

"Yes, sir."

"You're still my son despite all those things that didn't please me. You're a Peadlebody. No one will ever take that away from you! Even if you do decide to become human."

"Thank you," Gerald breathed a sigh. A tear welled in his eye and he wiped it away. His voice got all raspy when he tried to speak. "You'll always be my dad."

"And one final request."

"What's that?"

"I'd like an invitation to Raymond's wedding."

"I'll see what I can do."

"Very well!" Benjamin Peadlebody brushed his hands clean of any fouler play, folded his arms against his chest, pivoted on his heel, and with his velvet cloak swirling with him, he disappeared into a mist of blue.

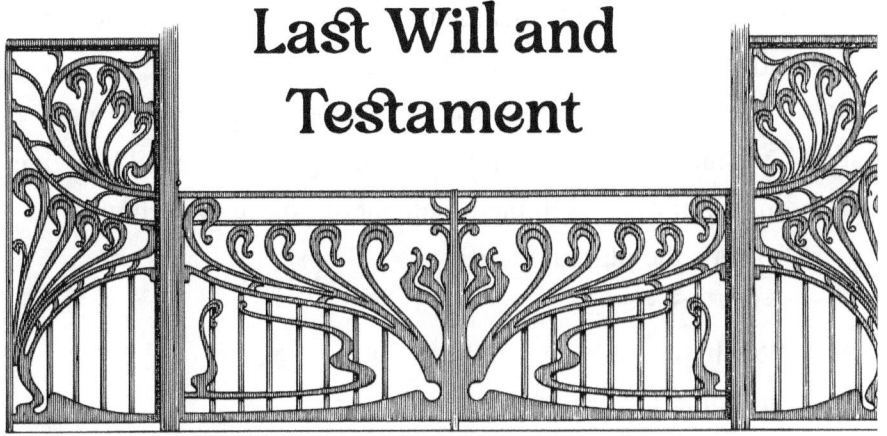

Last Will and Testament

Raymond untied Amber. There in the car's backseat they watched his grandfather, enchanted by the man's charisma.

"For a moment, I thought you were gone," Amber whispered. "It scared me. I realized what a loss that would have been for me." "Really?" He shifted his focus to her.

She wiped a clump of dust off his sweater and then took his hands. "I don't care about your relatives. I want to be with you. Forever, or for whatever forever means to us mortals."

They smiled into each other's eyes until Amber looked out the window again.

"Your grandpa looks like you, Raymond," she whispered in his ear.

"Very handsome."

"He's a full-blooded vampire, Amber."

"Yes. But he's very handsome."

"I'll take that as a compliment." He gave her a hug and a kiss on the cheek.

All the advice Benjamin gave to Uncle Gerald made sense. What Benjamin categorized as weakness, Raymond considered his uncle's strong points.

When Cottlebone lured Ellen into the manor with the mirror, and into Raymond's view, Raymond shuddered and turned away from the scene. He sank back against the seat of the car. "I looked at her and then everything went cold."

"She turned you into stone." Amber hugged him and he patted her hand. "So, I guess, that gorgon is going to be held captive in a room full of mirrors in the basement of your uncle's house?"

"That's the plan, I guess."

"Ew," she said.

"Yeah."

"Remind me not to live here."

"Don't worry about that. It was never my plan to move into the Peadlebody mansion."

"Did you hear him though?" Amber asked.

"What?"

"Your grandfather wants to come to our wedding."

"I heard. What do you think about that?"

"What do I think?"

"You're the bride. You send the invitations!"

She laughed, looked out the door again as Benjamin Peadlebody spun into a vapor. "I like the idea. It's kind of exciting when you think about it."

Raymond raised a brow. He had not expected that reaction. "Really?"

She smiled at him, her eyes emitting that special sparkle that he knew was only for him.

"I always wanted an eccentric wedding! Your grandfather's appearance would be totally unconventional!"

Acknowledgments

My critique group Pat Stricklin, Carol Caldwell, Penny Percenti and Jan Symonds who sat patiently listening to me read my first drafts. Veer West Screenplay Festival for giving a dramatic reading of An Unconventional Mr. Peadlebody before an audience and offering an award as Best Mystery! And to you, my dear readers who take the time to step into a completely zany world with me.

Please subscribe to my website to learn about upcoming events, new releases, sales and giveaways.

http://gardnersart.com

Find me on Twitter at https://twitter.com/DianneGardner

You'll find an audio book with the same title narrated by the talented voice actor Brad Wills.

Visit my website for more info.

OTHER WORKS BY D.L. GARDNER

Sword of Cho Nisi Series
       Rise of the Tobian Princess
       Fall of the Kings
       Curse of Mount Ream
       Silver Threads Companion short stories
       Darkness Holds the Son

Ian's Realm Saga
       Ian's Realm Trilogy
       Layla Born at Night
       Fallen Morning
       Diary of a Conjurer
       Cassandra's Castle
       Lost on Taikus
       Tale of the Four Wizards

Thread of a Spider
An Unconventional Mr. Peadlebody
Pouraka
Altered
Hoarfrost to Roses
Night Ice
Wind in the Wilds
The Far Side of Heaven
Where the Yellow Violets Grow
Dylan
Ferris Wheel
Sometimes Dragons Win